"Te⋯⋯⋯⋯⋯⋯⋯⋯if"

She ran her finger⋯⋯⋯⋯⋯⋯⋯ a⋯⋯ered h⋯⋯"W⋯⋯ werewolf ⋯⋯es out. You want to know what werewolves do? We seek to mate. Unfortunately there aren't many female wolves to satisfy my werewolf."

"So it needs a mate?"

"Yes." Holding her hand to his lips, he kissed her knuckles. "And I've found one."

Was he saying that if she was his lover that also made her the werewolf's lover?

"But don't worry. There are ways to keep the werewolf at bay."

"Such as?"

"Sex until I'm sated." She delivered him a wicked grin, and he added, "Though I've never tried it before. It would require a lot, from any woman, to satisfy me."

Though unspoken, the words reverberated in her head: *I'm up for the challenge*.

Available in September 2010

Mills & Boon® Nocturne™

Moon Kissed
by Michele Hauf

Last of the Ravens
by Linda Winstead Jones

Touch of Surrender
by Rhyannon Byrd

MICHELE HAUF

MOON KISSED

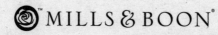

MILLS & BOON

All the characters in this book have no existence outside the imagination of
the author, and have no relation whatsoever to anyone bearing the same name
or names. They are not even distantly inspired by any individual known or
unknown to the author, and all the incidents are pure invention.

LIBRARIES NI	
C700421126	
RONDO	10/08/2010
F	£ 4.99
PST	

First publish in Great Britain 2010
Harlequin M
Eton House, 18-24 Paradise Road, Richmond, Surrey TW9 1SR

© Michelle R Hauf 2009

ISBN: 978 0 263 88774 7

89-0910

Harlequin Mills & Boon policy is to use papers that are natural, renewable
and recyclable products and made from wood grown in sustainable forests.
The logging and manufacturing processes conform to the legal environmental
regulations of the country of origin.

Printed and bound in Spain
by Litografia Rosés S.A., Barcelona

Michele Hauf has been writing for over a decade and has published historical, fantasy and paranormal romances. A good strong heroine, action and adventure and a touch of romance make for her favourite kind of story. (And if it's set in France, all the better.) She lives with her family in Minnesota and loves the four seasons, even if one of them lasts six months and can be colder than a deep freeze. You can find out more about her at www.michelehauf.com.

For Lyda Morehouse because she rocks

Chapter 1

The asphalt blurred under Bella's running shoes as she abandoned her casual evening jog for a lung-bruising sprint. In the tropical humidity this sweltering midsummer night, her chest, back and face dripped with sweat.

Aware of the frenzied breaths close in her wake, she forced herself to push through the pain of exertion.

Escape. Don't let them get you.

She wasn't familiar with this neighborhood, yet she knew it formed the line of demarcation where the suburbs met the industrial north side of the Twin

Cities. Not the best jogging spot for a lone young woman, especially with the streetlights out of order. The only light came from the distant neon of a string of nightclubs that peeked between four- and five-story warehouses.

Taking a long stride and ignoring her burning hamstrings, she made the curb. Thank God, she hadn't slipped. They'd be on her. To rob her or bite her or—

What *were* they? They had teeth. Long teeth. They had snarled and flashed fangs.

When she'd taken off running, they'd given her a head start, laughing, as a group of men will do when they wish to frighten a woman. She'd prayed they would simply stand there, not pursue her. But that prayer hadn't been answered.

Close by, the *ta-thum, ta-thum* of a train rolling over the iron track matched the heavy labor of her heartbeats.

She'd never be able to outrun them. But maybe hide?

To her right, a dark warehouse beckoned. The three-story structure mastered the corner of the block. The double-wide door gaped, a black maw.

Bella dashed inside.

Too late, she realized her mistake. She'd trapped herself. The entire block was dark. Who would hear her scream?

Lungs heaving, she struggled to stay upright on her shaky legs.

Darkness nudged up against her shoulders, making it difficult to even make out the walls around her. The windows were like glass-toothed open mouths against the dark sky. Dark masses of bulky objects—stacked, like lumber—forced her to tread carefully.

Her running shoe crunched on a loose board and she wobbled. Arms groping through the air, she swung blindly to stave off a fall. But equilibrium abandoned her.

Before she could hit the concrete, strong hands caught her about the waist and tugged her into darkness.

A man holding her breathed heavily, as if from exertion, like her. Warm breath wafted over her face. He smelled strongly masculine. Earthy. He was not one of her fanged pursuers. Yet she couldn't immediately determine if he was exactly a safe harbor.

His strong arms clasped about her arms and across her back. He took a step, dragging her deeper into the darkness. A boarded-up window, six feet to her left, admitted thin shafts of spare moonlight.

A piece of rough wood tore across her shoulder and a sliver snagged her T-shirt. Bella struggled. "Let me go. Who are you?"

"I've saved you from those wild idiots outside. No thanks?"

"If you let me go."

His nose brushed across her forehead, as if taking in her scent. "I don't think so."

His intense actions now frightened her more than being chased. Arms tight about her body, he studied her, as she did him. Face a breath from hers. Aggressive stance. Shoulders squared and hips firmly placed. He was twice as wide as she and a head higher. All brawn and muscle. Bigger than the many male dance partners she'd performed with over the years.

The thick muscles in his arms pulsed against her shoulders, squeezing her uncomfortably. He chuckled through his nose and continued his sniffing trail over her face, drawing down near her ear.

Repulsed, Bella squirmed, seeking a means to break the binding hold. Just as she felt a scream rise, a palm smacked over her mouth. She twisted her head, but he pressed so hard, her lips flattened against her teeth.

"Shh, pretty one." Her captor's voice was soothing and deep. It sounded far too nice—too attractive—for a man who might harm her. "They're here, preening about the doorway. You want me to release you and see how you fare with three instead of one? I bet they'll take turns."

A reedy moan escaped her throat.

Strong yet cautioning fingers dug into her bicep. "Listen."

Tears burning in her eyes, Bella listened. The three men entered the building, slowly, cautiously, their light footsteps landing randomly on two-by-fours scattered on the floor.

They'd all been taller than her; most men did rise over her five-foot-four frame. Dressed in black and looking more than a little Goth, the lanky trio oozed menace.

The supple thickness of her captor's leather jacket crushed her breasts and belly as he pressed his torso against hers. His solid muscles hugged her everywhere. Trapping her. Threatening her with each slight move he made.

A flicker of prudence cautioned her to remain still. Make no noise. Yet Bella slowly moved her fingers over the rough wood behind her. Must be a stack of pallets. If she could find a nail to use as a weapon…

A thin ray of moonlight struck the corner of her captor's forehead, illuminating dark hair slicked back from his forehead and over his ears. There was a pale shimmer in the one eye she could make out. Dark brown, wild and surrounded by shadowed flesh.

Had she stumbled into the arms of a homeless man? But he didn't reek of alcohol or body odor.

Still, she couldn't budge, and the hand over her mouth hurt.

A tinny clatter ratcheted up her heartbeats. Someone nearby stepped across the debris.

They would hear her thundering heart, she feared.

The man who held her forcefully nudged his nose along her cheek. His hot tongue dashed out to lick up a tear that fell down her cheek.

Though she wanted to retch, to scream, to kick out and fight for her life, Bella could only swallow the horror and pray she did not make a noise that would bring the others upon her. Four attackers would be unthinkable.

She heard feet shuffle nearby, and then a pallet of boards fell, nearly deafening her. The crash of wood connecting with Sheetrock released the odor of chalk. Apparently her would-be attackers were throwing things about.

"Where the hell did she get to?"

"Cool your heels, dude. She's in here somewhere."

A whimper tickled Bella's throat. Clenched tighter by her captor, she winced. Now both his eyes were visible in the slash of light, warning, teasing in a darkly macabre way.

He wouldn't toss her out to the others, would he? She sought his eyes to find the answer to that worry, but he tilted his head to listen.

"Did she run out the other side? The whole place is wide-open. Check that exit, will you?"

A wide hand explored her body from her back and around to her chest, slowly, without sound. When he squeezed her breast, she bit away a scream. A swallow put back the bile rising in her throat. Now he pressed his hand so hard to her mouth, his finger lay across her teeth.

"So sweet," he whispered in the calmest, most dreadful tone. "Your fear arouses me."

Woozy darkness toyed with her brain. *Don't pass out.* She had to stay alert.

Or would it be better if she didn't know how this night might end? Her life hadn't flashed before her eyes yet, so did that mean there would be only torture and pain?

Come on, Bella, she coached inwardly. *Where's your usual cheery optimism? You are safe. Just remain in this man's arms.*

Nausea coiled in her gut. When her leg muscles gave out, her captor tilted a hip into her to press her against the stacked pallets.

"Hold on, sweet," he murmured. "They may be hungry for your blood, but they can't scent a skunk in a garden."

Hungry for her blood? Did that mean they were—

No. Things—*creatures*—like that didn't exist.

They were a gang of wild, drunk men out to torment a woman.

The fingers at her breast found her nipple. It hardened at his touch. She was not aroused. It was the fear heightening her reaction to every touch, sound and smell.

A hard pinch snapped her thoughts to the moment.

"Stay with the program, sweet," he muttered. "They're at the other end of the warehouse. They'll give up soon, I'm sure."

She mumbled behind his hand, and he pressed hard but then relented. "Quiet. Or it's your funeral."

When he took his fingers from her mouth, it felt as if they were still there. She wriggled her lips and opened her aching jaw.

"Cosmopolitans, eh?"

Startled at his suggestion, she realized he must smell the drink on her breath. But how could he? She'd had one during an afternoon meeting with a potential client. That had been six hours earlier. Of course, she hadn't eaten since.

"Wh-what are they?" she managed.

He shoved her head against his chest, which effectively muffled her utterance.

"Vampires," he murmured. "And they're hungry."

She'd gotten that impression the moment the one

had flashed his fangs at her. This was so wrong. She didn't believe in vampires.

"They've left."

She struggled, but he quickly clasped her wrists before her. "They'll circle the building and roam the area. You're not safe yet, sweet, so keep calm. You can do that, yes?"

She nodded, conceding silently. He seemed willing to keep her protected and unseen, but why? For his own evil intentions?

"Mmm, but can I?" He again sniffed at her hair. A dodge of his head placed his mouth at her jaw. He licked it.

"I'm going to be sick," she whispered, hoping it would dissuade him.

Footsteps slapping the pavement outside the window alerted her. Her captor again pressed her head against his chest, smothering her breath against the warm, rough-woven sweater he wore beneath the jacket. He held her so fiercely, she thought he might break a bone. One of *her* bones.

"Here, pretty, pretty," came a voice from outside. A low whistle teased the evening air.

The sound pinched Bella's heart, like a stretched spring snapping to a coil.

He was right. They circled the building. How long would they prowl the area before giving up?

Could she keep from crying out when in the arms of another man who meant her harm?

A low growl, which sounded more like satisfaction than warning, preceded the press of his leg against her hip. He had an erection. The utter and sickening wrongness rent Bella's soul.

"Let's head back," someone outside shouted. "We'll find another."

Bella's spine straightened, her hope lifting.

"Give them five minutes," the man said. "Then they'll be far enough off for you to run."

"You'll let me go?"

"Of course. You don't think I'd take you right here in this dump?"

"You…you…" He'd said he'd let her go. The deal had been made. She wouldn't argue beyond it.

"I have your scent in my nose, sweet. No matter how far you run, I'll find you."

"No, please. You've saved my life."

"I've merely prevented you from getting raped and your neck torn to shreds. I suppose you do owe me, though."

And she could imagine what he'd desire as reward.

"You impress me, mortal." His grip on her loosened, but still his torso held her pinned against the pallets. "Other women would have pissed their pants in your situation. Are you so brave, or somehow beyond fear?"

She breathed through her nose, fighting her raging heartbeats. Her forehead dropped to his chest. So weak. Just…exhausted, and yes, beyond fear.

He'd called her *mortal*.

Bella curled her fingers into his sweater. "Are you like them?" she asked, not knowing where the question came from. Nervous energy. Macabre fascination.

"A vampire?" His chuckle vibrated against her forehead. "Human blood does nothing for me."

That didn't exactly answer her question. Bella leaned back, her head lolling across the wood pallets. She pressed her hands to his chest as a means to keep from collapsing.

"They've gone far enough now. Their scent is weak."

"Y-you…" Stress softened her voice to a whisper. "You can smell their distance?"

"Yes. Your fear is subsiding. Next will come shock or collapse. You'd best be off before you find you cannot move at all."

"Thank you." Yet another strange utterance when what she really wanted to do was kick the bastard and scream at him.

He stepped away, but they were wedged between stacks of pallets, and that kept him close enough to touch. Moving right, she tested his promise to allow her to leave. And when she tried the ground with her foot to see if it would be sure, a hand grasped her wrist and pulled her to him.

He wasn't going to let her leave!

"I'll take my reward before you flee."

"But—"

He crushed his mouth to hers with a violent and urgent kiss. It hurt, and it wasn't kind. But her mouth was already numb.

He pulled her into an embrace that lifted her feet from the floor and clasped her body against his like a monster picking up a child and ripping off its head.

But he didn't harm her. Instead, he groaned with pleasure.

Suddenly setting her down and pushing her away, he twisted his head and shook it fiercely, like a dog shaking off rain. "Go!"

She didn't need to be told twice. Sliding her hands along the boards to guide her, Bella found the doorway where she had entered.

"Go north," she heard him say. "They went south."

North, then. And she took off running.

Shoulders pressed to the pallets behind him, and eyes closed, Severo listened. Each of her footsteps poked at his muscles, as if to prod awake something long dormant.

He required no prodding. At this moment, he was more awake and alive than he'd felt in decades.

He'd been strolling the neighborhood, assessing the abandoned real estate, when he'd picked up the vile scent of longtooths on the hunt. Their obnoxious odor had triggered his gag reflex. Yet he had sensed the female's scent and had ducked inside the warehouse.

If he could save one human from the clutches of a vampire, then it was a good day indeed.

But what he hadn't expected was the way she'd made him feel. Or that she'd make him feel at all.

He had walked this earth for many decades and had given up hope of ever finding a true mate. Human females were so fragile, delicate, and not worth more than a few nights of pleasure.

This one was different. She was emotionally strong.

Could she be the one? A woman he could finally make his own. His mate. Forever.

Chapter 2

Sunlight woke her. Bella sat up on the couch and blew aside a stray fern from her face. An oblique muscle on her side ached, forcing her horizontal again. She stared up through the luscious green fronds.

"I slept on the couch?"

Her body ached. Her hamstrings pulsed. Her shoulders and ribs felt bruised.

She touched her tender lips. Tears slipped down her cheeks.

Something had happened last night to turn her world on its side and roll it off a cliff. If she put aside the possibility of near rape, there was the evidence that those bastards who chased her were…

Vampires.

And the creep who'd held her in perilous safety had confirmed her suspicion as if he knew it were the truth.

And he'd called her mortal, which put into question his own status.

"Oh, Bella, you must have bumped your head. You're thinking like a crazy woman."

Storybook creatures were not supposed to exist. A woman was supposed to fear serial killers, rapists and crazed gunmen loosed in city malls. Not men who looked human yet wanted to suck your blood.

Her heart began to race as swiftly as it had last night. Bella pressed a palm over her chest. She still wore yesterday's clothes. On the cotton shirt she saw a smear where his hand on her breast had dirtied the fabric.

A repulsive shiver chilled her from neck to hips.

Scrambling from the couch, she tore the shirt over her head and made a beeline toward the bathroom. Shedding her jogging pants, running shoes, panties and sports bra, she hit the shower, crying.

"Shake it off, Bella. That was a new street you took last night. You were not thinking straight."

She always walked to and from the clubs at night and had never once felt unsafe. A northernmost suburb of Minneapolis, her town was considered upscale and safe. She lived on a main strip where neat townhomes and lofts segued into a neighborhood of trendy dance clubs and restaurants. The dance studio where she practiced three days a week was but four blocks away.

Every other night she jogged five miles, usually down the strip, then through the city park that boasted manicured jogging trails and plenty of streetlamps. Never had she been attacked. The occasional catcall from a passing car or leer from a drunk huddled up against a storefront was to be expected. Heck, Benny the drunk, who nightly posted himself at the corner of Spruce and Second streets, always got a wave and a greeting from her.

She'd thought to take Declan Street last night, knowing it traversed a vacant section of older warehouses. She liked to explore. Her intention had been to go no more than a block, but once those men leaped out at her, her brain had switched from curiosity to flight.

Unfortunately, she'd run *away* from the safety of the well-lit strip.

"You put yourself in a bad situation. You dealt with it. You're safe and they didn't hurt you. Now get over it."

Spitting out warm water, she turned her back to the stream and reached for a bottle of shampoo.

Time to resume good old reliable Belladonna Reynolds mode. She was smart, stable, and could always be counted on to be responsible. Her Web design clients praised her creativity and precision. The dance studio was courting her to teach. Even when clubbing with friends, she was the one who quit drinking first, called cabs for everyone and made sure they got their car keys the next day.

Cosmopolitans.

He'd smelled the drink on her breath. Which was entirely possible. Bella hadn't eaten yesterday after that late business lunch. Not wise, because she had been straining during that last mile of running.

But to smell how far the vampires had fled? How could he possibly have known something like that?

Vampires.

Even thinking the word made her want to retch. Clutching the warm brass showerhead, she tilted her head to catch the water on the crown of her scalp.

Why was she so willing to accept what a complete stranger had told her?

She saw the fangs. Long and white, slightly curved, like a deadly blade.

But nothing could be worse than that hard, stolen kiss. He'd violated her in the sense that she'd relied on him for safety, and then he'd stolen it with his gropes and aggressiveness.

Bastard.

I have your scent in my nose. I'll find you.

"Don't think about it, Bella," she told herself. "It was a bad night." Should she call the cops?

What could they do? She hadn't clearly seen any of the men's faces. Once they'd flashed fangs, her better senses had vanished.

And she'd seen only parts of her captor's face. Though she'd never forget his lecherous growl. He'd seemed more animal than the vampires.

"Quit thinking that word," she admonished and flicked off the shower.

Stepping out onto the bamboo floor mat, she toweled herself off.

Today was Saturday. Though her Web design business allowed her to work from home, she followed her no-work-on-weekends rule. With nothing required of her today, she usually jogged on weekend afternoons at the park.

Nix that, she thought. Perhaps the video store down the block would offer some comedies to clear her thoughts.

The doorbell rang. Bella glanced to the LED clock on the toilet tank. It was noon?

She'd slept so late. Deservingly.

"Seth."

Her best friend had said he'd stop by with tickets for tonight's jam at the club. He DJ'd and they expected a sold-out house.

Tugging a white watered-silk robe around her body, Bella raced out to the door, dodging the overgrown bamboo plant at the end of the couch. Seth opened the door with his key first and entered.

"Oh, sorry, Bella. When you didn't answer, I got worried."

He swung the key ring around his forefinger a couple times and tucked it in his pocket. Seth was a recovering emo who still loved the fringy eyebrow-dusting bangs and slim, fitted clothing. Recently, he'd graduated to techno club music in protest of the dirgelike tunes he'd once embraced.

He leaned in to kiss her cheek. His lemony after-shave always made her smile.

"What's this? Did you fall and bump yourself? Your jaw looks bruised."

All the bravery she'd talked herself into during the shower slipped away now that she stood in the safety of Seth's arms. Bella burrowed her face against his shoulder and sobbed.

"Okay, something's wrong. Let's sit you down and— Bellybean, it's okay. I'm here. Talk to me."

"Oh, Seth, you'll never believe the horrible thing that happened to me last night."

"Hell, Bella. Do I need to call the police?"

He steered her toward the couch. His bright blue eyes studied her as he touched her jaw gently. They'd developed a friendship during ballroom dancing classes in middle school. That friendship had deepened in high school, after a medical-careers class in eleventh grade. Seth had been Bella's model for compassion.

"Are you all right?"

"Just a few bruises," she said, sniffling. "Physically, I'm fine. Mentally, well… I was chased by three men."

"What? Where? When?"

"Last night."

"Were you jogging?"

She winced at his admonishing tone. "Yes, but I took a new route."

"You know I hate you jogging at night to begin with, but you promised me you'd stick to the parks and well-lit avenues."

"I was bored with that route." Sucking in gasping breaths, she forced up calm and bent a knee to kneel on the couch by Seth. "I have to tell you this fast, because if I don't tell someone, I think I'll go crazy. But what I have to say is so crazy, you might think I've already achieved insanity."

"You can tell me anything, Bellybean. If someone hurt you—"

"They were vampires."

He closed his mouth. Seth's gaze searched her face. Not accusing or condemning, just listening.

"Three vampires," she said. "They flashed their fangs and chased me. Seth, I know it sounds strange, but the guy in the warehouse said they were vampires, too."

"The guy in the warehouse?"

"I ran into an abandoned warehouse to hide, but someone was already in there. He grabbed me. I thought he was going to hurt me, but he kept me quiet and hidden until the vampires gave up and left. He said he could smell them and I feel like he was some kind of creature, too, and— Seth, doesn't this freak you out?"

Head bowed and hands between his knees, he blew out a breath. "Not as much as you think it should. I'm freaked you were chased. The guy in the warehouse—he hurt you? Is that how you got this bruise?"

She clasped a hand over his when he touched her jaw. "He was holding his hand over my mouth so I wouldn't scream and alert the others."

"So he protected you. Huh." Seth put a fist to his mouth, thinking. "Did the guy protecting you have fangs?"

"Not that I saw. He said he hated vampires, that they smelled vile. He smelled things a lot. Seth, I just told you I was chased by vampires."

"I know, Bellybean. Don't worry. I've known vampires exist for a while now."

"What?" Surprised by that calm statement, Bella shot up on one foot, the other leg still bent on the couch. "You *know* about vampires?"

The chilling rush of blood leaving her head turned her flesh to goose bumps.

Seth shrugged. "I've been dating one for a couple weeks."

An openmouthed gape was all she could manage.

"Sit down, Bella. You've just discovered that mythical creatures exist, and not in a good way, either. Are you sure you're okay? None of them put their fangs to you, did they?"

She was still too stuck on the "I've been dating one" part to summon a response. Dragging her leg from the couch, Bella paced around behind the couch.

Seth was her BFF. They told each other everything. Shared good times and bad. He'd been the one to encourage her to begin dancing again. And he was always the first with a hug when she needed one.

He'd told her about a new girlfriend a few weeks ago over soup and sandwiches at Panera. Bella had been stunned how quickly he'd started calling this mystery woman his love. Seth never dated long-term and preferred to keep his dating schedule open for late-night pickups after a gig at the club.

And he'd neglected to mention this newest fling was a vampire.

"Whoever it was that grabbed you did good," he finally said. "If those vamps had gotten their hands on you they would have bitten you. I wonder if it was a were?"

"A were—as in werewolf? Seth, you're killing me here. First, you neglect to tell me your girlfriend is a vampire. And now you're so casual about the fact that creepy horror creatures actually exist. I don't know what to think."

"It's a lot to take in, but accept the fact that you have proof vamps do exist and move beyond it, Bella. That's what you do."

"Yes. Yes, I believe. I mean, how can a girl *not* believe when she's seen proof?"

He turned and propped his elbows on the couch. "And yes, I do mean werewolf. If he was scenting the vampires like you said, it's my best guess. Those things are like bloodhounds times ten. They can pick out a peppermint Life Savers in a city the size of New York. Put them on the scent, and set them loose."

"Oh my God." Again the nausea rose. Bella gripped the couch. "He said he had my scent in his nose, and that he'd find me again if he wanted."

"Shit, Bella, that's not good."

"No kidding. The last thing I need is a werewolf tracking me down to—"

Finish what he'd wanted to start last night in the warehouse?

Bella sank to her knees. Seth bounded over the back of the couch and lifted her so she sat on the back of it. He nudged between her legs, his hands to her hips and his head bowed to her forehead.

"Just lie low, Bella. It's going to be okay. Last night was a fluke. Don't ever go down that street again. And stick to jogging during the day, will you? Vamps don't do daylight."

"Oh, mercy." It was too incredible that the silver-screen stereotypes were true. "And crosses?"

"Kill vamps dead. But only if they've been baptized."

"Christ."

"That's about the point of it. Oh, and stakes work pretty well, too, but from what I understand, you've got to burst their heart or else they'll bounce right back at you. Werewolves, on the other hand, can do daylight. So maybe I don't want you going out for a run at all."

"Seth, I'm freaked that you know so much and are actually dating a vampire. How does that happen? *Why* does that happen? Are you her slave? Is she sucking your blood?"

She grabbed his shirt and tugged aside the wide lapel to reveal a purple-and-green bruise on the side of his neck. "Oh, no, you *are* a slave."

"I'm nothing of the sort." He tugged his shirt collar to make it stand upright. Seth was all about fashion and the right haircut. "She doesn't take very much, and besides, it feels good."

"Good? To have some creature bite into your flesh and suck out your blood? Oh, Seth."

Bending and putting her head between her knees felt right, but instead Bella wavered before her friend. She wanted to hug him, but at the same time she couldn't touch him. A vampire had bitten him. What did that make Seth?

"It's all cool, Bella. I'm in love."

Panic strummed her voice. "Because she has you under her control."

"Because she is the most perfect woman I have ever met. She makes me happy, and I make her happy. Now, I want to be sure you're safe tonight, so this ticket will go to someone else."

"No, I want to go to the show. I've written it on my calendar."

"Heaven forbid, Belladonna Reynolds wavers from her schedule," he mocked grandly.

"Seth! I'm not going to hide in the dark like a mushroom. I can deal with this. Maybe. After I've wrapped my head around it. Vampires? Really?"

"Yes, Bella, really."

"Right. Really." She tucked her forefinger in his jeans pocket, where she suspected he kept the ticket. "I want a ticket, Seth. Please? It'll be good for me to dance the night away and not think about other stuff."

He shoved a hand in the pocket and produced a Day-Glo green ticket and relented before she could take it. "Promise you'll take a cab to and from?"

"Maybe."

"Bella."

"The club is down the street, less than a mile. The street is well lit, and there are always clubbers and cars out well past midnight, so it's not like I'll be alone."

"Bella, among those clubbers are vampires. They are out there. And so are werewolves and demons and faeries and all other sorts."

"Oh, just stop, Seth. I haven't gotten sick yet, but you keep talking like you're such an expert on all those woo-woo things and I may hurl. Button up your shirt. I can't believe you'd let someone do that to you."

"Don't worry." He tossed her a charming wink as he tugged at his lapels. "She's very careful. If she took too much, I'd die."

"What?"

"That's not going to happen. She may even give me immortality. But that's my choice."

"You're not helping my need to hurl."

"Right. So tonight?"

"Is *she* going to be there?"

"Maybe. You want me to introduce you?"

Come face-to-face with another vampire after last night's adventure? "No."

"I understand." He lifted her hand and kissed the back of it. "So you should go shower again, and maybe once more before you go outside today."

"Why?"

"I'm thinking you can wash off whatever scent you were putting out last night. Or, I know, wear that sexy perfume you have, the one that smells like cloves."

"You think the werewolf will smell me from… anywhere?"

"Don't start to cry, Bellybean. I just think it would be a good precaution."

His hug felt great, yet at the moment Bella felt

her arms would never be able to grasp the reassurance she needed. Everything in her world had changed. How could she return to the cheery, stress-free, well-ordered life she enjoyed?

"Wh-what do werewolves do to people, Seth? I mean, if vampires suck blood, what about…"

"I'm not sure. They wolf out when the moon is full, I know that, which makes them into hairy creatures. Or so I've been told. I think they're real sex freaks, too. But again, it's only hearsay."

"Sex freaks," Bella muttered mindlessly. "When's the next full moon?"

"Couple weeks. Look, should I try to find out more info? Maybe I'll ask around if anyone knows a wolf in the area, see what you're dealing with."

She nodded. "That sounds good. But maybe it would be better to drop it all. Maybe he didn't like what he smelled."

Not judging by how he had groped her last night. And that kiss, so hard, and yet wanting. If she hadn't been freaked out of her gourd, she might have found it alluring.

An alluring werewolf?

"I think I do need another shower," she added.

Seth kissed her on the forehead. He was in entirely too good a mood after everything they'd just discussed.

Bella wondered if being bitten by a vampire released endorphins into the man's bloodstream. He had been extremely happy of late, so much so that she had briefly wondered if he'd been doing drugs. Seth was so against drugs, she'd not dared ask him about her theory.

The truth was worse than drugs.

"Come up and bang on the glass when you get to the club," he called as he strolled toward the door. "Love you, Bellybean!"

She waved him off and headed toward the shower.

What kind of scent had the wolf picked up from her? She'd been a sweaty mess last night.

And really, did she believe Seth's guess? The man had been a *man*. He wasn't a werewolf. Wouldn't he have seemed wolflike to her? Although, he had a beard and lots of hair…

"No, he wasn't. Couldn't be," she said as she turned on the shower.

But if she could buy the vampire bit, that meant she had to get on board with the werewolves, too.

Chapter 3

The music pummeling the innards of club Silver leaked through the open back doors. Graffiti scrawled across the brick walls had gotten a recent freshening up, and the bold colors glowed in the night.

A small group who couldn't gain access danced in the lot behind the elite club. The bouncers kept watch but seemed to approve. It was this way every evening. The management was even considering serving drinks outside to the unchosen.

Severo paused at the front corner of the three-story brick building to watch the line out front as some were gifted admission and others slunk away, pouting, yet determined to return another day for another go at admittance. The back-lot dancers were too gauche for those who wished entry through the front.

Slipping a hand in the pocket of his brown leather jacket, he tried to catch a few words of the song, but the beat was about all he could discern. Didn't matter. He wasn't a fan of the erratic music the clubs played. Lynyrd Skynyrd was more his speed. But he did like the atmosphere. The noise and crush of bodies put him out of his thoughts and into a mindless place where nothing really mattered.

But until he entered the club, he was anything but mindless.

He strolled down the front avenue and noted the black stretch limo parked across the street. Vamps, no doubt. They scoured the clubs, but in a subtle send-out-the-troops manner that brought potentials back to the horde. The higher-ranking vampires couldn't be bothered to go inside and mingle with the lesser humans.

Nasty longtooths. Severo hated them all, save a select few with whom he had the opportunity to establish trusting relationships over the decades.

The August air stirred a frenzy of gasoline, heat-softened tarmac, spilled booze, cat piss and perfume. When so many odors combined, he could easily acclimate and move above them, so to speak.

They faded into the background as murk, allowing distinctive scents to rise.

One scent in particular surfaced. It was familiar, rich and enticing. He'd gotten but a taste of it, and he wanted more.

The shivery little rabbit who had fled the vampires and run right into his arms. She had seeped into him on an intoxicating cocktail of fear, adrenaline and—though she would deny it— arousal. Sweet, she still lingered on his tongue and in the pores of his flesh.

Bowing his head and marching forward, Severo gained entrance to Silver with a mere nod to the bouncers.

Seth spun Jayne's latest diatribe against the tabloids; she was the current "it" girl on the techno- funk scene. The crowd bounced, shimmied and jumped on the stainless-steel dance floor beneath epileptic-fit-inducing strobe lights.

Bella pushed her way down the entrance ramp, hung with thick black velvet curtains, and weighed the chances of getting up to the DJ's box. The dance floor was body to body. Seth was in his groove, fists pumping and head bopping. But she did manage to catch his attention with a quick wave.

She needed this night to lose herself in the loud

music and redirect her thoughts from other things. Things that had stabbed at her brain all afternoon. She was still shocked at Seth's confession. But tonight it was all good.

As soon as she sipped her first cosmopolitan.

The shortest route to refreshment was straight across the dance floor. Finding the beat seductive, Bella slinked her way into the crowd. Ballroom and flamenco might be her preferences, but she could shake it with the best of them.

She inched her red spangled skirt up at her thigh and shimmied before a sexy dancer. He matched her move with a suggestive shake of his shoulders. It was all in fun. And man, did his teeth sparkle.

Spinning, Bella insinuated herself between two women. They bumped their hips to hers and that made Bella laugh. She raised her arms above her head and decided the drink could wait. Surrendering to the beat took her to a great place.

Masculine hands stretched down her arms, and she rotated her hips. Together she and Mr. White Teeth rocked in a wide circle. It was overtly sexual, but she didn't feel the threat level she had last night. Even the flutter of fingertips tracing the swinging hem of her short skirt didn't offend her.

She was in control here. No one was going to chase her or try to take advantage of her. Not unless

she wished it. And she would never ask to be controlled. Control was hers. Her life didn't function
without it. And tonight she intended to take it back.

No wonder Seth was always so naturally high.
Music did something to people. It moved them
beyond the norm and opened their hearts and minds,
even their souls. It was why Bella had navigated her
way back to dancing after a five-year absence.

The smell of alcohol, something fruity like green
apples, reminded her that she did have a goal.
Dancing her way through the crowd, Bella spied an
empty space at the bar and slid onto the slick silver
plastic seat.

She knew the bartender and smiled at him. He
shot her an acknowledging wink and set about
making her "usual."

This club served the best cosmopolitans, and no,
Bella did not have *Sex and the City* dreams of
landing Mr. Big and wearing designer shoes. She
was happy with her job as a Web site designer. And
while she liked sexy spike heels, she'd take a
healthy relationship with a stable man over Manolos
any day.

The bartender slid a shimmery pink drink into
her grasp and shook his hand at the dollar bills she
laid on the counter. "First one's free for you, Bella."

Cool. She'd take a free drink any day.

The cosmo was sweet with a bite of sour. Crossing her legs and twisting to watch the dancers, she shifted her shoulders to the rhythm.

Behind a Plexiglas barrier, Seth danced and pumped his fist to the tunes he delivered to the masses. He spiked his hair on the nights he DJ'd, and it went a long way in transforming his usual emo look.

Dating a vampire?

You're not going to think about it, Bella. Have another drink.

She was about to signal the bartender when he placed another pink drink before her. Pleased he was keeping an eye on her needs, Bella tossed him a wink. But when she dug in her purse for cash, a thickly veined, dark-haired hand slid a five-dollar bill onto the bar.

Heat prickled the back of Bella's neck.

A husky male voice whispered, "Told you I'd find you."

Chapter 4

He had found her. In seconds her heart reached Mach speed, and she choked on her drink. The bartender spun a look at her, and she gave him a silly smile and a shrug.

Though she didn't dare turn to look at the man, she recognized his familiar scent. That deep, earthy odor that was also sweet. What kind of kook had she become that now she was scenting out people like some kind of… *No, he can't be.*

The person next to her vacated her stool, much to Bella's dread. The man didn't slide onto it but inserted himself between the empty stool and her body. A strong, muscled thigh pulsed against her bare thigh. The spangles on her skirt pressed into her flesh.

"How did you find me?" she asserted.

"I followed you. From your home."

"From my—" He knew where she lived? "Please leave, or I'll get a bouncer and tell him you were threatening me."

"You won't do that." He reached for her drink and sniffed it. "That's how you smelled last night. Vodka and cranberries. You women and your pretty pink drinks. But your scent is different today. Lots of perfume." He sniffed at the air before her. "Cloves. Did you think to hide your natural scent from me?"

"Yes. No." Bella grasped her throat, so aware of her low-cut neckline. He'd noticed, as well. "I'm not comfortable talking to you."

"Good. I like a woman who is honest. And I'd hate it if you were one of those who hung on any man who will give you the time of day."

She pressed her hand on the cocktail napkin and inched up the wet edge. She was supposed to be safe here.

Bella looked aside. Seth was so close. Was he keeping an eye on her? A trio of scantily clad women danced before the DJ's box. Seth's mind was probably not on his best friend.

"Look at me," prompted the man who was sort of her rescuer. "Let me look at you. I could only imagine how gorgeous you were last night in the darkness."

She glanced at him and found his warm brown eyes. They were dark yet softer than they'd been in the moonlight. Not threatening. Even attractive.

"Your eyes are bright," he said.

Bella shifted her glance away.

To look into the man's eyes felt like complying with a request. And she didn't want to give him that boon.

You're in control of your own life, remember?

"You're not shy." Even amid the din she heard his low voice perfectly, as if they stood in a column of air set apart from the crowd. "Talk to me."

Hold conversation with a man who frightened her? Never. But she had to know…

"So are you really a—"

"A what?"

Still unwilling to meet his gaze, she toyed with the stem of her goblet. "My friend told me about vampires and how they really exist. And then he guessed you might be a werewolf." She whispered the word, as if she were swearing in church.

"Very clever, your friend. Is he the one in the box that you waved to when you first came in?"

"Have you been watching me?"

"Yes." The bartender stopped before the man. "Budweiser," he ordered. "So, you've recovered from your jogging adventure, I see. Wearing sexy sequins and flirting with men out on the dance floor? One would think you weren't so much traumatized by being chased as perhaps aroused."

"Bug off, creep."

She slid off the stool to find an escape, and as luck would have it, a path parted on the dance floor. The beat picked up and the entire crowd bounced, raising their hands over their heads.

Bella turned. Through the sea of waving arms, she saw no sign of the man. Or werewolf. Or whatever he was. Had she imagined speaking to him?

No, she could still feel the intrusion of his thigh against hers. Hot, solid, powerful. He'd marked her with his heat.

"Don't be stupid, Bella," she told herself.

She shuffled her way through the dance floor, intent on reaching the hallway that led to the back door and her escape.

She reached the ladies' room door just as a tall man in a leather jacket stepped before her and clutched her forearm. She hadn't noticed his clothing before. Just his presence. How did she shake this guy?

"You're in danger if you remain here," he said.

"No kidding? I'm in danger from you. Let me go."

He released her arm and put up his hands as if to say "I'll back off."

But he didn't back off. And though Bella could not see over his shoulder, she knew escape was but a dash away.

A couple of dark-haired men brushed roughly by her, and she had to lunge closer to the man to not get her feet stepped on.

"Vampires," he said close by her ear. "They're tracking you again."

"You don't know that."

"What? That they're vamps? Or that they're following you? They've had their eyes on you since you sashayed through the front doorway. What did you do to piss off the vamps?"

"Nothing. I didn't know they existed until last night. Now would you back off?"

"If I leave now, you're vampire prey. You want that? Fine."

He stepped around her. He favored one leg with a slight hitch. Within a few strides, he blended into the darkness.

His menacing presence gone, Bella could breathe now. The air in her personal space cooled.

She eyed the back door. The two *alleged*

vampires loomed before the doorway. Their eyes didn't glow. They didn't flash fangs. Besides the matching black business suits and slicked hair, they passed for average human men.

Over her shoulder and ten feet away, her self-assigned protector held his hand out to her.

Pressing a hand to her chest, Bella realized her heart was pounding. Yet it wasn't music pummeling her insides; it was fear. So much excitement in two days would surely put her over the edge. Could a person OD on adrenaline?

The men at the door crossed their arms before them, their gazes fixed on her.

What kind of horror movie had she stumbled into?

Now she had two choices: take her chances walking by two vampires or put her trust in a man she couldn't be sure wasn't as bad as the other two.

She remembered what Seth had said. *Vampires bite. Werewolves are sex freaks.*

Choosing the lesser of two evils, Bella stepped quickly and slapped her hand into her self-assigned protector's palm. He tugged her down the hallway. When they reached the main room, he pressed her against the stainless-steel wall.

"I am what your friend guesses. Does that frighten you?"

"Listen, buddy, the only thing that frightens me

about you is your need to shove your hard-on against my thigh. Give it a break, will you? I just took your hand to get away from those vampires. Now I'll be on my way."

"You need me to walk you out of here. There are vamps outside, parked across the street. Do you want to take a chance they are interested in you?"

"What is going on? What did I do? Twenty-four hours ago, you...you *people* didn't exist. And then my best friend tells me he's dating some vampire chick, and isn't at all surprised when I tell him I've seen three of them. And you're a freaking wolf?"

"I am a man. I only wolf out during the full moon, and I'll thank you to call it correctly."

Again he did that strange sniffing thing before her face.

Now Bella was getting angry. "Stop it. You're acting like a wolf, so I'm going to call you one. I'll have you know I don't like dogs."

He flinched, as if attempting to hold off a snarl. What? He didn't like being called a dog? *Then take a hike, buddy.*

Softening his expression, he shook his head, admonishing. "Just know that between me and those longtooths eyeing you up and down, I'm the one who won't feast on your blood."

"Yeah? What *do* you do? Shake me around like

a chew toy? Oh, mercy, I can't do this anymore. I have to leave."

"Let me escort you. This way."

Again he held out his hand for her to accept. Bella stared at the offering. This was so wrong. Much as she liked horror movies, she preferred romance and comedy and happily-ever-after. And she never left noisy bars with strangers.

"I'll hail a cab," she said but took the man's hand.

He led her toward the front door. "If you want to wait for a cab, that's your choice. But I beg your trust to allow me to escort you home. It's not as though I don't know where you live."

At the reminder Bella's world began to swirl.

He squeezed her hand. "Don't faint on me, sweet. Come."

The rush of air as the door opened smacked her to reality. He tugged on her hand, and she merely followed, moving around the waiting line of hopefuls.

The street was busy with passing headlights. The werewolf tugged Bella close to the wall and they walked along it. He walked with a slight limp, as if he favored one leg. When they had reached the end of the block, not far from the end of the line of waiting hopefuls, the man slowed.

"So your friend is dating a vamp? Did he mention her name?"

"No," she answered. "I don't know anything. And for that matter, I don't have your name. If you're going to stalk me, it would be good to have a name to give the cops."

He smirked and drew her close, more as a means to allow others to pass by as they headed for the line. "Severo," he said. "And you are Bella."

"What? Are you psychic, too?"

"I heard the bartender use it. See the limo?"

A shiny black stretch was parked five car lengths down from the club entrance. Dark windows did not reveal passengers.

"Vamps," he said. "And if my guess is correct, it's Elvira."

"You are so kidding me. Not the mistress of the dark?"

His smirk didn't touch mirth. "Her name is Evie, but I call her Elvira because she fits the cliché to a T. If she's the one your friend is dating, you may as well write his eulogy now. I wonder…"

"His eulogy?"

Again he shoved her against the wall.

"I'm getting so sick of you pushing me around." But as before, she was unable to wriggle free from his powerful grip.

Their noses touched when he leaned in. "How close are you and your friend?"

"Me and Seth?" Talk about intense eyes. They were deep brown but alive with wonder as he held her gaze. Not so much menacing as…attractive. "We've been friends for a long time. We're best buds."

"Any reason for Elvira to believe you two have been getting it on?"

"No! Seth is like a brother to me."

"Do you two hug and hold hands?"

"Why?"

"I think you may have pissed off the wrong vampiress. My wager says those vamps after you last night were sent by Elvira. And she's seeing you now. Give her a glance over my shoulder. Let her know you see her."

Bella dared a look at the limo again. Knowing now that there might be a vampire woman sitting inside, staring at her, lifted her anxiety level to a new high.

"Good girl," Severo cooed. "Now, we'll give the mistress of the night reason to believe you've no interest in that pasty human who spins discs in the club."

"How—"

He kissed her. And he manhandled her. Severo's hand slid up her thigh, raising her skirt. He pulled her against his body as he'd done last night. But this kiss wasn't as violent, only insistent and claiming.

Did he want to show the vampire woman across

the street that Bella was his? This wasn't what she
wanted. No matter who watched.

"Wait a second." She pushed against his chest—
it was firm, solid—but he wouldn't be dissuaded.

"One more, sweet. Give the curious vampire
bitch a show, or you'll have vamps on your tail for
longer than you wish."

"But I don't—" *Want to kiss you* didn't come out.
Because the protest didn't feel right. Did she want
him to kiss her? "This isn't going to work."

"Worth a try. This time open your mouth for me,
Bella. I want to taste that cosmo again. I think I may
develop a liking for them."

"You're a jerk," she said on a gasp.

"A jerk who's trying to protect your pretty little
ass."

With a protest stuck in her throat, he snuck his
tongue into her mouth. Before she could weigh the
possibilities of biting it, Bella found herself
reacting to the powerful and disturbing intrusion by
pulling him closer and matching his tongue dance
with her own.

God, this was so wrong. He was a stranger. He
could be dangerous. He wasn't even *human*.

But he could kiss.

He held her possessively, one arm behind her
back, his strong fingers splayed down to cup her

hip. Another hand caressed her torso, right up under her breast. He wasn't about to allow her to lead, and that should bother her, but it didn't.

"So sweet," he muttered into her mouth. "My Bella."

Okay, wait. The kiss was acceptable. But claiming her as his own?

"Let's go." He ended the kiss so abruptly, Bella thought he might have heard her crazy thoughts. He tugged her along, leading the way.

"You think Elvira got the hint?" she wondered breathlessly.

"Doubt it. Vamps are stupid, blood-hungry animals."

"And you're not?"

He swung her to an abrupt stop at the intersection, though the light was green. "I am not an animal."

"But you confirmed that you're a werewolf."

"Three days a month I howl at the moon, and yes, then I become an animal. But the other twenty-seven or twenty-eight days, I am a man. Got that?"

"Yep." She was not going to argue with anything that could howl at the moon and change into an animal, no matter how few days a month. "You don't like vampires much, do you?"

"I despise them."

Bella followed his swift pace across the street in time to beat the light. "I can walk by myself. I mean, I know where I'm going. You don't need to pull me."

He let go of her arm, and Bella walked faster, ahead of him. Normally she loved the sound of her heels marking her steps, but now they only reminded her how desperate this situation could become. Because if she thought she would be safe once she arrived home—accompanied by a werewolf—she must be ten kinds of crazy.

He whistled lowly, a satisfied sound. A comment on her back view, likely. She slowed to walk side by side. He did not meet her eyes, but she swore he wore a smirk.

So the man did have a soul. Maybe.

She flat-out asked him. "Do you have a soul?"

"That's an odd question."

"No more odd than your being a werewolf."

"Perhaps it is you, a human, who is the odd one. Yes, I do have a soul."

"Good. I mean, whatever. Do vampires have souls?"

"Yes. But they don't see their reflections."

They arrived at the door to her building, a three-story walk-up. Bella owned the upper loft. It was set into a hill, so her third level led out to the patio and the pool in her backyard.

"Here we are," he offered.

"Yes, I suppose you know that. I suppose every vampire in the city now knows, too."

"Exactly." He opened the door and strode into the foyer. "Which is why I'm seeing you right up to your door."

He knew she lived on the third floor? Dread curdled her saliva.

"I, uh, I don't think so. I'm fine now. I can lock this outer door after you leave. Just go, please?"

Stoic and determined, he stood on the bottom step. He was a head taller than her—and she was wearing four-inch heels. Broad shoulders squared the bruised leather jacket and caught his long, mussed brown hair, which looked clean but not combed. His dark beard was trimmed close and a mustache framed his mouth.

Bella didn't want to look at his mouth too long. She knew the feel of it. And it wasn't something she should be thinking about if she wanted to make the guy leave.

He splayed out his hands, but it wasn't a surrendering move. The man wasn't going anywhere.

"Fine." Bella marched past him, up the first few stairs, but stopped. "You go first."

"I prefer to bring up the tail. Easier to keep an eye out for intruders that way."

"But they could be lurking up ahead."

"I don't smell any," he answered plainly.

Bella sighed heavily, turned and marched up the stairs. So he was staring at her backside. She should appreciate the attention, but despite the wonderful kiss, it made her crawly.

Her mother had drilled the whole stranger-danger routine into her brain when she was a child.

So why had she taken a new route last night? It was as though she'd been looking for danger.

And she had found it. Rather, it had found her.

Now to get rid of it.

Sticking the key in her door lock, she decided too late that she should have waited. The man pushed the door open and prowled inside.

"I didn't invite you in. Now you're going beyond a protective walk home, and entering without permission. I thought you sorts needed permission to cross a threshold."

"'You sorts'?" He smirked and strode to the center of her living room, his limp more apparent now with the lights on. "Just the vamps, sweet. I can cross any threshold I like. Nice place. If a bit junglelike."

The loft had an open floor plan, the living room, kitchen and bedroom all open to share one huge room. Admittedly Bella had gone overboard with the plants, but she liked that they kept the air clean.

Severo's gaze followed the long white chiffon drape that hung from the cathedral ceiling to the floor, separating the living room from the bedroom at the far end.

Observing the wide planter with the massive blooming cactus, he strode to the patio doors and tapped the glass. "A pool, too?"

"Yep, living the high life. So, if you'll leave, I'll lock the door behind you and get out my garlic. I have a cross on the wall there that I can use in a pinch. So you see? I'm sure I'll be fine."

Bella kicked off her shoes and leaned against the kitchen counter. She wiggled her pinched toes, but her focus was not on comfort. The drawer with a butcher knife inside was a leap away.

"You won't be fine." He approached her so swiftly, the fear rose in her body and Bella felt it flush her cheeks. "They'll watch you all night."

"You don't know that."

"If my suspicions are correct, Elvira won't rest until she's satisfied."

"Meaning?"

"She must want you dead, or at the least, injured, if she believes you a threat to her latest snack."

"Seth is not a snack."

He backed her against the granite kitchen counter with an arm to either side of her. She should be getting used to his urgent obsession for uncomfortable closeness, but it still made her nervous. The plastic clicks of her skirt spangles made the situation slightly strange. His size made her feel small.

But she couldn't deny her interest in this overwhelming, in-your-face man who wouldn't take no for an answer.

"No human can ever be anything more than a snack to a vampire. Unless she turns him."

"Turns? You mean makes him a vampire? Oh my God, can she do that? Will he know?"

"He'll know. But he'll be too infatuated to protest." He dipped his head and ran his nose along her neck.

"Stop it. I want you to leave."

"Make me."

Bella swung her arm up and slapped the man hard across the cheek. The sound of flesh to flesh echoed sharply. He reared back, shook his head and delivered her a leering grin.

"Try it again," he challenged coolly. "Come, Bella, raise my ire. Stir my blood."

This time he caught her hand before it connected with his cheek. Gripping her wrist, he licked her palm from fleshy base to quivering fingertips. And behind the lascivious act, he grinned again.

"By now you should know your fear excites me, sweet."

"Don't call me that. I don't want you here. Can't you understand that?" Bella's glance to the phone, which was too far away, by the couch, stoked him to action.

He pressed a palm over her throat. Bella feared he might become violent. Finally he would do what he wanted to do last night. Why had she allowed him inside the building?

Because she really was worried about the vampires.

His eyes were so intense, they stilled her. She could only gasp as he slid his hand to the red spangled neckline. His thumb slipped behind the fabric and over the top of her breast.

The sound he made was sexy and wanting, a moan for something he desired but wouldn't take. Clinging to the counter, Bella reacted to the illicit touch with a whimper of her own.

"Bella," he whispered as he moved nose to nose with her. "You want my touch?"

She shook her head. A squeeze of his fingers rocketed a delicious twinge of pleasure from her breast to her belly and down to her loins.

"Then remove my hand. Push it away."

She grabbed his wrist with both hands but didn't move it. And in her pause, he bent to kiss the top of her breast while he massaged the nipple with his fingers.

She craved the way he made her feel. The dangerous aura of his presence. The uncertainty of what he would say or do to her next. The erratic pace of her heart was caused by fear and a discomfiting desire.

"Please," she whispered. What had he said his name was? "S-Severo. It's…not right."

"What? A man you just met touching you like this? I told you to take my hand away. And then I'll leave."

"No, you…" *You're a werewolf!* Why did that bother her more than being touched so intimately? "Please just go. I can't do this. I'm too freaked right now."

"I understand." His hand slid up to her neck again, and Bella regretted the lost touch at her breast. "I'll leave, but I won't go far. I'm keeping watch tonight."

"Fine," she said, not because she approved, but because she wanted him gone so she could be alone with her crazy self.

He opened the door and turned to her, but he didn't say anything. Dark, glittering eyes held her in his grasp. Right there, still under his thumb.

"Thank you," she said. "For looking out for me."

"You've fixed yourself to my senses, Bella. I can't get you out of my head. And I don't wish to. Sleep well."

He closed the door and Bella collapsed over the counter, her arms stretched out and her cheek smushed against the cool granite.

"Vampires and werewolves? Oh, my."

Chapter 5

Following a long shower, Bella padded through
the loft and switched off all the lights. The streetlights out front always cast a yellow streak across
the floor. Tonight it comforted her.

After her encounter at Silver and her unnecessary
escort home, she couldn't hit the bed fast enough.
But on the way, she stopped before the window and
tugged aside the blue chiffon sheer.

The connection of gazes startled her, but she
didn't turn away. Severo sat across the street on a
bus-stop bench, staring up at her. Her own personal
security guard.

Or her own personal stalker.

Who was a werewolf.

She should be horrified, but to be honest, all she could feel was relief.

She looked but didn't find any vampires lurking in the trees in the park across the street. Not that she would know what they were, anyway. Nevertheless, if they were out there, she was glad to have a protector on the beat.

Bella woke to sunshine. Because it was the weekend, she had all day to wonder over her strange new world.

"I have to call Seth."

She started for the phone but paused by the window to look across the street. The bench was empty. Vampires didn't do daylight, so her protector had left.

How could she be so accepting and calm? she wondered as she picked up the receiver and hit speed dial. Because she had proof.

Sunnyside Belladonna, Seth often called her when he wasn't addressing her as Bellybean. Always willing to see the good, even when standing amidst a muck of bad. And if shown the truth? She believed it. It was a waste of time to deny what she'd witnessed.

"Seth, how are you?"

"It's freakin' ten o'clock, Bella. How do you think I'm doing?"

"You're usually up by eight. Oh, no, are you no longer a morning person because of your girlfriend?"

"Can we have this discussion later?"

"Fine, but we do need to have it. Severo said something last night that makes me wonder about your girlfriend. I'm scared for you, Seth."

"Severo? Who in hell— Is that your werewolf?"

"He's not *my* werewolf."

"Yeah? Well, don't start sucking face with the guy. I've always imagined you walking down the aisle someday with a *mortal* man. And you know how scared you are of dogs."

"Tell me about it."

She had mapped out her jogging routes specifically to avoid any houses with dogs behind fences. Big dogs, little dogs, didn't matter. She didn't like any of them. Rather, it wasn't a question of dislike, but a real fear.

"Listen, Bella, let's meet at the Moonstone at six, okay?"

It was their favorite restaurant and was a few miles down the strip. "Deal. I'll see you later. Last one there picks up the check."

A brisk swim was in order. Releasing the latch

on the patio door, she slid it open to the gorgeous summer day. Birds chirped and the grass was so green, it belonged in a cartoon. Everything seemed right. Truly, she must have dreamed the world doing an upside-down flip.

Padding outside in her undies and T-shirt, Bella never worried that anyone would see. The six-foot-high fence, and the fact that she lived at the top of a hill, guaranteed privacy. And the first- and second-floor owners had but a view of the street on the other side of the building.

Tugging up her shirt, she stopped halfway over her ribs when something jumped the fence.

He landed deftly, one hand to the ground in a predatory pose. With a smirk, he noted Bella's jumpy reaction. Severo rose, stretching back his shoulders. He utterly dominated the small back-yard.

Her protector had returned.

Bella tugged her shirt down to her thighs to cover her spare pink underwear. She could make a run for it, but he'd probably beat her to the door. Then he'd crush her barely clad body against his and kiss her and—

"Good morning, sweet." Severo strolled to the padded lounge chair angled by the pool and sat. Stretching out his legs, he twined his fingers behind his head, though the leather jacket and biker boots were hardly pool wear. "Nice day for a swim. Don't let me interrupt. You were set on skinny-dipping?"

"Why are you here?"

"Still on the beat."

"But the vampires don't come out during the day."

"You're right. Truth is, I wanted one last look at you before leaving."

"Well, you've seen me. Now you can go."

"Your tits look great in that thin shirt. Makes me want to suck them."

She crossed her arms high over her chest. As crude as the comment had been, she lifted her chin and looked down through her lashes at him. He liked her breasts?

Stupid, Bella. You're playing with fire. This one is different than most men, who can tease without promising anything more.

His eyes strayed lower. It was either hug her arms across her breasts or hold the shirt down.

Bella decided to walk down the three steps and sit at the pool's edge. The water crept through her underwear and wet the hem of her shirt. The man's intent gaze hardened her nipples.

She plunged in. There. Now he couldn't see anything.

"I'm not going to perform for you," she said,

frog-stroking through the water, "so you may as well leave. Go home and get some sleep."

"You are insistent that I leave you. And after I've done you two favors."

"Two?"

"Saving your life and keeping said life safe. So I think you owe me at least a chat. Aren't you at all interested in learning more about me?"

Treading where the water dipped to eight feet, she eyed him curiously. Yes, she did want to know more. Like how he was able to track her merely by scent. Like why he felt that he had some kind of God-given right to intrude on her life.

Also, why it was that she couldn't simply call the cops and have him arrested.

And why was it that she found him more attractive today, in full daylight, than she had last night in the dark? He was still scruffy and unkempt. The beard and long hair framed his dark gaze and bold features. The look didn't so much say "Protector" as it screamed "Dangerous."

Ignoring her erratic thoughts, she dove forward and did an underwater somersault. Surfacing, she spewed water and slicked back her hair. The water refreshed her. Now, if she didn't have an audience, she would get naked.

"All I want to know is why you keep coming back."

"Like I said, you've stuck yourself to my senses. I can't shake you. So if I can't ignore the pretty woman, then I may as well enjoy her."

She flipped him off and did another deep dive. Touching bottom, she wished for the magical ability to breathe underwater. Not that it would make him leave. He'd probably dive in and try to rescue her.

Coming up, Bella found him squatting near the pool's edge. Why did that not surprise her? Had flipping him the bird angered him? She'd like to see him jump in, leather jacket, big, clunky leather boots and all, and try to wrestle her into submission now.

After abandoning dancing in high school, she'd joined the swim team to fill that need for movement and to physically challenge her muscles. She'd won a few medals for her back crawl and high dives. She could so take the guy if he were in the pool.

But thank God he was not.

Swimming backward, Bella landed at the opposite side. She stretched her arms along the tiled edge. If he was going to stare at her, she could do the same.

A trim brown beard traced his jaw, and stubble darkened the front and sides of his neck. Dark chest hair peeked out at the top of his shirt. Long brown hair topped off the deviant look. Talk about hairy. Made sense if he was a werewolf.

She'd never dated a man with chest hair or a beard. The look didn't attract her. And she had no intention of changing her preference now.

"Ask me," he prompted.

"Ask you what?"

"The question that burns in your bewitching green eyes. I'm not going anywhere, so you might as well make the best of it. There's nothing threatening about conversation."

Her legs floated to the surface, and Bella flicked her big toes, scattering droplets across the water's surface. "All right. If vampires suck blood from humans, what is it a werewolf does?"

"With humans?"

"Yes."

He clasped his strong, wide hands together between his bent legs, focusing across the horizon above and behind her. "We avoid them mostly. The less contact we have with the mortal race, the better. If humans haven't got proof of our existence, then you understand how much easier it is to survive?"

"I'll buy that. So why the continued contact with me? I'm a human. I have proof of your existence."

"I've already explained that."

"Right. You have my scent bouncing about inside your nose and can't shake it off. Peachy. So what about those three days around the full moon you mentioned?"

"In this human form I am called a were. *Were* means 'man,' you know? Then there is the wolf form, which is the caninelike animal most humans associate with wolves. The werewolf is the man and wolf combined. Understand?"

She nodded. The creature lesson was fascinating, in a stomach-curdling way. Shape-shifting and blood and fangs were not her idea of a good time, unless they were up on the big screen.

"During the full moon, the werewolf takes over as the moon peaks in the sky. All it can think to do is mate."

"Mate?"

"Have sex."

"With another werewolf?"

"If one is available. The female of our breed is rare. Which makes for a lot of frustrated males."

"They don't…try to mate with humans?"

"In werewolf form I should scare the shit out of you. Of course, during the day, when I take were form, as you see me now, I'm also horny as hell for those three days. That's when humans come in handy."

"I see." Seth's theory on the sex-freak thing was true. "So you basically live to have sex?"

"I live. And I have sex. They are two different functions, not dependent upon one another. But yes, I do like to have sex."

Yeah, she did, too. With humans. And at *her* pleasure, not on demand or forced because the moon was full.

"Would you have raped me the other night?"

"Never." A strong, sure answer. He tilted his chin up and met her gaze. "But I cannot deny I wanted you."

Bella peered into her reflection on the water's surface. "I know that."

She had sensed his want. Discussing it now, in a simple poolside chat, was strange, but that didn't dissuade her from seeking answers. "You don't have a girlfriend? I mean a werewolf girlfriend?"

"I've never had a mate."

"So you've not ever…"

"Not in complete werewolf form, no. And if we continue to discuss my sex life, I may have to strip down and swim over there. Being near you arouses me, Bella."

"I'd say that's good reason for you to leave."

"Make me."

Again with the bold challenge. She considered swishing a wave of water at him. Like that would deter the big, bad wolf. "What keeps back werewolves?"

He removed his jacket and tossed it on the lounge chair behind him. The black cotton shirt he wore stretched across his chest and shoulders, revealing powerful biceps.

"Silver. It must penetrate and enter the bloodstream, though. You can't simply press a silver spoon against my head and expect me to sizzle and burst into bits."

"So you don't eat people?"

"You must have watched *An American Werewolf in London.*"

"I saw an old video when I was a teenager. I'll never forget that scene with the dead girl and her throat ripped out."

"That's not going to happen. Unless you've tormented my kind, or are deserving of just punishment. Vampires are more likely to maul and kill humans than my breed will."

"That's weird, because I'd think the one closer to an animal would be more likely to do the mauling stuff."

"It hurts me when you label me an animal."

His confession stunned her. Men didn't reveal their feelings. Not most.

Sure, he looked like a man now. But he wasn't. Not really. And he'd explained he could be a *real* wolf. That was about as animal as a guy could get.

"May I join you?"

"Do dogs swim?"

"I am not a dog. I'm a wolf. And get that straight."

He began to unlace his heavy boots.

Dare she invite him in? That damned piercing gaze of his would not relent. Something about the challenge he pressed upon her excited her. And if she were the one to do the inviting, then she would still be in control.

"You're not going to leave until you've touched me, are you?"

"So quickly you learn my manner. I like that about you, Bella. Even as your heart races with fear, you aren't afraid to meet the next challenge. And no, I don't intend to leave until I've at least been allowed to stroke your soft skin."

Mmm, a stroke sounded nice. Romantic.

Bella's elbows slipped from the pool's edge, and she kicked to stay above water.

This was wrong. So wrong. And yet, part of her thrummed with anticipation. The man was growing on her. He wasn't shockingly handsome or charming, but something about his aggressively gentle approach intrigued her.

"Come on, then, but keep your distance."

He tugged the T-shirt over his head, revealing an

abdomen that would have made an abs instructor whimper. He kicked off his boots, and he unzipped and tugged down his black jeans.

"Keep your skivvies on," she said when he stood before her in nothing but black boxer briefs.

"Fair enough."

Damn, he was a sight. Powerful thighs and legs pulsed with his movement. The cut muscles on his abdomen emphasized square hips. The dark boxer briefs did little to disguise his erection. Bella had never seen someone so appealing, so utterly powerful and intriguing.

He jumped in, splashing her with his grand entrance. Coming up in the center of the pool, he treaded water and shook his head, spattering water across her face. "This is heated. Nice."

"Really nice on a cool evening."

"In the nude?"

"Only when I'm alone. So wolves can swim?"

"Faster than you, so don't get any ideas."

Right. Not safe, Bella. Don't forget that.

"You're all about the he-man stuff, aren't you? Me Tarzan, you Jane. You know that's not attractive to most women."

"You like it," he said with confidence.

"I do not."

"You're aroused right now, sweet."

"Don't call me that. You have no right to give me a pet name. And if you think I'm aroused because my nipples are hard, it's only because the water—"

"Is warm." His prideful grin told her he'd scored the point on that one.

Okay, so she was a little turned on. His incredible body, rippling with muscle, went a long way in making him more human and real. And while she wasn't attracted to the hairy look, she couldn't deny a hunger for some washboard abs.

He swam closer and Bella held her position at the edge. She'd let him approach and see what he had in mind this time around. If he kissed her, she would accept it, but she was asking for more than a mere kiss, and she knew it.

"So you haven't called the police?" He treaded water a couple feet from her but did not drift closer.

"Like they'd believe me. Hey, three vampires chased me, and now I've got a werewolf stalker. Send help right away!"

"You make light of it, but I know you're frightened, Bella. You needn't be scared of me."

"You insist on manhandling me every chance you get without asking my permission. What about that treatment should make me unafraid?"

"Again, you want it more than you know. I don't smell fear on you now. And though curiosity has no scent, I'd wager that is what you're feeling. You're curious about me. About us."

She was about to say "There is no us," but that was too easy. Instead, Bella lifted her leg and toed his chest, pushing him back about a foot. "Stay. Good boy."

The water rushed up around her face and into her mouth with his swift approach. He put her up against the tiled wall. Bella choked on swallowed water.

"Stop with the dog comments," he said. A low, throaty growl followed.

"All right, I'm sorry. Let me go. You're so damned sensitive."

"I want you to know the way of things." He positioned his body along the length of hers and dipped his head over hers, forcing her to look up at his face. "I will strike out against cruelty and wrongs, no matter who is responsible. But I can be kind to those I consider friends."

"You strike out…? What does that mean? Are you some kind of werewolf avenger?"

He chuffed a breath beside her cheek. "You think me an animal simply because I react to the way I am drawn to you?"

"I'm not trying to draw you. Hell, I just want you to leave."

"You don't want that, or else you wouldn't have

invited me into the pool. Oh, Bella." He nuzzled aside her cheek and kissed her water-slicked hairline. A shiver tickled her neck. "Why did you come into my life?"

"As I recall, I wasn't looking for a friend the other night. I was running for my life."

"You run often. Your body is sleek and gorgeously muscled."

"I'm a dancer."

"Yes, you looked right at home last night in the club."

His closeness warmed the blood in her veins. Had someone lit a fire beneath the cauldron?

"I—I prefer ballroom and flamenco, but any kind will get me moving."

"Being tailed by vampires gets you moving, as well. Will you let me kiss you?"

"Now you have the consideration to ask first?"

He lifted her chin so she could not look away from him. A tenderness she did not expect to find softened his gaze. He was a real man. A man who could be hurt with inconsiderate words and be tempted to rescue her at the first scent of danger.

A man she wanted to kiss.

Bella leaned forward. Water slopped around her shoulders and his chest. Their lips, wet and soft, pressed, then parted with the wavery ripples. The hairs on his chest slicked to dark silk under her exploring fingers. A sinus-clearing bite of chlorine entered her mouth as she parted her lips to push her tongue into his.

Yes, she moved in first. It was inevitable. The exotic being who held her invited the dangerous exploration.

She wrapped her legs about his hips. Severo moaned appreciatively and coaxed her to fit herself against the landscape of muscles ridging his torso.

They bobbed backward in the water, folded in an embrace. He steered them toward the steps until Bella's feet touched bottom and she was able to balance.

Kissing this man was like drawing air. It was a need, a natural act, something she required more and more of. The rough beard, wet under her fingers, teased, and she slid her palms down his neck and gripped hanks of his hair to keep his mouth on hers.

Severo's fingers glided up her thigh and over her behind, clutching, squeezing. The thin undies were but soaked tissue over her flesh. Every move he made was possessive, inciting. Bella fed his want with murmurs and small movements until she lay on top of his body, stretched out across the half-submerged steps.

Struck by what she was doing—lying on top of this man—she lifted her body but didn't move aside. "Oh, mercy, this is going too far."

"It's going exactly where we want it to."

"We?"

"This is not a one-sided embrace." He grabbed her hand and pressed it over his groin. Through the wet cotton, his hard shaft felt immense, wicked. Bella stopped herself before giving it a squeeze. "I need you, sweet."

"Why? Is the moon full tonight?"

"No, fool woman. You think you can touch me like this and not expect me to react?"

"But *you* put my hand on your—"

"You've brought me to some kind of pinnacle, and I don't want it to stop."

"It has to. This is happening too fast, Severo. Please?"

He released her hand and she grabbed the steel handrail.

"Very well. I promise not to push this any further. But just stay."

Bella knew herself well enough to know that if she stayed, she would want to go further. And she wasn't cool with that. Not yet.

"Sorry." She stepped from the pool. At that moment the phone rang. "I've got to get that."

Severo groaned as he sat up on the middle step and flipped back his head in a spray of water. He made a noise that was half growl, half agreement.

Bella scuttled into the kitchen, dripping wet. It was Seth. He had to change the time for tonight.

"Is it your vampire woman?"

"Bella, don't be like that," he complained. "I'll meet you around nine at the restaurant, 'kay?"

"Fine. I'll see you later."

She clicked off but held the phone to her chest and glanced out the patio door. Severo sat alone at pool's edge. His broad shoulders flexed as he pressed his palms to the patio floor and leaned back.

"Marvelous," she murmured. "Poor guy. Left him high and dry. I did play the tease."

Her soaked T-shirt clung to her breasts, hard nipples jutting. "Better change before I go out there."

The human woman had some kind of grip on him.

But he wouldn't force himself on her. He'd never do that to a woman. Besides, she had just met him and discovered the world was populated with paranormal creatures.

She was taking things well, as far as he was concerned.

He'd put himself in this situation; he should have

known better. But when he was near Bella, his brain softened to mush. And that was not his style.

Was she the one who could be his lifelong mate? Only time would tell. And, more important, the werewolf.

Right now he knew only that he wanted to be close to her. So close that their flesh slicked with sweat when they were against one another, their lips melded, their bodies joined.

He groaned and eased a hand over his wet boxer briefs. A glance to his dry clothes lying on the bench decided it for him. He pulled off the boxer briefs and wrung them out over the pool. He'd have to go commando.

Using the towel on the lounge chair, he dried off. Ignoring a hard-on took monumental willpower. Dressing and tying up his boots, he stalked inside Bella's home after finding the patio door unlocked.

So she wasn't keeping him out? Good girl.

He scanned the room, dodging the jungle of plants hanging from the ceiling and sprouting up from pots on the floor. She wasn't on the phone; the cordless sat on the counter.

The vast room was like a big studio, divided down the center by the flimsy white fabric. A big couch and a plasma TV designated the living room on one side, and on the other, against the wall, sat a low bed and a nightstand.

Bella appeared from what must be the bathroom, wearing a loose white top and pants. Some kind of yoga wear. It appealed to Severo because her nipples pointed through the thin fabric, and she did not wear a bra.

"What's that?" she asked.

He dangled his underwear in his hand. "Can I hang these in your bathroom to dry?"

"Uh, sure." She pointed over her shoulder and he took direction. "Will you leave, then?"

"I will if you want me to," he called.

Her pause gave him hope, but with a shake of her head, she confirmed, "I do want you to."

"Fine, but I'll return when the sun sets."

"Do you think that's necessary?"

He strode out from the bathroom and met her at the couch. "Yes, I scented vamps all night. They were prowling. Looking for something."

"Really?" Now the nervousness he recognized warbled her voice. A twinge of fear filled Severo's nostrils, acrid and hot.

"It'll be fine. Just keep that stake and cross close at hand. Holy water would be great."

"Oh sure, I keep a liter in the fridge for such occasions."

"Sweet."

"Don't sweet me. In what alternate universe do

you get to boss me around and expect I'll tolerate another of your kisses?"

"Another?" He lifted a brow. "You like my kisses."

"They're fine." She surprised herself with that answer.

"You wish to have one more before I leave? Be decisive, no maybes."

"Yes."

He did love this woman's daring.

Severo swept her into his arms and kissed her soundly. She accepted his command and answered with an eager reply. Plunging in deeply, he explored her, noting the texture of her tongue, the soft insides of her mouth. Her sweet breath. Every moan she murmured only made him all the more determined to possess her. To win her.

To get the hell out of here before he couldn't resist the desire to rip away those loose clothes and lave his tongue all over her flesh.

"Tonight." Severo kissed her on the forehead and walked out the patio door.

Chapter 6

Severo arrived home to find a turkey sandwich on the kitchen counter. Actually, it was like a Thanksgiving feast stuffed between two innocent slices of French bread. Stuffing, cranberries, gravy and loads of meat.

Heloise, the cook/housekeeper, had worked for him twenty years, and he dreaded the day she considered retirement.

Not only was she a great cook, but Heloise also understood his foibles and knew what he was. She knew when not to press and when a defiant tone would be tolerated. She worked Monday through

Thursday, noon to whenever, and would never move in, despite his frequent suggestion she do so. She had a family; he understood.

Demolishing the sandwich, he then tipped back a couple glasses of water. His appetite never waned. He loved meat. He ran off the calories nightly, so he needed not fear a gut. Besides, he was still young.

At ninety-some years, Severo was only about a third through the usual werewolf's life expectancy. Three centuries were more than enough. He wasn't immortal, and he was thankful for that.

He'd endured much in his near century of life. He'd seen unspeakable horrors, and he'd participated in the horror himself. He'd loved but once— an unrequited love. And that had taught him to be wary of future love.

Until he'd caught the lovely Belladonna Reynolds in his arms. He'd only intended to keep her safe from the vamps, then release her, never to see her again.

Setting the empty plate in the sink, he headed for the office.

Funny how life never follows the plans a man makes, he thought. He didn't need the distraction of a sexy human woman. He lived a simple life, yet he was always busy with real estate purchases. He systematically purchased forested land in the upper northern areas of the state. Much was state forest release.

If Severo had his way, he'd buy it all. But there were the Indian reservations, and he would not deny them their bid to reclaim some of the land. He was getting close to beginning construction on the wolf preserve. At this moment an architect in Minneapolis was designing the project to Severo's specifications.

A lifelong dream, the preserve would protect those he considered his closest relatives in the animal kingdom. The wolf packs were few in Minnesota, thanks to frightened farmers shooting wildly at wolves that strayed from the pack, and hunters seeking a prize to mount and display for friends.

If only there was a way to protect his kind from the vampires. Beyond their banding together in multiple packs and standing strong against the longtooths, or allying themselves with the bloody bastards, it was better that a werewolf kept to himself.

There were some packs who participated in the blood sport—a vicious retaliation against the vampires—but Severo did not condone senseless violence.

Though a member, Severo had not attended the Council for years. It was a conglomeration of representatives from the various paranormal nations.

Vampires, witches, werewolves, faeries, elementals and others. They tried for peace amongst the nations but accepted tolerance.

No humans served on the Council. Humans were but distractions to the paranormals. To be avoided by the werewolves. Few considered them a necessity, save the vamps.

And yet, Severo would not fight his body's attraction to the human female. He hadn't experienced such a powerful pull since, well, not even since Aby.

Aby had been different. Theirs had been a close, friendly bond, like family. Yet not. He'd been more sexually attracted to her than she had been to him. But she had felt it. He knew it.

Picking up the picture frame from the shelf behind the document-littered mahogany desk, he tilted it to erase the reflection from the window. Bold red hair spiked about a pixie face with a smile so bright, it hurt him to know she was no longer a big part of his life.

He tapped the glass over her face. "Miss you."

Aby was but a phone call away. Ten numbers. Three states.

And one wedding ring.

He set the picture down and heaved out a sigh.

Had he not walked this earth long enough that

love should finally be his? He did desire it. He craved the connection and emotional bond that accompanied what he believed love to be.

But most of all, he wanted to hold another in his arms and know he was loved in return. That he was not merely a friend.

Could Bella be the mate this tired werewolf had dreamed to find?

For a human, she impressed him with her acceptance, her teasing foray into discovering him. It was as if she dared herself to step over the cliff, to take the plunge into the unknown. He suspected she lived a neat, orderly life within her jungle of a loft. Yet she fed on adrenaline more than she realized.

He liked that about her. Any woman who got involved with him would need to be comfortable with the adrenaline rush. Introducing chaos into her life would please him immensely.

But it worried him that Elvira and her mindless sycophants might be after Bella. If her friend Seth was involved with Elvira, it made sense that the female vampire would seek to remove all human connections the idiot boyfriend had. That's how the longtooth worked.

Severo growled in disgust. He punched a fist into his open palm with a smack. He cared little for the man. But no one would harm a hair on Bella's head.

It mattered little what she thought about him. All that mattered was that he had to follow this feeling of desire. If she was the one for him, he would not relent until she was his.

An hour before she intended to meet Seth, teacup in hand, Bella peeked out the window. Like clockwork, he again was sitting on the bus-stop bench. Silently stalwart. Clothed in leather and looking like something no fool would want to mess with. A force not to be overlooked.

A force whose black boxer briefs had hung like a blatant you've-been-naughty flag in her bathroom. She'd plucked them down and folded them neatly. How did she return such a thing to someone she hardly knew? Discreetly slip them from her purse and mutter, "You forgot these"?

Bella rolled her eyes. Wasn't it usually the woman who slipped her underwear into the man's things? She bet Mr. Big Bad Werewolf would love to find her panties among his things. But not when he was dutifully guarding her from the other Big Bads.

She wondered about the relationship between vam-pires and werewolves. Severo had made it clear he didn't like vampires. But was that just him, or did they all battle and clash?

Either way, with vampires after her, she was glad to have a vampire hater on her side.

Although when he was around, no real sides existed. He had no respect for her personal space. He got close enough to breathe her air, and she his.

Initially it had disturbed her. Now it felt…nice.

Had she really gotten close to naked with him in the pool?

She didn't think she'd ever touched hard muscles like his before. And his kisses…

There weren't words for the way his kiss made her feel. Instead, a sensual shiver whispered over her shoulders, reminding her of his power.

Clinking her spoon against the porcelain teacup, she wandered across the room. It was the perfect evening to sit outside on the lounge chair and watch the sun disappear on the horizon. Glamorous light glittered across the pool. But she wondered if her protector would have her back if she was out of view.

Surely he'd smell them coming a mile away, she realized, and decided outside it was.

Three minutes passed before her fence jumper appeared. Bella didn't even startle. She merely glanced over the rim of her teacup at the imposing hunk of male.

"You shouldn't be outside at night," he told her.

"It's *evening*. The sun hasn't set."

"Do you always correct people, Bella?"

"I—" She did. It was a bad habit. "You can't keep away from me, can you?"

"I'm going to take that comment as an invitation. Mind if I join you?"

She slid her knees up on the lounge chair so he could sit on the other end. Naturally, he chose the middle, stretching his legs before him. A deft slide of his arm put her legs over his lap. He stroked her skin above the anklebone and grinned at her.

"Chai?" he asked.

"Good guess."

"I could smell the cardamom, cinnamon and honey from the bench out front. Anise, too, I think. Or is that your clove perfume?"

"Okay, you've impressed me with your olfactory superpowers. Tell me something I don't know. You tracked me to my home? So you can pick out anyone and find them if you have their scent?"

"Usually. Within a range. The suburbs are spread out, so the range is not so difficult. But in the city proper so many people are wedged into every nook, cranny, car and house that it takes a while to detect some."

"But you followed me like a bloodhound to the bone, eh?"

"Something like that."

He bent and kissed her ankle. The ends of his hair tickled the top of her foot. Bella curled her toes. Had she been thinking that long hair didn't attract her?

"You're more comfortable with my presence now." It wasn't a question.

"Apparently. I may even invite you in to watch a movie."

"I enjoy movies. But let me guess. A werewolf flick?"

"No, it's a romance I picked up the other day. Probably a tearjerker."

"And you want *me* to watch it with you? I'll take a rain check."

"Ah, I've uncovered a weakness. The man doesn't do emotional scenes."

"This man prefers action, gun fights and explosions. Besides, I don't need a movie. I'm plenty entertained sitting right here, watching you sip tea. Your lips purse and look like candy treats when you sip. I'd love to nibble on that thick upper lip right now."

"You'll spill my tea."

"Set it down."

"You're bossing me again."

"And you're going to listen."

He held his hand out for the teacup.

With but a two-second pause to consider her options, Bella set the cup on his palm. He set it on the patio.

The man's body glided along hers. His fingers raked through her hair and his mouth met hers in a soft collision. The throaty sound of his pleasure rumbled against her senses, bruising them, opening them to every soft breath, touch and sound. The air changed, as it usually did when Severo kissed her. It became light and heady and so unnecessary.

A dash of his tongue to the underside of her upper lip stirred up a pleasure-drenched moan from Bella.

"Angry you succumbed?" he asked against her mouth.

"When do I get to boss you around?"

"Whenever you wish, I shall do as you command. Except leave or stop watching out for you."

"*Anything* I ask?"

"Within the realm of the possible. I'll not humiliate myself for you, so don't ask me to do something silly." The brush of his beard across her collarbone drew a sigh from her. "And just so you know, I prefer anything having to do with touching you and making you feel good."

She did, too. But what could she ask of him?

What *dare* she ask of him? This was a fantasy come true. Only, she'd never fantasized about a paranormal lover. Just a commanding one. A man sure of himself and what he could do for her.

And wasn't that the opposite of how she envisioned herself? Bella Reynolds, strong, capable, not about to take shit from anyone.

Unless he asked with that mischievous glint to his eyes.

He still leaned over her. She touched the base of his neck where the fine hairs flowed down and across his chest. She twirled her fingertip among them, liking the silky play of them across the whorls of her skin. He stretched his neck, as if he were a cat coaxing her to stroke him.

"You like that?" she asked.

"I should not admit this, but your touch... It gentles me."

She liked the sound of that. Of taming a wild and wicked stranger. Because she still considered him a stranger.

Heck, she didn't know his full name. By now she should have looked him up on Google. Was Severo even a name? It was probably his last name. She couldn't decide if she wanted to know his whole name. Might spoil the adventure, which, he'd correctly guessed, she loved so much.

"Take off your shirt," she decided. Bella grinned, savoring the empowerment she hadn't thought he would allow her.

The small black buttons slid from their slots faster than she thought possible. Shirt abandoned on the ground before the lounge chair, her wicked stranger smiled in anticipation and waited for direction.

This was too easy. This wasn't empowerment. The man was just plain horny. He'd strip naked for her if she asked.

However, nothing was wrong with a better view of this guy's ripped body.

She ran her fingers across his chest, raking her nails over his tiny rigid nipples. He clenched his jaw and gave her quick kisses to her chin and at her earlobe.

"I've never touched a man with chest hair before. I like it. It's so masculine."

"Your touch renders me hungry for more, sweet. What is your next command?"

"Hmm, take off my shirt," she said, sliding up a knee to hug his hip. "And that's it for tonight. Deal? Shirts off, nothing else."

"Second base. I can live with that."

"You'd better not make me regret it."

"Never."

She lifted her arms as he tugged off her T-shirt.

The air swirled across her bare breasts, only to be quickly replaced by his hot mouth on her nipple.

Arching her back lifted her breast up against his mouth, and he answered her plea with insistent suckling and a gentle tweak to the other one with his thumb.

"Your breasts are gorgeous. I could feast upon them all day and night and never wish for more."

"Sweet talker, you. Oh, mercy, that's good. That tongue of yours makes me tingle all over."

"Tingles are for amateurs. I'm going to make you come, sweet."

"But we agreed second base was it."

"I don't need to go further." He lashed his tongue across her nipple and dipped his head to the left to pay the other breast its due. "Mmm, your breasts fit my hands as if they were made for them. I like them this size. Small yet so round."

With a hand behind her back, he lifted her and pressed her groin against his. The intense tugging and laving at her nipples sent exotic shivers scurrying through her body in all directions. He alternated between quick laps with the pointed tip of his tongue and long, sweeping tastes all about her rigid flesh.

Her breasts were so sensitive to a man's touch, but more so at Severo's attentions. Bella felt his tongue all the way through her body as the delicious sensations traveled up, down and everywhere in between.

He dizzied her with his talent. And he was making her so wet that she clenched her thighs to capture the feeling, to increase the intensity that hummed there.

"Yes, squeeze your thighs together to make it happen, sweet. Come for me."

No man had ever talked to her like that. But the words sounded so sexy coming out in his husky voice and in a wanting, deep tone that hummed against her flesh.

Pushing her fingers through his hair, she dug in and tugged.

He laved across her nipple slowly. "Hot and…receptive. God, you are so sensitive, Bella. Do you feel this in your—?"

He used a word that startled her yet at the same time made her gasp with desire. Because he was right on target. The man knew what his touch was capable of. He could make her come merely by—

Could he? She might have an orgasm if he slicked his tongue a little to the right.

A soft nip at the outer edge of her areola was what did it.

Bella cried out as an orgasm utterly blindsided her and swept her up. Her body shook beneath his powerful torso. His hands glided across her breasts. He kissed them slowly, dragging his tongue around them and then up to her mouth, where he caught her surrendering sigh in his mouth.

Bella clung to him, gripping his hard muscles, as if letting go would make her fall endlessly.

He let out a smirking chuff next to her ear. "You've never come that way before, have you?"

"Are you kidding? That was amazing. How'd you do that?"

"You're very sensitive to my touch."

"No shit. Oops."

He smiled against her breast. "You don't use language like that, do you?"

"Never."

"Do the things I say offend you?"

"A little. No. I mean, they sound good the way *you* say them. Oh." She moaned again, catching a lingering wave of orgasm. Muscles languid, she melted in his strong embrace.

"I like the sound of your pleasure. You cry out to the heavens. Feel how hard you've made me?"

Despite her resolve to stay planted on second base, she reached down and stroked his hardness through the snug leather pants.

Bella wanted to feel him. To stroke him. To give him return pleasure.

She unzipped his pants, but he caught her hand in a clutch. "What happened to second base?"

"I think I slid over the plate. I want to touch, to feel you."

"You can't *just* touch, sweet. You know how things work. You're a big girl."

"And you're a big boy."

He growled and gave her a bite on the neck, softened with his lips stretched over his teeth. "Very well, but you were the one to break the rules. I want that one to go on the record. Aaah."

She gripped his erection and tugged it out from the tight confines of his pants. He shifted his hips and pushed down his pants to offer her easier access.

He was big and Bella delighted at the feel of the soft velvet skin. It was like suede covering steel. The smooth head snuggled against her palm as she stroked over it lightly, gauging the funny little bobs and jerks it made with her every touch.

"You'd better mean business," he hissed at her ear. He nipped the lobe and sucked it hard. He pinched her nipple.

Bella gripped her prize firmly and stroked up and down. Flesh shrugged along the hard column. He breathed heavily against her neck, loving her work, which she knew from his lack of commands or comments.

Severo pressed both hands to the chair arm over her head. The flimsy wicker creaked. She didn't stop.

And he met her eyes, branding her with his deep, dark intensity, which still managed to frighten her, yet also gave her confidence. She stroked the beast, taming him to her command. He loved it. He touched her with his eyes. Pleading. Thanking. Promising. Daring.

Shudders racked his immense shoulders, and as he came, he maintained eye contact. His seed warmed her belly, over and over.

When he was finished, he reached for a towel and wiped off her stomach, then tossed it aside and collapsed on top of her.

"I like third base the best," he said on a satisfied huff. "Your turn?"

"I've already had a turn. That was…"

"Worth doing again?"

And again. The weight of him upon her made her giddy. This powerful man was so relaxed and comfortable with her. A man who was more than human.

"I hate to be a spoilsport, but I'm meeting Seth tonight. I probably should get ready."

"You have a date?"

"It's not a date. It's a 'what the hell are you doing dating a vampire?' kind of meeting with my friend."

"And what if he asks about your werewolf?"

"I'm not dating you. You are not mine."

"No, but we're involved in something here, Bella." He stroked her neck like a cat. The sticky head of his penis nudged her belly. "*This* is not two people being casual."

"You're my protector."

"And you—" he bent to kiss each breast and smoothed his hand down her stomach and adjusted his new erection so that it lay straight along her belly "—are my destroyer."

"I don't want to hurt you."

"It's a good destruction, trust me. I want it over and over, if you'll give it. But I'm not sure about you going anywhere alone. It's night. Will you allow me to escort you?"

"Do I have an option?"

Seth expected only her. But if Severo's guess about Seth's girlfriend siccing vampire slaves on her was anywhere near correct, then she'd like to have him along for support.

You want the werewolf to go along because you're not ready to say goodbye to him.

How could she after what they'd just shared?

Chapter 7

She'd dressed sexy to meet her friend Seth. A body-hugging black top and skirt with white polka dots decorating the double layer of ruffles at the hem. Bella claimed it was her dance-practice skirt. Whatever it was, it showed every curve!

She'd tugged her hair into a sleek ponytail that emphasized her sharp cheekbones and narrow face. And her eyes were all dark and smoky with makeup.

Severo wanted to eat her alive, suck her until she moaned for him to stop. He wanted to feel those short, glossy fingernails dig into his muscles again and to capture her climaxing cry in his mouth.

God, he loved holding her body when it shuddered beneath him.

But she gave him the excuse that she had to dance at the club this evening, after she met with Seth. Part of her dance-class requirements.

They strolled along the boulevard, heading toward the Moonstone. He knew it was a family diner that served well past midnight. Steaks, fries and lots of grease. Heart attack on a plate. His kind of watering hole.

"So I'm not invited to watch you dance?" he asked.

"You can come along if you like."

"But you'd rather I not."

"I didn't say that. Do you want to sit and watch me beat the floor with my feet? Or would you rather play security outside the back door?"

"Now you're taking advantage of me. Did you consider I might have something to do after your little meeting?"

"Like watching me?"

She had him there.

He didn't like being a third wheel. Just who was this Seth, and how had the mortal attracted attention from the likes of the insufferable Elvira? She normally didn't do mortals. Not for long.

"He's already inside. I can see him." Bella waved and then touched Severo's chest.

Severo knew what was coming. "I can stay outside if you prefer to keep your dog tied up on the leash."

"Now look who's getting snarky." She toyed with the collar of his leather jacket. The dark shadowing around her eyes made the green irises so bold, like sweets to be devoured. "I was going to invite you in."

"I'd like that. But?"

"But let me do the talking, okay? This is weird enough introducing you to Seth."

"Weirder than him confessing to you that he's dating the mistress of the night?"

"I suppose not. *Are* we dating?"

"I consider you the only woman in my life. But if we must do some sort of ritual involving movies and dinner and roses, I confess I've fallen short."

Her shy smile made him want to kiss her, to show the world how she had captured him. But they were in the parking lot of a family restaurant. He had a sense of decorum. Unlike vampires, he could control his animal instincts. Most of the time.

The hostess directed Bella and Severo to a table at the back of the restaurant that was lit by a flickering plastic Tiffany reject hanging overhead.

Already standing in wait, Seth hugged Bella and kissed her on the mouth. A quick kiss, but a kiss all the same. *Some friend.* Severo's hackles prickled, but he played the cool one, waiting until the jerk noticed him.

"This is Severo," said Bella, introducing them.

Severo offered his hand, but the twerp stumbled backward and landed in the booth.

"You didn't tell me you were bringing him along. Bella, what the hell? Three days ago you learn about paranormals, and now you're dating one?"

"We're not dating," Severo said as he slid onto the vinyl booth behind Bella. He made a point of leaning over to kiss her cheek, then tilted her jaw so he could kiss her fully on the mouth. He glanced to Seth. "We're just exploring mating possibilities."

The man's stunned gape served Severo a satisfying victory. "Christ, Bella, you said this guy almost raped you."

"I would never. Did you say that to him?" asked Severo.

"He's cool, Seth. And no, I didn't say you raped me. But I wasn't sure what you were capable of that night." She patted his hand. Severo didn't like the condescending move, so he pulled back his hand and slipped it, fisted, inside his jacket pocket. "Seth, Severo has been keeping an eye on me in case the vampires come back."

"What? Why would they? Like, come back for *you?*" Seth quizzed.

Severo did not like the tone in the man's voice. Hell, he was hardly a man. Lanky and pale, he looked like a teenager. Why did young men think that wearing their hair in their eyes was attractive?

"Has he been filling your mind with stupid fairy tales to get you to forgive his callous treatment?" Seth asked. "What's your deal, man?"

"You're a testy one, aren't you? Elvira's lovers are usually more subdued. Drained, actually," Severo replied.

Seth blinked. "Elvira?"

"He calls your girlfriend that," Bella offered.

"Her name is Evie," Seth snapped. "And how do you know her?"

"Oh, we go back a long way, me and the mistress of the night," said Severo.

"The mistress…"

Seth's sputtering affront did not impress Severo. The idiot mortal was caught up in the vampire's allure. Actually, he was probably heavily under vampire persuasion and unable to resist the long-tooth bitch.

"Just listen, will you?" Bella pleaded with her friend. "Tell him what you suspect, Severo. Why the vampires are after me."

He did not owe this mortal a thing, but Bella asked so nicely that he wanted to please her. "I believe Evie is jealous of you and Bella. That's why she sicced her sycophants on her the other night."

"Jealous? Of what?" asked Seth.

"Of your relationship with Bella," Severo said calmly. He scented the man's growing rage. It wasn't a normal reaction. The vampire bitch had been drinking from him; he could smell the vile longtooth oozing from his pores. "She's seen the two of you together, I'm sure."

"We're just friends," Seth hissed.

Severo nodded. "But you love Bella, yes?"

"Of course I do."

"Vampires are pernicious creatures. While they toy with love as if it were meant to be batted about like a volleyball, they will also smash it to oblivion if it serves their pleasure," Severo explained.

"Yeah? What about werewolves? I thought you guys were the ones who were so protective of your mates?" Seth challenged.

"We are." Severo slid a hand around Bella's shoulder and pulled her against him. "You want to try me?"

"Jeez, Bella." Seth shoved his glass of ice water to the center of the table and slammed his arms across his chest. "I don't want to talk to this creep." He sneered at Severo. "What made you think you could invite yourself along?"

"Because you don't have Bella's best interests in mind," Severo stated calmly.

"That's it, man. I'm out of here," Seth thundered.

"Back to your vampire mistress?" Severo asked as the guy slid out from the booth. He was but a kid. Couldn't be a day over twenty. Which made him wonder how Bella had ever hooked up with him in the first place. "She's seen you interact with Bella. My guess is she doesn't want the competition."

"Bella means nothing to me," Seth spat. He shrugged his fingers through his hair. "Well, you know, Bella. We're not like *that*. We don't 'explore mating possibilities.' Christ, now I'll never get the image out of my head of you and wolf boy here—"

In less than a breath Severo held the man by the shirt lapels. He didn't lift him so high that his feet left the ground. Didn't want to cause a scene. "You tell your mistress to back off."

"Severo." Bella's quiet plea calmed the elevating rage that threatened to obliterate Severo's patience.

Seth nodded agreeably, and Severo set him down.

"Call me, Bella," Seth said. "You're dancing tonight? I'm sorry, I didn't know. I've got plans."

"I forgot to tell you, Seth. You can catch me next time," replied Bella.

Seth nodded and vacated the restaurant quickly.

"Why did you have to do that?" she said as

Severo slid into the booth seat next to her. "Always playing he-man. Gotta be the alpha dog."

Instead of berating her for her uncouth word choice, Severo leaned in and kissed her silent. The high booth granted them privacy. The kiss did the trick, and he enjoyed it much more than chastising her. Her fingers slipped between the buttons of his silk shirt and he felt her nails dig into his chest. *Yes, hurt me. Mark me.* Mmm, she was exquisite.

"Still feel the need for dancing?" he asked.

"I have to. It's part of dance class."

"Would you entertain the idea of returning to your home and allowing me to undress you, starting with those wicked shoes, and lick my way all the way up to your mouth?"

"I think I've lost the mood. I'm still angry with you for being so mean to Seth."

"Very well."

With a resolute sigh, Severo toyed with the flatware that had been placed squarely before him. His thigh touched Bella's thigh, and his shoulder hugged hers.

Her presence did not cease to still him like a muzzle on a raging beast. He would have liked to shove the idiot Seth through the window, but Bella had gentled him again. What a wonder.

Tilting his head, he laid it upon her shoulder. A

smirking breath escaped her. She slid a palm along his cheek. It didn't matter if she was angry with him. This quiet moment meant the world to him. Just him and Bella together.

Must he wait for her to dance before taking her home and having his way with her?

He asked, "How about now? Change your mind about being angry with me?"

"Yes, werewolf." She laughed softly. "You win. Let's head to the club and get this dance over with."

Severo was familiar with the flamenco style of music. He enjoyed the intricate guitar rhythm and understood some Spanish words the cantor sang. But he'd never watched a flamenco dance performance before. Bella hypnotized him.

She danced with a female partner, each mirroring the other and then at times breaking off to do their own thing upon the small wooden dance floor. The intensity between the two blazed through the small room.

He sat in the back of the club, which was no more than twenty feet from the makeshift dance floor.

The craggy-faced man next to Severo reeked strongly of menthol. He clapped his veiny, long-fingered hands in rhythm, matching the others in the crowd, who encouraged the dancers with their clapping and occasional shouts of olé.

Settling against the wall, he observed through narrowed eyes as his woman seduced the crowd. *His woman.* Dating wasn't necessary. Claiming her was, though. He'd already learned her climax. But he wouldn't truly claim her until he'd made love to her completely.

And then there was the werewolf. That part of him would provide the final test of whether or not Bella could be his true mate.

A rapid *rasgueado* by the guitarist brought the women together in a floor-pounding explosion of stomps and hand claps. The crowd's enthusiasm increased.

The man next to him voiced his approval, and Severo found the beat with all the rest.

Bella strode ahead, leaving Severo to close the door behind him. She opened the patio door. A soft night breeze drifted through the screen, tickling the chiffon that hung from the ceiling down the center of her loft. A flowery aroma steeped the air, but she couldn't guess what it was. Mrs. Jones had a wild and abundant garden on the other side of the fence. Wolf boy might know.

She chided herself for thinking of him that way. He was a man, as he'd explained. But she was curious about the wolf part. Yet curiosity led to dread. Vampires with sharp, shiny fangs were bad enough. What would a fully wolfed-out werewolf be like?

Maybe she wasn't so curious, after all.

"Want something to drink?" she offered when he wandered back and forth before the couch. "I have vodka and Sprite."

"No beer?"

"I'm not into the icky stuff."

He grinned. "I'll take a swig of vodka, neat. But don't slip any of that fruity stuff in there."

"Gotcha. One anti-cosmo coming right up."

Tossing his jacket on the couch, he dodged the bamboo plant and stretched his broad shoulders and flexed his arms. He didn't stop moving, striding across the floor as if he were measuring for a marriage bed.

Oh, stop, Bella. That's the wrong image. A caged animal was more appropriate and intriguing.

Was he nervous now that they were alone and sex might be the next step? Full-on sex, that is. Wasn't like he hadn't already rocked her world.

If he could bring her to climax merely by licking her nipples, Bella could not guess how wondrous getting naked with him would be. On the other hand, she could imagine such a scenario. But why imagine when all the elements to the fantasy were at hand?

Severo had told Seth that they were "exploring mating possibilities." But it hadn't sounded as disgusting to her as she thought it should. Mating? With the virile man who filled the room with his presence?

Bring it on.

Vodka straight had never appealed to her, but she took a sip before handing the tumbler to Severo. He downed it in one swallow, set the tumbler on the birch coffee table and tugged her into his embrace.

"I needed that," he said.

"I have difficulty believing you require a drink to loosen up."

"Oh, I'm loose."

"I know that. I saw you doing *palmas* while I was dancing."

"The what? I wasn't doing anything untoward, sweet."

She smiled at his teasing allusion. "*Palmas* is the clapping of hands, which are as much a musical instrument to flamencos as their feet."

"Ah. Yes, I think I picked it up." He tapped a rapid rhythm with three fingers against her collarbone. "Yes?"

"Very good for a newbie."

"You dance often?"

"Couple times a week at the studio. Then I try to

pick up at least one performance a week at the club. Next week I have an important audition at the studio. If I can pass, I'll become an apprentice. After a few years of intense study, perhaps they'll allow me to start teaching."

"Impressive. You are a marvelous dancer." He swayed, prompting her to move with him. "But I thought that wasn't your job?"

"It isn't. I do Web design to pay the bills. But teaching a couple days a week would be awesome." She shifted her hips into a sway and the ruffled hem of her skirt swung out. "You dance, Severo?"

"Nope."

"Never?"

Without a word, he tugged her to him and traced a finger along the low-cut V-neck of her top.

"Not in all your... How old are you, exactly? Are you immortal?" With the slightest push from him, Bella spun out and did a half twirl.

"Close to one hundred years," he said. "But not immortal."

"A hundred? I'm dating an older man."

"So we are dating?"

"I think so." She did a double *golpe* foot stomp to punctuate her decision.

"Works for me."

She stepped out and twirled up to him. Her skirts

spun wide and crushed against his legs. His fingers glided through her hair and he drew the veil of soft brown tresses across his face.

"I want to dance with you," she said.

"Oh, we'll dance."

The skim of his fingers down her midriff stirred a rhythm in her blood similar to the insistent beat of flamenco. Bella palmed his hands and guided his movements up, over her breasts. He glided his palms across the sensitive swells, cupping them and thumbing the nipples.

"I don't like it when you wear a bra. Harder to get to the sweets." He nipped her breasts through the fabric.

"I have to when I'm dancing. Don't want to be jiggling all over."

"Mmm, no. Only for me."

Bella's appreciative purr drew him closer.

At her neck he kissed the heat of her pulse. Once, twice. A dash of his tongue sent shivers across her flesh.

A tilt and twist of her hips spun her about, so that the pulse of his heart beat against her shoulder blade. Bella pressed her derriere into his groin. His wanting moan gave her a smile.

He caressed her breast, cupping it, squeezing. His low sigh vibrated against her back. The sound of a man's pleasure proved a delicious aphrodisiac. Alone, in a room lit only by the low bulb over the kitchen stove, Bella danced with the only man she desired.

Spinning, she placed her hands on his shoulders. The dancing shoes only put her eye level with his mouth, so she lifted *en pointe* to claim a kiss. Vodka tainted his breath. Desire quickened his motions.

He lifted her with ease and turned her around to set her upon the back of the couch.

It felt right, the two of them coming together in this strange dance that was not quite human and not quite sane.

That thought put her off.

Bella slid from the couch and walked a few steps, the nails pounded into her shoe heels clicking precisely. Severo caught her hand and spun her to face him. The aggressive alpha that she'd experienced most often was not present in his eyes. Instead she saw a gentle pleading and knew that he silently wondered why she was so reluctant.

She knew the answer. It pounded in her heart.

"I'm afraid," she replied, "that I could fall in love with you."

"What's so wrong with love?"

"Nothing. Only, I'm not sure I'm looking at this rationally."

"And the rational viewpoint would be?"

"One mortal human fooling around with one nonmortal werewolf. How far off the sanity scale is that one?"

"Are you disgusted by me, Bella?"

"Not at all. Well, you initially put me off. I mean, I was freaked that night the vampires were chasing me, and you did come on strong and a little creepy—but not anymore. Now? I find you the most attractive man I've ever known."

"You mean that?"

She nodded. "You're so sexy. Every time you're close to me, it's like my body responds before my brain can process the information. I hunger for a glance from you. I ache for a touch. I want you, Severo. And that scares me."

"The werewolf isn't going to intrude upon our liaisons, Bella, if that is what concerns you."

It did. And it didn't. Honestly, she was unsure about how quickly their relationship was moving. Sure, she'd had a couple of one-night stands before. Sometimes two people came together to have sex, nothing more.

But her and Severo? It was much more than one night of sex to serve a need. It had to be.

"You're thinking too much, sweet. I won't hurt you."

"I know you won't." It wasn't physical hurt she

worried about, but the emotional pain he might cause. Could she, a mortal woman, do this?

"Take off your clothes," he said.

Yes. Just surrender. Let it happen, Bella. You want him.

Bella bent to pick up his tumbler, saying over her shoulder, "You want them off? Come and get me."

She wasn't sure how he made it to the kitchen counter before she did, but Severo met her there, took the tumbler and placed it in the sink, then lifted her into his arms. "Your wish is my command."

When she thought he might carry her to the bed, he stopped at the couch and set her on the arm. Okay, this was good. Not as much pressure as she would have endured if he had gone to the bed. They were easing into things slowly.

A stroke of his hand slipped the sleeve from one of her shoulders and then the other. His hot breath skimmed her skin from the top of her arm to the base of her neck, burning into her, marking her.

Grasping for an anchor against the dizzying pull of his command, Belle grabbed his shirt in her fists.

He remained focused on her, kissing the bodice of her top and tugging the stretchy rayon lower with his mouth. His hand glided down and slid her skirt high up her thigh.

She began to slip off her shoes, but he said, "No, leave them on. I like them. They're so powerful."

He pulled the top to her waist. Her bra clasped in front, and with but a flick from Severo's fingers, it snapped open and the straps slipped to her elbows. He took her nipples with hungry precision, and Bella arched backward. Mercy, she loved his mastery of her body.

With one strong hand across her back, he lifted her and wrapped her legs about his waist. The wide flamenco skirts splayed along his legs. He ripped off his shirt and then unzipped his pants, and she tugged them down his hips.

Once she saw the prize, her inhibitions fled. It was thick and heavy in her palm. Bella gripped it firmly.

"You're in a hurry." Not so much a question as an agreement. "I still haven't landed on third base." He reached down and struggled with the many yards of skirt fabric. A toss spilled ruffles over her stomach and breasts. "Let me get your panties off."

Elastic ripped as his urgency ignored caution. He mumbled, "Sorry," but there was little care in the word.

Bella wrapped her legs tight about him, hugging his hard, hot shaft against her stomach. As she moaned, he pumped against her, sliding his erection over her bare flesh.

He kissed her across her collarbone, the base of her neck, the rise of her breasts. She put her hands on the couch and took his bruising kisses with abandon.

She ground her mons against his erection. The head of it poked against her stomach, insistent, the proverbial sword ready to slay her.

"Do you have condoms?" he blurted.

"I'm on the pill."

"Good. I can't wait any longer. Say it's all right, sweet. Let me come inside you."

He wanted permission? The man was a dream. "Yes, please."

He hooked one of her legs with his arm and stretched it over his shoulder. Not awkward for a dancer. Bella trusted he wouldn't let her fall backward. Supporting herself with her hands to the couch, she cried out as he entered her. Hard and heavy and thick, a perfect fit. Every slide tugged at her; the friction brought her to a frenzy.

"You were made for me," he growled, echoing her thoughts. Always he held her with his eyes. And she wasn't about to look away. He looked into her as he slid into her. He filled her, mind, body and soul. "So right, sweet. It's never—" he tensed, his jaw clenching, and she knew he neared the verge "—been like this before."

Remarkably they climaxed together. The world fell away and the two of them remained, locked together in a bond that defied anything either had known.

Later they lay on the rumpled bedsheets in the gray shadows of early morning. Severo's lover traced his chest from nipple to nipple in a lazy dance. She smelled like sex and vodka.

"So, earlier," she said in a sex-softened voice, "you said it had never been like this. You mean the sex?"

"God, yes, Bella. I've had great sex over the years, but the first time I put myself inside you it was like I'd found my place. You are the only one. You are my mate."

"Your mate? Is that like calling me your girl-friend?"

"Yes, I suppose so." He chuckled and pulled her on top of him. He had a raging erection again. "Fit yourself where you belong, sweet. Mmm, right there."

He was too relaxed to move. Didn't matter. Feeling her wrapped about him, her fingers dancing across his flesh and the tips of her long hair dusting his wrists was enough to make a man come. And he did.

Her laughter alerted him, and he dodged through the overgrown thicket of field grass, his paws beating the ground to find the source of mirth. The day was new after he'd spent the night wandering the countryside.

The world was different when he was not standing on two legs. Better this way.

Rounding the trimmed hedge, he bounded onto the tiled patio area, tracking her summertime scent to one of the lounge chairs.

"Oh, Sev! Your nose is wet and cold. Stop licking me! You're always so playful in the mornings. Go inside and shift, and put some clothes on. I have work to do today, and I want you to meet the witch who'll be invoking the demon."

"Aby!"

Severo sprang up in bed. It wasn't his home. And Aby was far from his arms.

Bella woke to find Severo sitting alert. He'd called out something. A name? He didn't seem aware that she was awake, and for a moment she merely observed him as he sniffed the air. He got off the bed and reached for his clothes.

"What is it?" she whispered.

He shushed her and pulled up his leather pants.

"You're scaring me, Severo." She sat up and tugged the sheet over her breasts. The patio door was still open and the room had cooled.

The door was open? But there was a screen.

Before she could curse her stupidity, the screen flew inside and two dark figures crashed through. The patio door cracked, and glass shattered.

Chapter 8

"Stay right there," Severo called to Bella as he dashed into the fray.

The first vampire swung out at Severo and missed. Severo, while dodging, tilted his torso and snagged a glass shard from the floor. He swung his arm up, slashing the glass across the vampire's neck. Blood beaded the air in a long chain and splattered the white chiffon drape hanging nearby.

"I thought you said the wolf wasn't here?" the other vampire shouted and ran for Severo's back.

The first vampire didn't answer. He fell to his knees, clutching his spurting throat.

Bella gripped the sheets and found herself crawling to the end of the bed to kneel there. Huddling in fear was the furthest thing from her mind. This was exciting.

Her lover stretched out an arm and delivered a fist to the second vampire's skull. The hit only made the vamp blink. He cracked a bloody grin and charged Severo. The two landed on the floor in a crush of flesh and bone. They rolled across the hardwood, exchanging punches to vulnerable body parts.

A wolflike growl preceded a masterful kick. The vamp flew backward, shoulders hitting the wall with a crunch—but he wasn't down.

Severo stood and shook out his shoulders. He growled, vicious and violent, his fingers curving to angry claws. Every muscle across his back bulged and tensed. The tendons in his forearms pulsed with movement. He was marvelous. A beast of power and strength. Bella couldn't be afraid for him, because somehow she knew he would defeat the opponents.

Meanwhile, the bleeding vampire collapsed on the floor, arms out and face down.

Severo slid across the floor, colliding with the glass shards. He gripped a long piece of glass and lunged for the fallen vamp. The glass pierced the vamp's back, blood gushing up from the heart.

And then something remarkable happened. The

fallen vamp shuddered, his entire body reacting to the injury. Within seconds, he was reduced to ash, piled upon the bloody pool.

Scuffling with the remaining vampire, Severo shoved him against the wall. His powerful thighs flexed. He forced the vamp's shoulders into the wall. The Sheetrock cracked. A cloud of chalky dust flew about their heads.

His eyes fell upon the cross on the wall. A gift from Bella's grandmother, who had passed a decade earlier. He grabbed the foot-long cross and slammed it against the vampire's face. Smoke hissed and the vampire yowled. The cross burned through to his jawbone.

Severo dropped the vamp at his feet. He flicked away the cross, sending it clattering across the floor.

"Damn, that was real silver." He shook his hand and stalked about, surveying the bloody mess.

With intense focus, he marched up to the bed.

Now Bella did cringe. His eyes held the same intensity she'd seen when he'd made love to her, yet it had darkened and grown deeper, if that were possible. Was he in a rage? Some werewolf state that made him violent toward anyone?

He gripped the bedpost and yanked it off. "Mind if I use this?" He wielded the serrated wood stake. "Holy wounds take forever to kill," he commented as he strode back to the suffering vampire. Plunging the stake into the vamp's heart brought his struggles to an end. Another ash reduction and the room fell silent.

And Bella let out a breath she must have been holding since the vampires charged through the patio door.

Severo wiped his bloody hands on the white chiffon drape. He looked over the destruction and winced. When he glanced to her, Bella rushed to him.

His bare chest rose and fell roughly. It was spattered with blood, which she didn't want to touch. She took his hand, which he displayed palm up. A deep burn from the cross reddened his flesh.

"Will it kill you?" she asked.

"No. But it'll hurt like a mother for a while. Get back on the bed, sweet. There's glass everywhere."

Realizing the danger, Bella complied, backing carefully away until she climbed onto the bed.

Though barefoot, her lover stood still, surveying his destruction. He must have taken cuts to his feet, yet he appeared only angry about the intrusion, and not at all concerned about his wounds.

"Sorry. I'll have someone come clean this up." He dug a cell phone from his pocket and made a quick, mysterious call. When he hung up, he said, "Stay right there. I'm going outside to check the periphery. You okay?"

Okay? In what sense? A glance to the piles of vampire ash made her wonder if she was safe. Nothing could come back from the ashes, right? "No problem," she managed.

As soon as he marched outside, Bella ducked her head and muffled a scream against the pillow. She didn't want to look at what lay on the floor. It smelled so strongly of blood and ash, she didn't need to look.

The sight of the vampire's slashed throat had been seared into her eyes forever. The blood-spattered chiffon. The ash piles that had once been living men.

But he'd saved her. Again.

Now she wanted him back. Holding her. Protecting her. Sheltering her.

"Severo," she whispered. "Please hurry."

He'd woken from a dead sleep to the scent of those nasty longtooths. Not soon enough to prevent Bella from witnessing the bloody killing. He hated himself for that. But that he'd kept her from harm meant he'd accomplished his goal—to protect Bella.

Protect his mate. The one woman he connected with on a visceral level. Even Aby he hadn't connected with like this.

You woke from a dream, calling her name, he thought.

Why had he been dreaming of Aby while lying

next to Bella? And after they'd made love. That disturbed him. He and Aby had never had a sexual relationship, though they'd been close on other levels.

But he wouldn't think of that. He must not. Bella had captured him by the tail, and he liked that just fine.

I'm afraid that I could fall in love with you. He remembered her words.

How could he erase her fear of him? He knew it was because he wasn't human. Did she fear his werewolf?

He'd been careful not to change when the vampires had attacked. Had he shifted, he could have taken both out with one swipe of a taloned paw. Vampires were no match in physical combat with werewolves. Yet Severo's strength was not to be disregarded while in mere were form.

With one last scan across the horizon from the roof of Bella's loft, he satisfied himself that no others were in the neighborhood. He scented vampires at a distance—probably five miles to the north—but their presence didn't agitate him.

Had the bitch Elvira sent the vamps to kill Bella? That was going too far for jealousy. He owed the mistress of the night a visit.

But first, he had to get Bella safe. She would

probably balk at such an idea, but he wouldn't take no for an answer.

Jumping to land before the pool, Severo surveyed the damage as he strode inside the home. The patio door would need to be boarded up, which the cleanup crew would do. As well, they'd sweep up the vamp ash and clean the blood. The flimsy drape was a loss.

During the height of the war between the vampires and witches, which had ended only a few years earlier, the need for discretion had grown paramount. As a result, most paranormals carried the number to a reliable cleanup team. No smart wolf left evidence for mortals to peruse and wonder over.

Bella waited on the bed, as if afraid to leave the safe island amid the blood and destruction. She plunged into his arms and he held her tight, the sheet wrapped about her and her limbs shivering against his body.

"Sorry," he whispered. "I heard them coming, just not fast enough. You shouldn't have had to see that."

"You were so brave," she said. "I love you, Severo."

That confession knocked him over, so he had to lean against the wall as he held her. She loved him? It was a wondrous confession that he'd never hoped to hear from a woman—let alone a *mortal* woman—in his lifetime.

He'd given up on love after Aby.

"You weren't frightened?" he asked.

"Yes, but watching you took away the fear. How is it that you are so much stronger than vampires? Are werewolves on top of the heap?"

"Not always. When I am in were form, I'm a match in strength to a vampire. As a werewolf… well, look out. But they were idiots. And I did have the cross."

He splayed open his hand. The burn was now a red indentation, as if he'd gripped the thing tightly for a long time.

"It's already fading," she observed.

"The silver didn't enter my veins. I'm fine. Just a burn. You're still clinging like a koala, sweet. Sure you're not afraid? It's okay."

"Of course I'm afraid. But I think it's that I want to be sure you're solid and real, and that I didn't just lose you. Kiss me."

Her lips quivered at his mouth as they connected gently. He wanted to indulge that tremor of her fear; it was what had first attracted him to her.

He wasn't human, and he was different from her. He fed upon the different, the unusual. And Bella's fear fed him.

"Your skin is goose bumpy," he whispered as he slid a hand up her back. That induced a real shudder from her, but he sensed it was a sensual reaction to his touch.

"I want to make love again," she said. "Right now."

So the adrenaline rush had the same effect on her as it had on him? Unfortunately, they couldn't indulge right now.

"I called for cleanup. They're usually very prompt. And I don't think you should stay here any longer than it takes to pack. You're not safe here, Bella." He tucked her hair behind an ear and kissed her eyelid where it tasted like soft woman. The flutter of her lashes tickled his mouth. "Come stay with me."

"At your house? Where do you live?"

"About twenty miles north of the city. You'll be safe there. I have protection wards against vampires, demons and others. No one messes with me out there."

"Leave my home? I'm not sure."

She glanced about the havoc, still clinging to the sheet wrapped about her. She was still frightened, he knew, but too proud to admit it. She impressed him with such bravery.

"I have my work, and tomorrow I practice at the studio. This is all happening so fast," she said. "I've only known you a few days."

"It doesn't take a lifetime to fall in love, Bella."

"Love. Yes. I said that, didn't I?"

Maybe he had been too quick to grasp for the untouchable. "It's the adrenaline talking."

"No, I…I think I meant it." She stroked his beard and kissed him again. "But is it because I've fallen down the rabbit hole?"

He quirked a brow. "The rabbit hole?"

"Alice's tumble into the wild and weird. First there's you—and believe me, that's all good. But now vampires want to kill me and my best friend?"

"And they will if you don't take action. You cannot beat them here, unprotected and vulnerable. You need my protection to stand against them. Will you take it?"

She stared at his outstretched hand. Once before she'd accepted that offer.

Could he win her? She'd confessed love, and that felt splendid. But she hadn't fully entered his world yet. And indeed, it would be a tumble down some kind of rabbit hole.

"You can do your work from any computer, yes?"

She nodded.

"Come with me, sweet."

Bella slid her fingers over his. "Yes."

The cleaners arrived as Severo toted Bella's suitcase out the front door. He paid them in advance and shuffled Bella out before she could see their equipment. They were not overly respectful of the dead. A Hoover vacuum picked up vampire ash "real swell," as one of the cleaners commented. Severo was cool with that, yet he didn't want to push Bella over the precipice she'd been forced to toe this morning.

There was yet a good amount of tumbling down the proverbial rabbit hole to be done.

The sun dashed a thin line of orange across the horizon as they stepped out onto the sidewalk.

"Where's your car?" she asked, yawning. They'd had about an hour of sleep after a night of making love.

"I don't normally use it. We can hail a cab." With a suitcase in each hand, he headed a few blocks up, closer to the businesses.

She followed, clicking along beside him in the high heels she'd tugged from her closet. He loved that she was a practical woman who did unpractical things, like slipping into spike heels at dawn.

"You don't drive? But how do you get from your house to town?"

"I drive on occasion. Gotta take the Mercedes out for a spin once in a while. But usually I walk or run."

"As a wolf?"

He chuckled. "No. When I change shapes from

wolf to man, I'm naked. The clothing doesn't change with the rest of me."

"So what if you wolf out during a fight with some vampires? Does that leave you…?"

"Naked, but successful. I tend to carry extra clothes with me in my backpack." He looked up the street. "There's a cab. You can sleep as soon as we get to my house. You need it after the night we've had."

Chapter 9

Bella woke to find herself eye level to a tray with orange juice and breakfast sitting next to the bed. Warm, buttery toast, and fresh-picked strawberries sat atop the ramekin of sweet jam.

She didn't remember much after arriving at Severo's mansion in the country. Exhausted after a long night, Bella hadn't taken the time to look around. Her lover had carried her to his bedroom, like some kind of knight delivering a princess to her slumber.

The last thing she recalled was him kissing her on the forehead, her chin, her breasts, and he must have navigated lower, but she had nodded off by then.

Long dark velvet curtains, half-closed, allowed but a narrow strip of bright afternoon sun down the center of the room and across the bottom of the bed.

The bedsheets were soft white and the comforter was a deep navy satin. Piles of pillows supported her as she sat up and reached for the orange juice.

Cold and freshly squeezed, it hit the spot.

She took her first opportunity to look around.

The simple room was huge, as big as her whole loft. The walls stretched to a barrel-vaulted ceiling painted with pastoral scenes. All the overstuffed, overlarge furniture was upholstered in the same navy velvet as the curtains.

A painting on the wall opposite the bed attracted her interest. Looked like birch trees. The face of a wolf was cleverly hidden among the birches, so a glance might have never picked it out.

At the end of the room were two doors—the closet and the bathroom. Bella went to shower.

After the shower, with a towel wrapped around her, she found Severo waiting at the end of the bed. He wore boxer briefs and no shirt. Daylight surfed across his broad chest, glinting on the dark hairs.

"Waiting for the shower?" Bella asked.

She boldly stepped between his legs and he eased his hands about her hips. His hopeful gaze pleased her.

"I would have liked to join you, but I just got in. Will this work, then? You staying with me?"

"I think it will," she said. "You're unsure?"

"Only because I don't want you to feel forced into anything. I would never do that."

"Oh, really, Mr. I Like To Tell Bella What To Do?" She smiled and kissed him. "I'm here of my free will."

"Good. If you should ever change your mind—"

"I'll be gone before you can argue otherwise. So! After that nap, I'm starving. I don't think a piece of toast is going to cut it."

"Heloise is making something savory right now. She's my cook and housekeeper."

"Does she know what you are?"

"Yes, and she's a faerie, so she's cool with that."

"A faerie?" Bella chirped in an entirely too wondrous tone. "Does she have wings?"

"No, she's more of the brownie persuasion. You'll meet her. She's great. Been with me for years. If you need anything, just ask Heloise. You don't mind staying in my room? There are other bedrooms, but I'd prefer if you slept with me."

"Of course you do. You like to be the one in control. The man on top."

"Is there any other position?" He clasped her wrists before him and squeezed.

"I think you'd like it rough, wouldn't you?"

"Mmm, Bella, you would be pretty tied up." His eyes glittered with desire.

The suggestion startled her, but only because she didn't react offensively to it. Tied up and at his mercy? Warmth spread up her neck and hardened her nipples. "I won't rule anything out with you. But let's take things slow, lover."

"You undo me with your acceptance, sweet. Why are you so accepting?"

"I'm not sure. I just... I said I love you earlier."

"You made me feel like I'd been given the greatest gift."

"And I mean it, even if it still feels a little crazy to fall in love so quickly and with a man who isn't even the same species as me."

"There's a lot you still don't know about me. Things you haven't seen."

"Like the werewolf?"

"Yes. Your tumble down the rabbit hole has only begun. The full moon is in three days. I'll want to get myself far away from you before then."

"Why? I want to see you as you are. Is it the wolf? Would you, or he, or whatever you call it, be violent toward me?"

"I don't suspect so. When I am the wolf, I am in canine form, but I, this man, am in there, as well.

But I don't ever remember what the werewolf has done after I've shifted."

"Really? So the werewolf can go out and do something and you wouldn't know?"

She straddled his legs and ran her fingers through his chest hair. "It's interesting that you talk about this other part of you as another entity."

"I do and I don't. I have a subtle influence over the werewolf. I mean, part of my were mind is present in that form, but it's mostly instinctual. Bella, listen to me."

Again he gripped her wrists, but gently, and kissed her knuckles.

"When the full moon is out, the werewolf comes out, too. You wanted to know what werewolves do if they don't drink blood? We seek to mate. Unfortunately, there aren't many female wolves to satisfy my werewolf. Let's say the werewolf has been going through a dry spell—an exceedingly long one—and is very frustrated. I sense it lashes out and does other things that I wouldn't be proud of."

"Like killing?"

"Not humans. Rabbits and such."

"So…it needs a mate?"

"Yes, and…" Kissing her knuckles, he held them to his lips. "I've found one."

"And that means the werewolf…?" Bella swallowed. She didn't want to think what she was thinking.

"Yes. It would expect as much."

"Ah."

So if she was Severo's girlfriend, that also made her the werewolf's girlfriend. Which disturbed her on a new level. Because if the were part of Severo enjoyed mating with her, well then, it was likely the werewolf would, too.

"Don't worry. I'll keep it from you. I promise. If I can be away from you the day preceding and following the full moon, we'll have beaten it for the month."

She nodded, not having words to say anything hopeful or promising. *For the month?* So that meant this would become a monthly thing.

"Though there are ways to keep the werewolf at bay entirely," he said, his tone becoming less serious and more playful.

"Such as?"

"Sex until I'm sated."

She delivered him a tight but wicked grin.

"It's true. If I have copious sex on the day preceding the full moon, then the werewolf will be kept at bay. I've never tried it before. It would require a lot, from any woman, to sate me."

"You don't think I'm up for the challenge?"

"I'm sure you are. But there's always the risk of what would occur if we were not successful."

The werewolf would come out to play.

Bella could deal with the man. She didn't want to deal with the animal.

"So, what's to eat?" she asked.

He leaned in and nipped her earlobe. "Besides you? I think Heloise has stew simmering. Let's go check."

With his bare feet propped on the black granite coffee table, Severo settled in the overstuffed easy chair and nursed a plate of beef stew. He never sat at the kitchen table. Too formal. Even the bar stools before the counter held no interest for him. Heloise could huff about his messy eating habits all she liked.

Bella did sit at the counter and had the neatest manners. It was fascinating to watch her interact with the elder servant.

Heloise was short, dark skinned and jolly. Cleanliness was a vocation to her kind, and she cooked as if she were a four-star chef. But she didn't approve of profuse thanks. That would result in his white shirts being laundered with a red towel in punishment. House brownies were hard workers with little pride. A simple thank-you went a long way.

After a taste of the delicious stew, Bella wanted

to know what the brownie had put in it. She didn't fawn but seemed genuinely curious, which, instead of bothering Heloise, brightened her disposition even more.

The brownie was currently showing Bella the fridge full of beef cuts she'd picked up at market the other day.

"Filet mignon!" Bella called to him and displayed the plastic-wrapped meat cut. "I'm in heaven."

And he was, too.

Suddenly life seemed bearable. Beyond bearable. He could venture to label it *right*. It hadn't felt this way for a long time. Since Aby.

He glanced to the wall beside the plasma television. Photographs hung in gold frames, put there by Aby. The one of him and Aby still hung there. He wouldn't dream of taking it down. He hadn't spoken to her for months, and he…missed her.

Friends were not easy to come by, especially for a man who'd been born and raised in a pack. The pack mentality did not allow for companionship, only constant competition and attempts to become the alpha. He'd been the principal alpha in the Northern pack for decades. And while they'd had their scuffles with the vampires over the years, Severo was proud his leadership had seen the wolves protected from humans.

After finding Aby, he had left the Northern pack. He'd found what had been missing from his life. Compassion. Companionship. And infatuation.

He had been more than willing to make Aby his mate. She had not.

Bella's giggle redirected his thoughts. She sat before the counter, soaking up the stew gravy with a slice of freshly baked oat bread.

To think, he had Elvira to thank for sending her thugs after Bella—and pushing her into his arms.

That was as far as his gratitude reached toward the vampiress. Today he would locate the mistress of the night and determine exactly what her intentions were toward Bella. And if Bella cared about the milquetoast Seth, he'd see about him, too.

"You have a pool, too," Bella said as she settled into the oversize chair alongside him. He set his plate on the floor and pulled her onto his lap. She wiped some gravy off his beard and stuck that finger into his mouth. He licked it clean. "Want to go for a swim tonight?"

Perhaps Elvira could wait.

Severo had told Bella that Heloise spent her evenings in the basement, laundering clothes, and usually left in time to get home for the late news. Still, Bella had been reluctant to strip naked and dive into the pool. Until her lover had done the stripping for her. With his teeth and tongue.

Now she surfaced in his arms and received a long, wet kiss. The weight of his embrace begged for entrance, so she wrapped her legs about him. His shaft slid into her, filling her. Severo was strong; he could tread water in the middle of the pool, allowing them to keep their heads above the water, while he pumped inside her. It was like floating and drowning at the same time.

They came together. Bella stretched her arms out across the water's surface, releasing her climax in a shivery cry.

"Severo," she murmured and then repeated his name.

He nipped at her chin. "Yes, love?"

"Is that your real name? It's so interesting."

"Strange, you mean?"

She gave him a nodding smile. "Is it your first name or last?"

"My surname, but I've never used my first. You don't think it suits me?"

"It does. Is it Italian?"

"It is. My parents immigrated at the turn of the twentieth century."

"What's your first name? I promise I won't tell if it's Percival or Eugene."

"It's Stephan," he offered. "But I don't use it, because it reminds me of my father. That was his name, as well."

"Your father? You have parents? Well, of course you do. Were you born a werewolf?"

"Yes. Both my mother and father were of the breed."

"Are they still alive?"

"No." He released her and swam backward.

The water temperature fell at the loss of contact with his warm flesh. She'd said something wrong. His parents must be a sore spot with him.

"I'd prefer you didn't use my first name," he said and heaved his body up to sit on the edge of the pool. Reaching back, he snagged a towel and sopped at his hair and chest. "Unless it's important to you."

What memories could he have of his father that made him want to renounce his name? She wanted to ask but sensed he'd put up a wall. "Severo works for me."

Bella dove deep, leaving him alone. The water muffled her senses, and the depths, which glowed aquamarine before her eyes, blocked out the world.

Here she swam, deep within the rabbit's adventure. Would he see her as a mere rabbit if the werewolf managed to find her?

* * *

Severo drove Bella to town for dance practice and promised to return for her in two hours. He shifted the Mercedes into Drive and rolled slowly down the street toward Minneapolis proper.

He wasn't sure where to find Elvira. She moved about the country but made her home in Minneapolis. Probably because she'd be laughed out of vampiredom in any other metropolitan area. He couldn't figure out if the chick knew she was copying the television personality, or if she genuinely believed the mistress-of-the-night look worked for her.

Vamps. He'd never figure them out, nor did he want to.

It had felt great ripping those two vampires apart in Bella's home last night. They'd had it coming, and he hadn't felt his energy like that for a while. The werewolf took a lot out of him during the three nights a month it reigned.

That was probably why he was so forceful with Bella. He needed an outlet for all that aggression. Sure, sex helped some, but he'd never lie to himself that romping the countryside as the wolf wasn't the ultimate.

With the full moon so close now, the dilemma arose of leaving Bella for three days, or remaining and seeing if he could sate the werewolf into submission. But he'd want to do that only for two days, the ones preceding and following the night of the full moon. The werewolf did need to roam at least once a month, and he wouldn't deny it.

That meant endangering Bella. Because Severo sensed that should the werewolf be anywhere within a sixty-mile radius of Bella, it would recognize her scent and seek her out—and then attempt to claim her as its mate.

And wouldn't that be grand? Finding a mate for the werewolf was all he could hope for. The culmination to a quest most males never achieved. Females of the breed were rare, and mortal females, well, they were too fragile. And to be approached by a werewolf for sex? Mortal women would run screaming.

Would Bella?

She'd wanted to quickly change the conversation about that. She might not think it, but much as she liked to believe she could accept him in his werewolf form, she never could.

He'd leave her this month. He must if he wanted to keep her.

Parking, because he preferred to walk outside and scent the surroundings, Severo got out and locked the car. Walking along Washington Avenue, he perused the bar offerings. A couple of strip joints flashed sexy pink neon. He could only feel pity for the women who danced inside.

Vampires were about this evening, both male and female, indulging in blood and lust. Their scent was nasty, like regurgitated blood.

Spying the black limo, he congratulated himself on an easy job. He wondered if Seth was inside the nearest bar, spinning discs. Probably. Which meant a confrontation was now or never.

An erratic techno beat filtered outside and must have disguised Severo's near-silent approach, because the two thug vamps in dark sunglasses standing outside the limo didn't turn until he was upon them.

The click of a semiautomatic alerted him, and Severo raised his hands in compliance but didn't stand down. "I promise I can break your wrist before you can pull the trigger," he offered slyly.

The thug glanced toward the back passenger window, blacked out with dark film.

"I want to talk to your mistress." Severo held up his hands in placation. "No funny stuff, promise."

The vamp snarled, revealing a yellow fang.

The back window rolled down and the scent of cheap perfume assaulted Severo's olfactories. "What does he want?" snapped the female.

"To chat," Severo said. He put down his arms and leaned over the window. "Mind if I join you?"

Her pale breasts, stuffed with silicone and barely concealed by the tight black sheath dress, rose and fell with a huffy sigh. Long black fingernails waved him around to the other side. The door unlocked and Severo gave the other thug a sneer before sliding inside.

Christ, but he wouldn't last long in this boudoir of perfume and vampire reek. Rolling down his window, Severo kept his distance from the vampiress, not because he suspected she'd slash him with those nails, but because he required the fresh air to keep his senses clear.

"Severo," she drawled with a classic night-mistress burr. "Long time. Thought I'd seen the last of you after that bloody debacle in the seventies."

He'd thought the same, but the woman was far from subtle. He caught wind of her whenever she blew into town, though he had to give her credit for keeping her messes to a minimum and being quick to clean up those that were not.

"Guess why I'm here?" he prompted.

"I saw you groping the mortal female the other night. Since when does one of the most powerful werewolves in the country stoop so low?"

He'd relinquished that "most powerful" title years ago to Amandus Masterson, after he'd left the Northern pack. No longer did he get off on conflict and pack politics. Nor could he conceive of indulging in the blood sport the wolves participated in. He was a lone wolf, and happy for it.

"She's mine, not the boy's—Seth, your plaything. The mortal woman poses no threat to you."

"They have a certain relationship that disturbs me."

"Leave her alone. Or next time I smell vamps around her, I'm coming after you."

She pursed her glossy black lips. "You're such a bully, Severo. Sexual frustration tends to do that to a man. Makes him rigid and aggressive." Fanning a black-nailed finger down her cleavage, she cooed, "You sure you don't want to try some luscious vampire flesh?"

He eyed the white breasts, which seemed to glow in the darkness. "Not if my life depended on it. Your kind is vile, Elvira."

"Don't call me that. It's Evie."

He sighed. "So will you comply? The woman is his friend. That is all."

"Make them stop being friends, and I'll consider it."

What a pouty, insolent vamp. "Just get over it, longtooth. You don't want the hurt I can promise you, so be smart and suffer your new toy his mortal friends. You know he won't last much longer. The thing is so drained, you can read by his flesh."

"I'm turning him."

Hell. Not good news for Bella or for the guy. "Haven't you enough sycophants?" he asked.

"I like this one. He's humorous. You know our sort can be so dreadfully dreary."

Like the chick next to him, clad in black and looking the queen of the Goths?

"I've said what I have to say. Whether or not you choose to take my words to heart will determine your fate. Nice talking to you, Elvira."

He swung out of the car and gasped in the night air to clear his senses. Striding away, Severo fisted his hands and growled. This was not over. It was just beginning. And much as he savored the fight, he did not favor waging war with one to whom he owed a debt.

Evie leaned over and plucked a long hair from the leather seat. She studied it, sniffed it. "So nasty."

And yet… There could be a use for this remnant from the werewolf.

She curled the hair about a forefinger until the pale flesh grew deep purple. "I will never bow before a dog."

Chapter 10

Severo had left the mansion last evening. He wouldn't tell her where he intended to stay for two nights. While Bella appreciated that he was only trying to protect her, after only twenty-four hours she missed him desperately.

Was this how it would be if their relationship continued? Him disappearing for three days every month? Certainly she could manage the distance. It was only three days. And what relationship wouldn't grow deeper with that time apart?

But her love for him was so new. Bella felt raw and uneasy as she lay alone in the king-size bed, her fingers gliding across the sheets on his side. Where was he? And in what form?

Tonight the full moon would shine brightly in the August sky. A harvest moon, which the weatherman had been encouraging everyone to go out and look at.

Bella flipped off the television and padded out to the patio. She slipped off her silk robe and dove into the pool naked. She'd gotten used to Heloise's schedule, and she tried to not strip when she knew she might run into her. The brownie was doing laundry and she usually left in the evening without a goodbye.

The pool was heated, which was a necessity in Minnesota. Floating on her back, she giggled as a falling red maple leaf landed on her belly. She let it lie there. Like a leaf floating in a pond, she was carried around the pool by the gentle current.

This could be the life. Living in a mansion with a housekeeper, gourmet meals and an attentive lover. What lottery had she won?

Okay, so the lover was not completely human. And though Severo had intimated that he'd like to support her, Bella could never allow that to happen. She liked work. It exercised her brain when her dancing was not moving her body.

Miss All About Control needed the independence

of supporting herself. But that didn't mean she couldn't work from her own office here at the mansion. She had a choice of plenty of extra rooms.

One of the patio deck lights flickered. Bella's heart did a sudden dive. She treaded water in the center of the pool.

Severo had given her explicit instructions to go inside and lock all the doors after 10:00 p.m. The werewolf knew where home was, and while it rarely ventured close, it might come sniffing about.

He did say that early morning usually found his beastly form reduced to a regular wolf, and if she wanted to look outside on the third day for that, she could.

"My lover, the wolf," she said. Her heartbeat resuming normal pace, she continued floating. "And Seth loves a vampire."

Severo had not said what had gone on between him and Evie, but he did say he'd given her an ultimatum.

Evie. *Evil,* spelled wrong. Which was what she sounded like. A self-obsessed vampire whom Severo laughingly referred to as Elvira.

Bella wondered if Evie truly resembled the tall, beehive-coiffed mistress of the dark. She wasn't sure she'd be able to keep a straight face if she ever met her. How far off Seth's scale was she? He normally went in for flirty, stupid and shallow.

A tap on the patio door alerted her. Heloise gestured. Bella dropped her legs and sank into the water to conceal her nudity. The housekeeper opened the door and made a dismissive gesture, as if she'd seen it all before.

"It's almost ten, mistress," Heloise called. "Best be getting inside."

"Already?" She hadn't thought it was that late when she'd come out here. "Yes, fine. I'll be right in. Are you turning in for the night, Heloise?"

"I go home. I have nice little house, given to me by Severo. Good night, mistress. You stay inside, yes?" She left the patio door open.

"Night." Bella swam over for a towel and slid up onto the ledge of the pool.

The open door taunted her. *Come quick, before it's too late.*

The housekeeper didn't stick around during the full moon? And she was a faerie. She should be more comfortable with the whole paranormal realm and all its dark shenanigans than any mortal.

Did that mean Bella should be treating this night as more ominous than she had last night?

Skittering across the flagstone tiles, she hastened inside and locked the door behind her, dropping the Charley bar, as Severo had taught her. The sky was dark and there, above the treetops, the fat harvest moon sat low and proud.

A canine howl sounded in the distance.

Bella's heart fluttered.

"I'd better check all the doors and windows."

Doors locked? Check. Windows locked, all fitted with special security bars that locked into a steel casement? Check. If the high security didn't give her the willies, then nothing else should.

It was nearing 1:00 a.m., and Bella sat in the middle of the bed, the soft shirt she'd picked up from the floor clutched to her chest. It was Severo's and it smelled like him, so she'd pulled it on after a quick shower to wash away the chlorine.

And here she sat, as she had last night, staring out the window. Severo's house sat at the bottom of a valley. The countryside rose in the distance. Hundreds of acres of forested land, he'd explained, all belonged to him. The moon had tucked itself out of view, but the sky was luminous against the black tree silhouettes.

An owl hooted. A dog howled. The wind picked up. And now branches scraping the windows kept her alert. Any little noise set her heart to a jackrabbit kick against her chest.

In the horror movies, it wasn't the gross creature

or the blood that got to her; it was the anticipation of evil.

"He's not evil," she whispered.

Their romance had been fast and more than furious. He'd captured her from day one, literally, and Bella appreciated now that he had not relented his pursuit of her. Never had she been with such a man. Virile, strong, attentive and, yes, commanding.

And much as she'd never wanted to be controlled, she didn't feel controlled by Severo. But an edge of domination existed, which she willingly surrendered to.

Because with Severo's control, she also received safety and a feeling of contentment.

Even sitting here, listening to the night spooks, she had to admit she was safe. The windows were secure, as were the doors. Surely the wolf wouldn't attempt to break through?

Part of her wanted to see the werewolf, to know her lover in all his forms. Another part thought it fine and dandy that she sat inside and it was outside.

Eyelids flickering, Bella yawned.

A squabble between worm-seeking robins outside the window woke her hours later. She'd made it through the second night, which, as Severo had pointed out, was the most perilous of nights, because during the full moon the werewolf most felt the call to mate.

* * *

The werewolf howled a long, lonely cry to the moon.

Bring her to me. Give me what I have wanted for so long.

It sensed something had changed. It had no notion that when it was not stalking the countryside, it could be in any other form than this man/beast shape. It knew only that humans were to be fiercely avoided.

And yet, a new scent clung to its form, the taut muscles that stretched its legs and forearms and twined within its flesh. It smelled human, and like a sweet plant it had once scented so many years ago.

Where did it come from? And how to find the source?

The werewolf wanted to know it, to feel it. To lick it and taste the sweetness that the lingering scent promised.

Yet the strange inner caution that often kept it from wandering onto private mortal land again held it back. Made it cower, for fear of revealing itself to the world.

It would not seek the scent. Not yet.

Night three. A glance to the clock revealed it was 2:00 a.m. Severo had said it would be safe after three on the final night. Anticipation kept her vigilant.

Bella had never been a dog lover. She didn't hate them, but she did fear them, for rational reasons. A dog had once bitten her. Another time, when she was a teenager, a huge rottweiler had chased her down an alley.

A wolf must be ten times more dangerous than a dog.

Bella smirked and tugged up the loose shirt for the countless time to draw in Severo's scent. Now she understood how he could take pleasure in scents. Scents reassured and excited her.

She slid the shirt across her bare stomach and glided her fingers lower to press upon the rise of her mons. There was where he mastered her with his tongue, flicking and pressing and teasing her to a climax that always made her see stars.

She'd never had make-me-see-stars sex with other men. And she couldn't get enough of the constellation Severo.

A loud noise outside, in the patio area, stiffened her shoulders. Bella waited, her neck straight and ears perked. A hot streak of fear stretched along her collarbone. She didn't know what to expect. A shadow crossing outside the window? A monstrous shape creeping before the shrubs?

Time passed slowly.

The next time she looked, the clock flicked to three forty-five.

Exhausted from sitting alert all night, Bella longed to fall asleep. But a niggling curiosity pushed her from the bed.

She scampered down the hall and across the vast marble foyer in the shirt, her legs bare. The house was still and illuminated with moonlight shining in through the sunroof three stories overhead.

Heloise took joy in revving up the floor polisher and going at this marble expanse. Bella wished she could get the housekeeper to come to her loft once in a while.

Severo had reported that the glass in the patio door at her place had been replaced and the floor and curtains cleaned. What he'd not said was that he wanted her to move back to town. Until he asked, she was content here. As long as she didn't miss practice or the audition in a few days.

Approaching the patio door, she scanned outside. The maple trees about the pool filtered out the moonlight. If a beast lurked in the shadows, she wouldn't be able to see it. And she'd never pick up its scent, as Severo did so well.

Still, she released the door latch and stepped

outside. Burned peat sweetened the air. She had seen the fires that afternoon and had guessed that they were about two miles to the west. Farmers burning brush in the ditches, no doubt.

The flagstones were cool underfoot. Clutching the shirt at her breasts, she scanned the circumference. Nothing.

Sitting carefully at the pool's edge, she decided not to dip her feet in.

A breeze flirted with her hair, blowing a few strands across her cheek. The soft touch reminded her of Severo's kisses when he was being lazy after they'd made love for hours.

Because normally everything about him was aggressive—go, go, go, and don't stop until you've gone beyond. She liked that about him. It made her strive to keep up, to release some control and let chaos reign.

She smirked at the notion that she'd relinquished control to a man. An incredibly assertive man who would not allow her to forget he was in charge of her pleasure. A charge he fulfilled beyond her dreams.

A click sounded to her side. Animal claws on stone.

Bella swallowed down her fear, and bravely turned to find a dark-furred wolf staring at her. Her heart seemed to stop beating. Her stomach loosened, while her neck muscles tightened.

It stood six feet from her. Black markings on its face made it blend it into the murky, predawn surroundings. Only the paler belly fur made it stand out. It was a big wolf, perhaps the size of a monster German shepherd.

Don't think about monsters. It's just a nice puppy. It's not going to hurt you.

To turn and dash inside might startle it. The wolf might think she was being aggressive and attack.

Don't be silly. He said his were mind is also present when he is the wolf.

Inhaling, Bella drew up courage. She could do this. She wanted to do this.

She held out her hand, not sure if she was offering friendship or her scent for it to smell. Probably both. Just so long as it didn't find her tasty.

It? No, this was her lover. That same piercing dark stare took her measure now. At the corner of its jaw, one canine tooth peeked out. It wasn't snarling at her, though. She hoped.

And then it bowed its head and lifted a paw to its jaw.

She didn't know what it was trying to convey.

"Severo?" She leaned forward on her elbows and the wolf padded closer. "Come to me."

The wolf whined lowly and padded up to her. It sniffed at her hands, then at her hair. When its nose grazed her ear, she flinched and cautioned herself not to make any quick moves.

Closing her eyes, she wished it gone. Why had she thought this a smart idea? It was smelling her. Probably wondering how easily it could rip her up for dinner.

No, don't think it. He is Severo. There must be some part of the wolf that recognized her and wanted not to harm her.

A nudge of its nose to her wrist made her wonder if it wanted her to…touch it?

Bella lifted a hand, and carefully, slowly, she reached to smooth her palm over the short fur between its ears. The wolf nudged her wrist again in an encouraging manner.

It didn't seem to be hungry or to have a carnivorous intent in mind. Bella released her breath and relaxed.

She ruffled her palms through its soft fur. It was thick and silken, unlike that of any dog she'd ever accidentally touched. And it didn't threaten her at all.

"You're gorgeous, lover."

Chapter 11

He awoke with a start. The air breezed across his back with a cool kiss of oncoming autumn. The night had died and he lay on the patio tiles, naked, scratched on the forearms and legs. And hungry, as usual.

A soft murmur made him turn over. Bella smiled, coming up from a sleep of the angels. "Morning, lover."

She'd come out to meet the wolf? *Brave woman*.

But not the bravery that meeting his werewolf would require. And he did want that to happen. The urge had struck last night. The werewolf had *known*.

A potential mate was close by. It had taken all Severo's influence to keep it away from the house.

"I love the wolf," she said on a sleepy smile.

And he bowed his head against her breast and held her tight.

"How's it coming along?" Evie strode into the brightly lit laboratory and traced a finger along the stainless-steel counter. "Was the hair sufficient?"

Ian Grim glanced up from a grimoire he'd been poring over. His dark hair hung over one pale eye and he licked dry lips. "Excellent actually. I've almost figured out how to deactivate the protection wards."

"And the binding spell?"

"I'll need another week for that. Patience, my lady. You've been dreaming of this revenge for decades. Another few weeks will only make the reward much sweeter. I don't understand your goal, though. Why not kill her?"

"Think about it, Grim. Of all the paranormals in this realm, what two species most clash and hate one another?"

"Used to be we witches and the vampires."

"Yes, but now that the Protection spell has been lifted, I've no fear of your blood. So you know what that leaves."

"It is an interesting prospect. I wish you the best."

"I don't need your wishes. I need your spells. Back to work, Grim."

The studio was small, lined from a mirrored wall to a cement wall with raised hardwood flooring. Off in the corner, a guitarist strummed as a female dancer breezed through a routine of stomping feet and twisting arms and hips.

Tonight was the audition session Bella had told him about. It was important to her, so he'd wanted to be here for her.

Severo wasn't interested in any of the women waiting for their chance to dance. He grew alert only as Bella took the floor, her arms moving out gracefully and twisting above her head to assume a beginning pose.

The black skirt hugged her legs and the heavy white ruffles fell above her ankles. A fitted black leotard put her breasts on display and made him jealous that two other men stood in the room.

He lowered his head and observed through his lashes as the music began.

Bella's body, sinuous and sleek, captured the music and spoke to his most feral desires. Below the waist she was forceful and loud. Above, she wove a sorrowful story with her arms and dramatic twists.

And then a man approached her, cocky and stiff, as if he were a bull approaching the cape. Which, Severo guessed, was the purpose of the dance.

He didn't like this man. The dark hair that slicked over his ears and the focus he gave to Bella raised Severo's hackles. He stomped out a rapid array of footwork, which stirred the other dancers to a cheering rhythmic clap.

Bella bent backward, one hand clutching her skirt up high, so a half arc of ruffles swirled from wrist to ankle. Fiercely determined, she snapped her wrist to a hip and spun about to mirror the male dancer as he tormented the floor with his heels.

The man charged her with the dominating steps of a bull. Shoulders thrust back and body sleek and straight, the man focused his attention on Bella's face. His feet tortured the wood floor as he stomped about her, claiming, defying. Owning.

Severo exhaled. Hell, he was jealous of the man wearing dance shoes and a gold-spangled bolero jacket.

But he checked his anger. If he was jealous, that could only be a good thing. That meant he wasn't obsessing about Aby. The realization made him momentarily sad, but he chased the feeling away with a try at the *palmas,* or hand clapping.

It didn't work. His focus remained on the mere inches of space between the male dancer and Bella.

The air was charged with pheromones, and the scent of their dance disturbed Severo. And then the man reached up to stroke the side of Bella's face—

"Enough!" With two strides, Severo insinuated himself between the two.

The guitarist stopped. The male dancer swore in Spanish and stomped off. Bella's look cut Severo sharply, but the small pain did not squelch his anger.

"You're leaving now," he barked.

He tugged Bella from the room and slammed the door behind them.

In the hallway she wrestled her wrist from his grip, then shoved him in the chest.

"You ass! What do you think you just did?"

"I didn't like the way he was touching you."

"Touching? *Touching?*"

"He was marking you with his scent."

"His scent?" She let out a frustrated groan and, grabbing her duffel from the assortment of bags on the floor, marched away. "You've embarrassed the hell out of me and made damn well sure I never dance at this studio again. Marking? Get a clue, wolf boy. We were dancing!"

He rushed after her, but she eluded his grip. "Don't touch me."

"Bella, he was being aggressive with you. You may not be able to perceive such subtle cues, but I can. He had more in mind than dancing."

She spun and swung up a palm. The slap to his face cracked loudly. Severo retaliated with a growl and he clasped her throat with one hand.

"You are an animal," she said. He dropped his hand then and, turning, she stomped off, the metal on her heels clicking angrily.

"I'm not an animal." He swallowed. His hand was still clenched and ready to choke anyone, anything. "Oh hell. Am I?"

Chapter 12

Bella stomped inside her loft and barely took time to unbuckle her dance shoes before kicking them across the rug.

The violet suede shoes were her lucky shoes. "Lot of good they did. That idiot wolf!"

Heading directly for the shower, she squeezed past the overzealous bamboo plant, shedding her skirt and top on the way. "He thought Tony was putting his scent on me? What kind of freak is he? Oh right, a werewolf freak."

It was good to be home. It had been nice at

Severo's estate, but after tonight, she wasn't in the mood for his raging alpha hormones.

At least he had taken a hint and had not followed her home.

A shower and scrub with lots of lemon bath gel refreshed her, but Bella stayed under the water stream for half an hour, till the water got cold. Lost in the patter of water, she allowed her thoughts to flee and she found a tolerable medium between anger and peace.

That the man could so easily toy with her emotions troubled her. And then she knew it was because he meant so much to her. If she meant half as much to him, shouldn't he have known his actions would destroy her?

The sun had set by the time she exited the steamy paradise. Tugging on a silk robe, she padded into the kitchen to browse the fridge. A few nonperishable items remained, though none appealed to her. Not even the half tub of milk-chocolate frosting.

"I miss Heloise's cooking. Oh! What is it with that man? He's always so…macho. So controlling."

She'd thought she liked that about him. But how could she after what he'd done tonight? He'd ruined any chance of her getting the apprenticeship.

She didn't know how to deal with his possessiveness. How did a girl date a wolf and make it work? "Mom never had any advice for that one," she told herself aloud.

Diana Reynolds, who had headed off to Tunisia a month ago to work with a charity organization, would have told her daughter to face the challenge head-on. *Don't let it upset you. Look at the reason why it's in your life. To teach you something.*

Teach her? But what?

To be less controlling? But in exchange for being controlled?

That didn't jibe.

To be more accepting of those unlike her? She'd always been open-minded. *Prejudice* was not a word in the Reynolds household.

To love? She loved. Many. But Bella had never loved deeply like this before.

Was romantic love supposed to ache as well as feel good?

Scratching her head, she surveyed the room. She didn't feel in the mood for a swim. The computer sat silently mocking her lack of attention.

"I should check my e-mail." It had been over a week, and though her current clients didn't require immediate attention, she never knew when a new client would contact her.

Booting up the Mac, she waited while the Entourage program downloaded 220 e-mails. That would take a while to sort through. And she was still too frustrated to sit quietly and do work.

Instead, Bella went to the Internet and searched Google for *werewolf.*

Wikipedia called them lycanthropes, humans with the ability to shape-shift into a wolf or a wolflike creature.

The *loup-garou* in eighteenth-century France was a feared and hunted creature, blamed for killing dozens of men, women and children.

Their weaknesses were silver and wolfsbane. And the idea of a werewolf bite transforming a mortal into a werewolf was purely a fictional creation.

Weren't werewolves themselves supposed to be fictional?

And yet, knowing they were real wasn't so awful. Just…

"Pissed," she muttered sharply. "So pissed at him."

She clicked to another site and another. They all rehashed the lore and legend and featured artists' renditions of the creature. But none of the sites told her about the man she was dealing with. She searched Google for *wolf.*

According to the Internet they usually ran in packs of six to eight. Yet, she thought, Severo had never mentioned other werewolves. The site also said a wolf could be an alpha, but to do so, it must find an unoccupied territory and a female to mate with.

Bella clutched her throat.

She read more. The wolf's sense of smell was about one hundred times greater than a human's. She knew that. They also marked their territory. So it was an ingrained thing with Severo, she realized. Was he worried Tony was marking his territory?

That still didn't explain his reaction at the studio.

She read more. "A wolf may growl to indicate warning or dominance."

Severo growled a lot. And it always turned her on if they were making out. He was dominating her.

A shiver traced her shoulders and arms. A good shiver.

A rap on the patio door made Bella sit up, alert. It was getting late. Who could that be? A vampire? In her anger, she'd forgotten the danger, the reason Severo had coaxed her away from her home in the first place.

Would a murderous vampire knock first? she reasoned as she walked over to the door. Through the long white sheers she saw the shadow outside— a big male shadow who wore a leather jacket.

"Go away!" she called through the glass door.

"I'm sorry," Severo said, his voice calm and low. "Please, can we talk?"

"I'm not in the mood." She peeked through the curtain, found he stood with his back to the door, and then dropped the curtain and paced around the living room.

This seemed to be his MO. Stalk her when she hated him. Overwhelm her with his caveman aggression and awkward charm to win her over.

"It's not going to work tonight," she muttered, with a glance to her abandoned dancing shoes.

He could have no idea how much earning an apprenticeship with Tony meant to her. Web design was fun, and it paid the bills, but it required one's butt in the chair all day. Dancing? Well, Bella couldn't get enough of the motion, the freedom, the utter abandon.

"Bella, please."

"Don't say my name," she whispered. She clutched her arms across her chest in a less than reassuring hug. "Just go away."

He couldn't hear her soft, trembling plea. But if he was so keen on picking up her scent, why couldn't he also hear through walls and windows? Shouldn't paranormal sorts be able to do all kinds of fabulous things with their senses?

And yet, his sense of propriety was off the scale.

"Wolves are protective of their mates. They mate for life," she said, repeating the information she'd read online. "And werewolves are creatures, not humans."

With a shudder, she paused before the patio door. His shadow was not there, but she could see a figure now standing before the pool's edge.

"He's not going to leave."

Resigned to make the best of it, at least to try convincing him to leave, Bella pulled the door open and slipped outside. He remained before the pool, looking down.

At an amazing sight.

Bella joined Severo at his side. Dozens of white water lilies floated on the surface of the water. The streetlight across the alley shone over the water and glinted in the droplets dewed on the pale petals. Gorgeous. And fantastical.

Bella swallowed and looked up at Severo.

"Roses are so common," he offered. "I figure you've received dozens from previous suitors. These caught my eye. They're a pitiful apology, but they're a start."

Her anger dissipated. The tenderness in his voice struck her. He knew he'd done wrong. She wished it hadn't been such a devastating wrong.

"The pool man is going to have a fit," she said,

and bent to sit and dangle her legs in the pool. Lifting her toe, she caught a bloom on top of her foot and balanced it there. The bright yellow center winked at her as it bobbled. "This doesn't begin to make up for what you did earlier."

He knelt, one leg stretched out to the side, hands clasped between his thighs. He hadn't yet met her gaze, so she knew he was feeling remorseful. *Good.* Mr. Big Bad needed to be knocked down a few pegs.

"I should not have accompanied you to the audition. I'm sorry. I just… You can't understand what it's like for me to stand by and watch my mate interact with another man."

"It's called dancing. People do it all the time without falling down and having sex."

He swiped a hand over his face and gritted out, "But you're mine."

"I don't belong to you. I don't want to be owned by you."

"You're my mate, Bella."

"Is that how it's supposed to be for a werewolf's mate? Secluded away from the rest of the world, never allowed to hold a conversation with another man for fear he may look at her the wrong way or, heaven forbid, shake her hand?"

"Please, Bella." He clenched his hands into fists, fighting aggression. "This is new for me. I'm trying not to be the he-man, as you call it, and to make this relationship work."

"New?" She tipped the flower off her foot and cast her toe about in search of another. "You've never had a mate before?"

"No."

"But you've had sex with women."

"Doesn't make them my mate. I explained this. You are the only one for me. You've met the wolf, and it accepted you. No other woman has met the wolf."

He was trying, she could tell. It must be killing him not to simply grab her, kiss her and drag her home by her hair.

Home. She'd just considered Severo's mansion to be home. She'd known him but a short while, and already she felt as if he was a part of her life. And some parts of life weren't always fun and joyous, but occasionally sticky and downright meddlesome.

"Severo." She breathed out and closed her eyes, drawing in the lilies' scent. "Despite the fact that this is the strangest relationship ever…and that you are not a gentle or compassionate person…and that you insist that everything goes your way…*and* that when you find someone you want, you take them, no matter their concerns… Despite all that, a part of me is in for the ride. I mean…"

She sighed. Was she going to admit this after only moments ago reveling in her anger?

It was futile to resist.

"This feels right. And I do love you."

Smiling a careful smile, he reached in to the pool and plucked a blossom. He tucked it over her ear, and a few droplets of water ran down her cheek. He traced one droplet down to her jaw.

"And yet, I don't want to sacrifice my life to be a part of yours," she added.

"You needn't."

"But dancing means a lot to me. I had hopes of getting that apprenticeship. It would have advanced my studies and allowed me to teach part-time."

"I'll call the studio tomorrow. No, I'll go there and apologize in person."

"No, don't. It's over. I'm sure Tony has already selected an apprentice. I don't want you going anywhere near the studio."

"I will not, then. Good thing for Tony."

She smirked. "He's gay, big boy."

"Really? But he moved so sensually with you. Ah, I don't have that… What is it they call it?"

"Gaydar?"

"Yes, that. I'm sorry, Bella." He removed his hand from her cheek, but she took his palm in hers.

"Apology accepted. But I have a life, which you need to accept if you want me in yours. And I have a job."

"You needn't work, Bella. I will take care of you."

"But I like my job, and I like to work. It gives me a sense of purpose. Heck, it's a means of communicating with others."

"I have an office at the estate. It is yours to use when you wish."

"I know." She sighed again.

She would get nowhere arguing about her need to keep hold of the real world. Not the weird, marvelous world at the bottom of the rabbit hole that Severo occupied. That world was interesting, and she liked being a part of it. But rationally, she knew she had to cling to her world as long as possible.

His presence, so immense and overpowering, was softened by the flowers' perfume. At once she hated him, and she did not. He was a lost soul, roaming the earth in search of another soul who could fulfill him, make him happy, erase his pain.

She hadn't thought she needed a relationship, but feeling needed did something to her idea of remaining single. It obliterated the idea.

And if that didn't do it, Severo's kiss did.

He tilted up her chin and leaned in to kiss her.

So gentle, lingering, not a hint of the intensity his kisses usually wielded. I'm sorry, the kiss said.

And then it was gone, and he sat next to her, stretching his legs out to the side so they wouldn't dangle in the pool. Bella snuggled her cheek against his chest. "I want to make this work," she whispered.

He stroked her hair and simply held her. His silence was the best thing he could have given her.

Bella hung up the phone and rubbed her palms along her bare arms.

"Something wrong, sweet?"

She turned to hug up to her lover on the bed. They'd retreated to the bedroom. Last night she had agreed her loft in the city wasn't safe and had gone home with him after they'd made love beside the flower-filled pool.

They spent most nights making love. It was as if they couldn't get enough of each other. He was her air, and she his. The man was insatiable.

"That was Seth." She rested her head against his shoulder and stared up at the ceiling. "He wants to talk."

"And he couldn't do it over the phone? Bella, how did he sound?"

"What do you mean?"

"It's been over a month. There's no way he could have survived as Elvira's blood slave. She must have turned him."

"He would have told me."

"Maybe he intends to tell you when you meet. You can't go see him. I won't allow it."

"I'm not asking your permission." She slid out of bed, thinking it was time to get dressed. A woman could not survive on sex alone. Breakfast was in order, even if it was two in the afternoon. "I'm going to see him."

She tugged a loose sundress over her body and took off.

"Then I'm coming with you."

Heloise was not in the kitchen, and Bella was glad for that. She wanted an apple, and a few minutes to think about her friend without the wolf bellowing at her.

Peace was not to be had.

Her lover padded in, wearing jeans and a frown. His limp was always more noticeable when his mood was foul.

"Last time you came along, Seth clammed up." She bit into a juicy green apple.

Don't look at the half-dressed werewolf's muscles. You can't stay angry at the man's ripped abs, and you know it.

"You're staying home, if I have to find a leash," she said.

He snarled. So she'd used one of the bad words. Get over it.

"And if I lock you in the bedroom?" he challenged.

"You wouldn't dare."

"I will if it means keeping you safe."

"He's a friend, Severo. Seriously, I'm adjusting to the possessive stuff, but you take it too far sometimes."

"You have no idea what his mind-set is. And if he is a vampire, he is not the same friend you used to know. Don't be stupid about this, Bella. You know better."

She did know better.

Setting the apple on the counter, Bella stretched her arms along it and laid her head on an elbow. "I don't want to believe it." She stared at the framed picture tucked behind the toaster. "Don't you have friends you worry about? Family?"

"I have no family. And friends are few and far between."

"So who is this?" She tugged out the picture and displayed it to him.

His intake of breath made Bella stand up straight. In the picture, a pretty red-haired woman snuggled up to Severo, beaming, as was he. Which had startled her the first time she'd seen it. Severo was not a smiley fellow.

He seemed ready to grab the photo away but wasn't sure how to do it.

"She means something to you. What's her name? And why haven't I met her? Is she an old girlfriend?"

"Enough!" He snatched the photo and studied it for long seconds before tucking it into a drawer. "She's someone I used to know."

"Really? Her picture is everywhere. Over by the TV, in the hallway. Down in the laundry room."

"When have you been to the laundry room?"

"I like to chat with Heloise. Which has nothing to do with the question you're trying to avoid. If she was a lover, I'd understand. We both had lives before meeting one another. I want to know who is important to you, Severo. Is she to you as Seth is to me? Talk to me."

He drew a hand over his mouth and jaw, delaying a reply. Looking about, he paced. Always he became antsy when he was riled or scented something wrong.

"She was a lover," Bella decided and took another bite of apple.

"She was not," he hissed. The ferocity in his stare made her choke on the apple. "And this conversation is over."

Chapter 13

Bella sorted through her few dresses in the large closet, which, surprisingly, held only a few items of Severo's clothing. The man did like his dark jeans and shirts. She guessed that made less work for Heloise. But if he'd lived for so long, surely by now he should have collected a wardrobe.

Or maybe not. Though the house was grand, the man lived a simple life, which she admired.

Yet she still wasn't sure what he did. Something related to buying forested real estate to create a wolf preserve. But how did he make his money in order to do that?

Feeling only a little guilty about leaving for town tonight, she decided she had every right to go out by herself. And it was to meet a friend. He couldn't begrudge her that.

Though she knew he meant well, wanting to protect her. But she needed to keep her life, as she'd hoped she'd made clear to him. It wasn't as though he didn't have a whole life she wasn't a part of.

That woman in the pictures. She had to have been a lover. Bella could feel it, no matter how much he denied it. And he had called out a woman's name that night the vampires had attacked in her loft.

Did she have a rival for Severo's heart?

Jealousy flushed her chest. And then she realized she was behaving like him, getting angry over something that likely wasn't a problem.

Though she had to admit, Severo's jealousy did make her feel special. No man had ever been so fiercely protective of her. There he went again, making a girl feel like a princess.

The bedroom door opened, and Bella didn't bother to turn around. She wore spike heels, panties and a bra. Let him ogle.

"Her name is Aby," he said.

Bella lowered the red dress she held and turned to him.

Severo, head down, limped a few paces. "She lived with me for ten years before moving out last year. She was...everything to me."

Ten years? And they *hadn't* been lovers? Now this was interesting. But his edgy tone cautioned her. *Don't rile the beast, Bella. Leave him to simmer.*

"Sorry. It seems a sore spot with you. I shouldn't have asked."

"You need to know. I shouldn't hold things back from you, Bella. Know that I try to be as forthright as I'm able."

"I know you do. I trust that you'll tell me what you think I need to know when the time is right. So thanks for giving me that part of you."

He nodded. "I'm going out to look at the car before you leave."

And with that, he was gone.

Bella stared at the open doorway. She had grown accustomed to her lover's constant presence, and so his swift absence pricked at her heart.

She stepped around the bed and pulled open a dresser drawer by the bed where she knew he kept a photo of the woman.

Ten years.

She traced the woman's face and Severo's beaming smile.

"Will you ever smile so big for me? Or is she always in your heart? What did she mean to you if you weren't lovers?"

A child? A friend? A relative?

"Maybe Heloise would know?"

He held the Mercedes' keys and waited for Bella. She had insisted on going into town to meet Seth without him. He knew she'd meet trouble.

After their argument this afternoon about Aby, he did owe Bella further explanation.

It hadn't been an argument. More like him clamming up and not knowing how to face the feelings he'd kept buried for more than a year.

For ten years he had shared his life with her. Now Aby was gone. Stolen by another man.

He'd given Bella what information he could about his and Aby's relationship. It wasn't much. Perhaps he could give her more. But how did he release the feelings that sat in his chest like a black mass unwilling to be pried out?

It was generous of her to say she would accept what he could give her when he felt right about it. "Bella. My Bella."

"You're not coming along?"

Surprised he'd not caught her scent, Severo hardened his frown. She wore red, and that angered him. Seth was just a friend, he reminded himself. Just as he and Aby had been friends?

He attempted to remain stoic. "No. I promised I would not."

"You won't follow me?"

Well, he hadn't promised that.

"At least stay out of sight, if you do. I know you will follow me."

"I loved her," he said and clutched the keys tightly. "Aby. I loved her. I could have made her my mate, but she didn't want that. I respected her for that."

Bella dropped her purse on the front seat and gave him an expectant look. "You don't have to talk about this."

"I need you to know me."

"Thought we were taking it slow now. I won't meet the werewolf until the next full moon. I don't need to meet the old girlfriend. Ever."

"She wasn't my girlfriend. She was my..." Even after all these years, he still didn't know how to describe their relationship. "Aby is a familiar. Do you know what familiars are?"

She shook her head.

"They are bridges for demons from their realm to this one. She is a tool. And she's a shape-shifter like me. But familiars shift to cats."

"Really?"

He could read her thoughts and answered them. "Cats and wolves do not get along, nor should werewolves and familiars. But I found Aby when she was a kitten—rather, the wolf did—and led her home. She had just begun a new life. Familiars have nine of them. They forget their experiences, though, from one life to the next.

"Aby grew up here, and we were like friends and relatives and lovers. Though we never made love, I wanted to have that relationship. And there were times I could sense the same desire in her, but mostly, she thought of me as a brother figure."

Bella didn't speak, which made the confession easier. Or maybe not.

"She fell in love last year. With a good man. A demon hunter. Someone I did not initially care for, but now I'm glad she loves him."

"Someone you didn't care for? The poor man. I can imagine the rough time you must have given him." Bella's smile soothed Severo's anxiety. "It must have been hard for you."

"It still is. I miss her. She doesn't call often enough. It's been months since I've spoken to her."

"Maybe you should call her."

"No, she's on the road all the time. She and her highwayman."

"Highwayman?"

"He's a demon hunter. Bit of a celebrity in the paranormal realm. I didn't like his cocksureness when I first met him. I felt threatened. But we've come to an understanding."

"Sounds like you've decided to accept him, if only because he means so much to Aby."

"That's about it."

He bowed his head, and Bella stroked his cheek. He loved her touch. The warmth of her, standing so close, yet not threatening, felt exquisite. She accepted him.

"Aby is who the wolf thinks about when he howls to the moon, I am sure. They used to get along, the wolf and the cat. It's bizarre to imagine, but we were happy."

She kissed him, barely touching his mouth. "Is it all right, then, with me? I don't want to step on her memory."

"You never could. I try to keep the two of you in different places in my heart. You are my mate, Bella."

"But will I ever be as close to you as you were to her?"

"I hope so."

She understood what he could not put into words. Bless her for that. And it gave him all the more reason to try his damnedest never to allow Aby into that place in his heart that Bella now occupied.

"I suppose you should be going?"

She eyed the keys he held out. *Please change your mind. Stay away from the vampires, and make love with me tonight.*

She took the keys. "Remember what I said about staying out of sight."

"I bow to your command, sweet. But know, if all hell breaks loose, I'm going to be there, loud and proud."

"Deal."

Scarlet was a local bar that catered to Goths and, now that Bella thought about it, probably paranormals, as well. She'd been here only once previously, with Seth. The entire place was lit in red: the booths were red vinyl, the dance floor was lit underneath by red bulbs, the windows had red stained glass and even the toilets were red.

An appropriate place to meet vampires, she supposed. If one wanted to meet a vampire. Which she did not.

"Please don't let him be a vampire."

Thankful they were meeting in public, she parked the Mercedes in the lot and hopped out. Wearing red might be overkill, but she never failed to dress the part when clubbing.

Though consciously aware of her surroundings,

she didn't spot a werewolf lurking in the shadows. Of course, Severo would be discreet. She smiled to think he was out there somewhere, keeping an eye on her. And it didn't feel like she was being stalked, only that she was loved.

Her black velvet stilettos clicked on the sidewalk, and she had merely to flash the bouncer a smile for admission.

It took a while to adjust to the atmosphere. The red tricked her eyes and painted the faces around her.

Dirgelike music surprised her. Seth liked the funky techno stuff. He'd call this stuff a snoozer.

"Where are you, Seth?" She sipped her drink and scanned the crowd and the upper level. Seth waved and lifted his drink.

With a glance to the door—would Severo make good on his promise to follow her?—Bella headed upstairs.

Seth rose and kissed both her cheeks and mouth. Lemon, cologne and beer—the scent worked on him. His hair seemed darker, the long fringy bangs hanging over his eyes. A couple of silver rings flashed on his fingers. Seth had never worn jewelry; bling, he said, was for posers.

Bella slid into the booth next to him. He held her hand, so she had no choice but to sit close. That was usual. He seemed to be the same old Seth, except for the rings. But a turtleneck in this weather?

"I've missed you," he said close to her ear so she could hear over the music. "You look great, Bellybean."

"You don't look so bad yourself. You dump Elvira?"

"No bitchy stuff tonight, Bella. Please. She's my lover, and you're going to have to accept that."

"I can, but does that mean you're a vampire?"

"Why do you ask?"

"Severo said you couldn't have survived this long without her turning you."

"You still hanging around that bastard werewolf? Is that why you're never home?"

"I had to move out to his place after vampires tried to kill me. Did you hear that, Seth?" She leaned close to his ear. "Vampires tried to *kill* me. She's doing this, you know. She's jealous."

"I don't want to get into this argument again. You're being brainwashed by that dog."

"Don't call him a dog. He's a wolf."

"Yeah, and I'm Renfield." He slugged back the beer.

Bella stroked the stem of her cosmo goblet. She had no appetite for alcohol right now. Or for snotty friends.

"Hey," he said in a calmer voice, "we started on the wrong foot. Let's just chill and catch up, okay?"

"Is that why you wanted to see me?"

"It's been so long, and I know I've been ignoring you. So you've moved? Permanently?"

"No, I still have the loft. I'm not sure about moving to town right now."

"Fair enough. What about the audition? Wasn't that a few nights ago?"

He'd remembered. Good old Seth.

"I didn't get the apprenticeship." She shrugged. "I'll give it another go next time."

"Bella, I'm sorry." He hugged her and kissed her jaw. Beyond his usual scent, he smelled like something darker. Blood? She didn't want to think about it. "Want to come to a party next weekend?"

"At your woman's house?"

"My house. But she'll be there. I'd like to introduce you. Sans wolf, of course."

Next weekend was the full moon. Bella didn't want to go anywhere. Nor did an invite to meet Elvira sound particularly intriguing.

"Can I take a rain check? Severo's got some things going on."

Seth laughed and a jerk of his arm spilled the cosmo across the table. "Ah, shit. Sorry. Just push it all to the other side. That's cool." He pressed his nose against Bella's hair and kissed her hard on the neck, lingering too long. "Let me guess. Full moon coming soon? He's going out on the prowl. Does the werewolf fuck you, Bella?"

She hauled off to slap him, but the small booth wouldn't allow her to get her arm around. Seth caught her fist and kissed it. His wicked smile disturbed her.

"You're crude, Seth."

"Yeah, but you know what they say about werewolves, don't you?"

"What?"

"They aren't happy unless the werewolf has a mate. That it's the monster, not the man, who needs to get boned every full moon. I can't see you screwing a hairy beast, Bella. It's so not you."

"Like letting some Elvira wannabe suck out your blood is any more sane? God, Seth, just…sit back. You've changed."

"So have you, Bella. You're uptight now. More so than usual. Bet if I asked you to dance, you'd make an excuse not to."

"My shoes are wet with cosmopolitan."

"See?" He grabbed her wrist when she stood and roughly tugged her back to sit by him. "Don't go yet, please? Or is your master here, lurking in the shadows?"

"Is yours?"

His drunken smile cut into her heart. "Touché. As a matter of fact she isn't. I wanted it to be just us tonight. Let's go to my place and watch a movie and make like old times again. Would you like that?"

His eyes were bloodshot; she could tell that even with the red lighting. And he was so pale. He was a vampire. He had to be.

Severo had said he could scent vampires. Bella wished he'd taught her to pick up that distinctive odor.

"Tell me one thing before I decide. And it has to be the truth, Seth. You know I can tell when you're lying."

"Very well, Miss Uptight. What truth do you need?"

"Are you a vampire?"

He smirked and mumbled a lackluster, "No."

Seth always mumbled his lies. God, what had happened to him?

"I've got to go. Bye, Seth." She leaned in and kissed his forehead. This time he let her go and tilted his head toward the dance floor, not even watching her leave.

Bella's feet raced as fast as her heart as she shoved through the club.

Severo was sitting on the passenger side of the Mercedes when she arrived. Bella got in, and before she could sniff away the tear, he reached for her cheek and wiped it away.

"I'm sorry," he said. "It was inevitable."

"At least he won't die now," she murmured. Forced optimism didn't work this time. Gripping the steering wheel, she closed her eyes and tilted her head against the seat. "Is there any way he can change back?"

"Impossible."

What she'd suspected.

"Will you drive home?" she asked.

"Climb over me, sweet, and I'll take you away from this nightmare."

The drive home was quiet. He didn't ask her what she was feeling. Bella sensed he knew her thoughts. She could understand Severo hating vampires now.

Halfway home he took her hand in his and pulled it onto his thigh. His silent reassurance made her cry. A gift he couldn't realize meant so much to her.

God, she loved this man. She ached for him. She loved him for the compassion he would never admit to possessing. For the domineering spirit that always erred toward protection over humiliation.

And she loved him for his humanity, for the fact that he loved and lived as she did, and was the same as her, except for the one small thing about his ability to shift shapes.

They pulled into the garage, and the radio shut off with the engine. Severo reached to open the door, but she told him to stop.

Bella climbed onto his lap, straddling him, and he inched over to the middle of the seat. She was grateful it was an old car, the kind without a floor shift and with a full front seat.

He found her mouth with a fierce kiss. She moaned into him, releasing the last remnants of sadness and surrendering to the desire that had built during the drive home.

Shucking off her sleeves, she tugged down the front of her dress and lifted her breasts to his mouth. He sucked at each one, again and again, drawing up the intense coil of climax with expert precision. It took no longer than a few minutes before she came, long and loud and crying out in the confines of the car.

"You're mine," he growled.

Bella eyed his fly and he tilted up his hips so she could unzip him. "And you are mine, wolf. I need you now."

"Tell me you want me, then. Where do you want me?"

"Inside me." Yes, she could use his rough language, because she trusted him. "I'm so wet for you."

He sucked in a hissing breath as she fitted herself onto his hardness. They clung together, moving little, for she squeezed him with her muscles, milking him to a fierce and triumphant climax.

This wolf was hers. And though he might think he controlled her, Bella knew otherwise. He was hers to command. And tonight she wanted him to serve her.

Sliding from his lap and lying across the seat, she put her heels on his thigh, pushing him away.

"I want your mouth on me, lover," she said.

Severo opened the door and stretched out his legs. He pulled her hips up and entered her with his tongue.

With her shoulders deep into the seat and her heels on his broad, muscled back, it didn't take Bella long to find the stars a second time.

Chapter 14

Bella's shoulders hit the wall, her arms stretched above her head. Her lover clasped her wrists, pinning her roughly. His greedy smile thrilled her. Every part of her was hot and wet for him.

He dove for her jaw, nipping along it up to her ear, where he sucked in the lobe. His erection ground against her bare thigh. He was naked, too, and had been since that afternoon, when they'd started making love.

Tomorrow night the moon would be full. Which meant tonight it was waxing and the werewolf would come out if it was not kept at bay with sex. This was a challenge Bella met eagerly.

"I've said it before," she murmured as his kiss found her mouth. "You like it rough."

"You do, too, sweet."

"Your strength is an aphrodisiac."

She tried to wriggle her wrists from his hold. It was loose, but she didn't want to be set free. The faux containment only made her more eager to satisfy his insatiable desires.

"Someday, sweet," he whispered in the harsh growl that accompanied his frenzied quest for sex, "I will bind you with ribbons and fall on my knees to worship you."

"I'd like that."

"Bella, my sweet, you own me. Know that."

He lifted her by the thighs and fitted her onto him. It was a slow, sure glide as he found a familiar position deep inside her. He pounded into her, with one hand at her hip, the other holding her hands against the wall. His determination was fierce, the fire in his dark eyes intent.

With a growl, he bent his head to suck in one of her nipples. He tugged at it, not biting hard—he never would—but his technique matched the force of his need for climax. He'd already come half a dozen times, as had she. Wrapped in each other's arms, they vacillated between urgency and a sweet, lazy lingering.

The clock struck midnight. So long as he kept making love to her, the werewolf would not show.

By now, sated and achy, Bella could no longer sense when orgasm neared. Instead it attacked without volition, ripping through her core and forcing out her pleasure in an unabashed cry. She dug her fingernails into his shoulders, which were already raw from her fantastic struggles.

"Yes," he hissed.

She dug in deep, sure she would draw blood, but knowing the wolf could take it.

Swinging his arms, he laid her on the bed and pounced upon her as she floated down from the climax. He was randy and frisky, like a puppy eager to play all day long. The more sex they had, the more alive and vigorous he grew. Bella sensed she would collapse from exhaustion soon. But what a delicious collapse.

Severo reached for the water pitcher Bella had placed near the bed hours earlier and drank right from it. Water glistened down his chest and splattered Bella's stomach.

"It's still cold," she said in surprise. "Share some of that with me, lover."

He dove in to kiss her, his mouth filled with cool water. It trickled out the sides of her mouth, and some she swallowed. Drinking from him, she giggled. He slashed his tongue across hers, performing a dance they both knew well.

Every touch stirred her. Every look devastated her. Every time he withdrew from her, she died a little, only to be resurrected when he entered her.

He nuzzled his bearded chin under her jaw, tickling her roughly. "Getting tired?"

"Not if the werewolf has in mind to make an appearance."

"I think you're close to putting it off," he replied.

"Really? I don't believe that. You're not near being sated. You could do this all week, couldn't you?"

"With you, sweet, I could. Once more?" he said with such enthusiasm, Bella laughed and tugged him down on top of her.

She didn't get to sleep until six in the morning.

Tonight was the night. He'd known Bella two months. He loved her. She loved him. When he'd asked her to have sex with him to keep away the werewolf, she'd gladly done so. Even when he'd known she was exhausted last night, she'd kept at it, stroking him, teasing him to another and yet another orgasm. The woman was a marvel.

But now the true test of both his and her love would be put to them.

Could Bella love the werewolf?

Rather—and more important—could the werewolf accept a human mate?

Dropping his shirt on the flagstone patio, Severo hissed in a breath as Bella embraced him from behind. Kisses down the back of his neck and spine ignited his libido. Not that it needed jump-starting. He'd been frenzied with her in bed this morning. It was as if the werewolf sensed that tonight would be its turn.

All his life he'd had to deny the werewolf's instinctual needs. He'd become accustomed to riding out that ache for what was missing, content to serve his werewolf's needs in other ways, through hunting and racing the moon through the night.

Was it really about to happen tonight?

The idea humbled him. Maybe he asked too much of Bella? She could be agreeing just to please him. Not that Bella did anything simply to please him.

"Are you sure about this?" he asked over his shoulder.

"I want to meet the werewolf." She slid a hand around his waist and stroked him over his pants, toying with the zipper.

"The werewolf will want to do more than meet."

His erection pulsed for attention, but he would not have her now. Not yet.

"I know. You've prepared me."

"But *are* you prepared? I don't wish to harm you, Bella, and I will not. As I've said, I'm not completely myself when I'm the werewolf."

"The werewolf wouldn't harm a potential mate, would it?"

"No, but I can't imagine…"

How the beastly part of him perceived a human woman. It was the most dreadful thought, and yet it focused him and made him more eager to call down the moon.

He knew that some of his breed took humans as mates, and had sex with them. When in werewolf form he was mostly shaped like a man, with arms, legs, torso, rib cage and a penis—but with a wolfish head and shoulders. And fur, lots of fur. But he'd never spoken to a single werewolf who had had a successful long-term relationship with a human.

They were a lonely breed, forced to find satisfaction with human females, which was never the ultimate mating.

"I'll be fine," she offered from behind him.

Bella's delicate embrace would never fit around the werewolf's torso; he knew that much. God, he didn't want to scare her away from him forever.

"Maybe we should wait until next month."

"Who's more afraid?"

"I am." He hugged her, pressing her head to the base of his neck. Her skin smelled of cloves, along with wine and the strawberries Heloise had left in the fridge for them. "I admit it, Bella. I'm terrified about the shifting tonight."

"Does it hurt?"

"No." He kissed her hair. "The werewolf instinctively knows it'll be allowed to come up to the house. I can't do this."

"You can and you must. I want to know all of you, Severo. Isn't this what you want? Besides, if the wolf could romp around with a cat, then I think I'll survive."

He knew she meant Aby. "That was different." The werewolf hadn't had sex with the cat, nor would it have considered such a vile act. In fact, his werewolf had rarely gone near Aby. "Bella, it burns in my heart to worry about you."

"Then don't." She kissed his chest, gliding her fingers through the fine hairs. When she snuck her fingers under his waistband to toy with him, the swollen head of his erection bulged, desiring release.

The worst part of it all? He wouldn't recall what went on tonight between the werewolf and Bella.

Could he be jealous of himself?

"The sun's almost set," she said. "Are you going to…stick around here?"

"No, I'm off. I'll return. If you get frightened or change your mind, don't hesitate to lock yourself in the house."

He clutched her arms, lifting her to her tiptoes. "Promise me you'll not put up a brave front?"

Her mouth tasted like strawberries. Never would he tire of her kisses. He would die fighting an army of vampires for another of Bella's kisses.

"Promise," she whispered, and he swallowed her sweet strawberry breath. He'd take that part of her into the wilds tonight.

And pray the werewolf did not steal her breath forever.

As the clock struck twelve, Bella sighed. She sat on a wicker chair, dangling her bare feet over the grass where it met the patio flagstone. Her white silk nightgown did little to protect her from the chill in the air. It was late September, a cool night, instead of the Indian summer she'd wished for. A sweater sounded great, but she hadn't yet brought her winter clothes over from the loft.

She tugged the terry-cloth towel from the chair and wrapped it around her shoulders.

The canine howls in the distance soared across the horizon, as if the animal paced, unsure which way to go. She couldn't know if it was her lover, but her heart sensed that it was.

Was the wolf unsure? Or was Severo so focused on maintaining control that even in wolf form he exerted enough influence to intimidate that part of himself that he referred to as the werewolf? What form was he in right now? Was he the caninelike wolf or the man-wolf creature?

Anticipation kept her awake. She wasn't fearful in the least. Okay, maybe a little.

More than a little.

She'd met the wolf. Despite her fear of dogs, she'd handled it remarkably.

But tonight? This was like an introduction to the last part of a man she loved, the one part of him he kept hidden from others. The core of him.

He wanted to share this part with her, to have her know him completely. She understood how difficult it was for Severo to do this. He couldn't know what his werewolf would do to her.

And how would she react? Would it be as that night when she'd first been chased by vampires? She'd fled out of fear of what she'd seen. And that had merely been fangs.

"Be brave," she coached. "He is your lover."

She would look at Severo, no matter how beastly he appeared. He'd explained to her that all the important parts were still like those of a man, though his head and shoulders sort of wolfed out. She'd not watched many werewolf movies to know what to expect. But then, coming to this with an open mind and no expectations was best.

If he wanted her, she would give herself freely, no matter what it entailed. She trusted him that much.

Standing and pressing her feet into the cool grass, she closed her eyes. The night surrounded her with clean, heady air and a hint of sap from the maple trees. The last lingering hedge roses released a surprisingly sweet aroma. She spread out her arms, and a breeze tickled her beneath the thin silk, sending shivers across her flesh and raising goose bumps.

And then the world changed.

An animal noise pierced the darkness. Not quite a growl. More a throaty murmur.

Bella stepped out a few paces. The house loomed twenty feet to her left, and the hedgerow six feet behind. Lush grass blades speared her toes.

Eyes closed, she could feel a presence. Not human. Feral, perhaps. Predatory, yet cautious.

Brisk air cut her cheek. She started but knew better than to make a sudden movement.

She heard the sound of a great weight crushing

the grass, limbs bending, stretching out, sharp and clear. Were they feet or…paws?

Breath spilled hotly over her shoulder. Bella turned abruptly.

The dark shadow cringed but did not flee. She couldn't immediately make it out in the shadow of the maple tree, but it was big. It breathed heavily, panting like an animal.

It had to be four heads higher than her, and its shoulders, silhouetted against the pale brick house, were wide. It was not a man, though it stood on its hind legs and long, muscular hands hung near its muscled thighs. The chest was wide yet deep.

It was too dark to make out details and the fur was black, so while she knew it wore no clothes, she couldn't see anything below the waist.

A glint of talon caught her eye as the werewolf approached. It bared its teeth and shook its head, which ruffled the thick dark mane from head to neck. Not like a man there. The face of a wolf peered at her.

When she thought a scream imminent, Bella realized it smelled her. It read her as Severo so often did, trying to figure her out.

Drawing back her shoulders, she closed her eyes and allowed the curiosity. She understood its world was navigated by scent.

Severo had said the werewolf had on only a few occasions encountered humans. He sensed his werewolf had feared them and hadn't gotten too close.

But it seemed at ease now, if that was what she could call the sniffing. Perhaps it simply knew it was at the top of this short food chain.

If it smelled her fear, would that excite it as that did her lover? Or make it aggressive and her position perilous?

She trembled as she stood before the werewolf. And yet, her fear did not prevail. Rather, the atmosphere felt…provocative. And, dare she say, safe?

Maybe. She dared to believe it.

The werewolf came closer.

Bella exhaled and her heartbeats slowed. Sudden calm lifted her courage.

Curious, she put out her hand, as she had to the smaller version, to allow it to sniff. Which it did.

Thick black fur covered its head, shoulders and chest. Though the rest of the body was dark, almost black, its torso was lighter. It was colored like the fully furred wolf.

"Severo?" she said softly.

The werewolf opened its jaws to expose teeth. Longer than vampires' teeth, and so many more of them, all sharp.

Severo had said nothing about it biting her. Would it bite?

A reedy moan escaped her, and Bella pressed her fingers to her mouth, holding it back.

She could do this. This was *her lover*. A man who loved her. This werewolf, this creature, if it had wanted to harm her, would have done so by now.

Suddenly it stretched out its massive bulk and howled. The night air echoed with the coarse, low-range howl. In the distance a few short yips answered. Was it a real wolf fearing the cry of what it knew was something larger and stronger than itself?

And when it lowered its head to look at her, Bella stared into a fierce gaze. *His* clear brown eyes. Looking into her. Seeing her.

"I love you," she said firmly. "I'm not afraid of you."

She put out a hand to touch its muzzle, but it jerked away from the shaky touch. "Sorry. I'm new to this. Not sure what to do."

Another howl silenced her. It must want her to be quiet. She could do that.

Her legs shook, threatening to bring her down. Bella focused on inhaling deeply and exhaling slowly. The scent of roses was so heady, she thought she might be drunk.

Wobbling, Bella did fall backward, catching herself with her elbows on the soft grass. It was like a half faint. She wasn't so much embarrassed as relieved to not have to stand on her weak legs any longer.

The werewolf reached down with a clawed hand yet did not touch, only lingered above her stomach. It was more a hand than a paw. Longer than anything human, yet finely boned and articulated, with a tuft of fur on the knuckles.

It studied her so intensely, she felt sure it must be struggling with Severo's interior warnings while it wanted to meet its own purposes.

Mating.

A talon slashed before her so quickly, Bella hadn't realized what the werewolf had done. Until the front of her nightgown fell open, exposing her breasts and stomach.

The werewolf growled lowly. She understood it as a gentle growl, perhaps approving. As Severo did so often while they made love and after he'd climaxed. The werewolf pressed a hand to her shoulder and she winced.

I'm not ready for this.

Then again, how could anyone be ready for this?

"So what's next?" she said, forcing a casual tone. "First dates are always so awkward, aren't they?"

The werewolf sniffed her face. Its fur brushed her chin as it moved lower, lingering over her breasts and down her stomach, till it sniffed at her sex.

Claws pricked her hip, but briefly. At the werewolf's touch, she turned over onto her stomach. She understood what it wanted.

Rising onto all fours, she flinched as a heavy hand hit the grass next to her and its torso touched her back.

The claiming had been quick, frantic. Once satisfied, the werewolf had loped off across the valley. The silhouette of her masterful beast had crested the hill and transformed itself into its smaller wolf size. It returned, loping up like a playful puppy and lowering its head to nuzzle her open palms.

Now she curled against the wolf's soft fur and snuggled up to it in the thicket of grass. The night had grown quiet. No longer did the ferocious huffs and grunts from the beastly werewolf echo in the air. Nor did she feel it inside her, moving so quickly she couldn't keep track of how many times she'd orgasmed along with the werewolf.

Initially, it had been frightening.

The first time it entered her, her body had ached.

And then, everything had changed. The werewolf had not spoken or looked into her eyes, for she'd remained in the doggy-style position. Yet, as it had taken her, Bella had forgotten it was the werewolf and had known only that Severo, the man she loved, was inside her.

Severo woke in the grass and jerked abruptly to a stand. Bella lay on the matted grass in a torn nightgown, her dark hair strewn across the grass blades. Sunshine toyed with her toes. Dirt and grass streaks marked the tattered white silk and her palms and knees.

"The werewolf did it," he said, not sure what exactly he felt.

Horrified? A little. And shocked. But surprised? No, the werewolf had been waiting for decades.

He was also worried for Bella's well-being. What the hell had she been put through last night? Would she be mentally scarred from this?

He reached out to touch her, but his nakedness suddenly felt so overt. He called her name, but she didn't rouse.

Forgoing running inside for clothes, he lifted her into his arms. She slept soundly as he carried her inside to the bedroom and as he laid her on the rumpled white sheets, she woke and smiled at him.

She grasped his hand and pulled him to sit beside

her. When he wanted to ask her if she was all right, she put her fingers over his mouth.

"I love the werewolf," she said, and closed her eyes and fell to sleep.

Must be something about having sex with a werewolf that'll put a shine to a girl's smile. Bella posed before the floor-length mirror, turning from side to side to check the brown jersey dress that hugged her curves.

She had showered and hadn't yet seen Severo. She figured he might feel strange about approaching her today. He shouldn't.

Stepping into her low-heeled mules, she sought breakfast.

Heloise was off for the three days, so she scavenged a kiwi and a banana and cut them on a plate. An English muffin would hit the spot, but she couldn't find any. Oat toast it was. The guy was into fiber and meat.

From around the corner Severo appeared. Rather, he lingered, like he was unsure about approaching her. He was clad in dark running pants and no shirt, and his tight six-pack drew Bella's eye. Head bowed and thumb to his lip, he looked up through his lashes at her.

"Come here, lover," she urged him.

"I…" He remained in the doorway, the sunlight upon his shoulders. He rubbed the heels of his palms together. "I didn't harm you, did I?" He winced as he said it.

"You did not. Besides being well and thoroughly sexed. But that never harmed a girl before."

"The werewolf had sex with you?"

"Yes. You don't remember?"

"You know I can't." He slid onto a bar stool across the counter from her.

All she wanted to do was hug and kiss him and show him how much he meant to her, but she sensed his apprehension and would allow him this slow approach. He had to struggle with the right and wrong of it. He was that kind of man.

"Do you want details?"

He winced again. "Not sure. Was it…terrible?"

"Not at all. You're magnificent as the werewolf, Severo. All muscles and growl."

"You weren't horrified?"

"Honestly? A little scared at the beginning. Okay, a lot scared. But the werewolf was gentle."

"Really?" He let out a breath.

"As gentle as it could be. I don't have any scratches or bruises. I checked. I want to do it again," she said.

"Y-you do? Should I be jealous?"

She slid around the counter and climbed onto his lap. Spreading her palms across his chest, she nipped his lower lip. "It's the same guy. One's a lot more intense than the other, and not as handsome."

"You think the werewolf's hideous, don't you?"

"Not at all. Just not as cute as you. There's no competition over whom I'd pick from looks alone. Besides, the werewolf has back hair."

"You make light of everything."

"Severo, it's fine. The werewolf and I got along, and we had sex like bunnies."

"Like bunnies? I don't want to know. Yes, I do. Did you…enjoy it?"

She nodded. "Might be achy today, but that's nothing given all the orgasms."

"Christ, how many?"

"Maybe you're better off not knowing some things."

"Tell me, Bella."

"I stopped counting after six."

He huffed out a breath. Then he laughed and kissed her. "You're cool with it, really?"

"I think you've got yourself a mate, lover."

Chapter 15

She did need a rest from sex after three days and nights of endless passion.

Heck, a girl could only take so much pleasure. Seriously. So tonight Severo ran Bella a hot bath and sprinkled rose petals from the hedges out back in the water. He lit candles and left her to soak.

He spoiled her. Was it guilt at subjecting her to the werewolf's overwhelming sexual needs? Bella hoped he'd get over that. She could handle it. On the other hand, being spoiled was nothing to complain about.

Blowing a handful of bubbles through the air, she settled into the water and closed her eyes.

* * *

Life had a way of tossing you the good stuff, then pulling the rug out from under your feet when you least expected.

It was after Severo overheard Bella talking to Seth that he fisted his hand and put it right through the Sheetrock.

Bella hurried out from the bedroom, eyed the hole and his fist. "I know he's up to something this time. I'm not stupid. He wants me to come to a party."

"Elvira will be there, as well as other vampires."

"I know. I told him I couldn't come." Her cell phone rang again, and Bella stared at the screen. "Seth's number. I thought I'd made myself clear."

"Let me talk to him."

"No." She hit the answer button. "Seth, I said I didn't want to come."

Severo heard the female voice over the phone and tore it from Bella's grip. "Elvira, what the hell are you up to?"

The vampiress laughed.

"I warned you about starting this with me," he said. "If you want a war, you got it."

"Then let the games begin," she snarled. "You can start by retrieving the head of your bitch's dead friend. I've already put the body out in the sun, but you know the new ones take so long to ash."

Severo sucked in a breath. Bella stood beside him, intently watching his face.

"It's not about them anymore, is it?"

"It never was," the vampiress said. "It's been so long since we've dallied, Severo. I look forward to the match this time. Oh, I've such plans!"

The phone clicked off and Bella took it from him. Severo swung around and punched the wall again. And again.

"What did she say? Would you stop tearing the house apart? Is Seth okay? What's going on?"

"Stay back, sweet." He rubbed his knuckles. "This isn't the time."

"It is if it's about my friend. Where is he?"

"It's between me and Elvira now."

"What does that mean?"

"He's dead," he snapped. He should not be so cruel, but he had never been one to couch the truth in euphemisms. "She killed him out of spite. It's me she's been after this whole time. She wants to twist the knife as deeply as it will go."

"Seth is dead? B-but I just talked to him."

Bella's body wavered. Severo caught her as she collapsed against his chest.

"Bella, I'm sorry." His world had finally caught up to hers. It wasn't fair.

"Why is it you?" she asked. Her wide green eyes sought the truth from his. "What did you do to her?"

She deserved the truth, and she'd get it.

"Seventy years ago, I killed her family. She owes me this."

"You've killed? You said you'd never…"

Yes, he'd told her he'd not harmed humans. Unless it was necessary. And those deaths had been necessary. It had been too long since he'd thought of that time in his life. The memory filled his nose with an acrid odor.

"But Seth means nothing to you. Why would she go after him?"

"In war one always kills off friends, family and loved ones first. That's how it works."

"What? But that means—"

"She'll come after you next."

Bella's shoulders shook. She rubbed her arms, attempting to fight off the shivers. He had frightened her and her fear scent filled him with shame. He shouldn't have said anything. But not telling her would have blemished the trust he had earned so far.

She settled at the edge of the couch. Severo touched her hair tentatively. He wanted to take her in his arms and make the world go away. To make it all better.

He fisted his fingers. That power was not in his hands.

"So," she said softly, so faint he had to lean in to hear, "you killed her family?"

"Her brother and father."

Sitting on the couch, he pulled her lithe body onto his. She tucked her head into his neck and cuddled as he wrapped his arms about her. He wanted to be a safe harbor for her, but he feared her trip down the rabbit hole was only just beginning.

"Before Elvira—Evie—had blooded her teeth, her family used to hunt werewolves. At one time, in the nineteen fifties, the United States had a bounty on all wolves. Paid something like a dollar a pelt. The nation went into a hunting frenzy."

"Mortals hunted you?"

"No, they hunted the real wolves. Mortals were—and are, for the most part—unaware of our breed. But noting the hunting frenzy, the vampires took it upon themselves to hunt werewolves. They didn't get paid for the pelts, but it didn't matter. It was for the thrill of the hunt. They captured my parents."

He had to swallow, to digest this cruel memory, which he'd thought to press back, far from reach. It hurt in his heart to recall it, as if the steel trap crushed his muscles all over again.

Bella's fingers played across his chest. So fragile.

And yet she was far stronger than him, for she had stood boldly before his werewolf.

"Do you know what happens when a werewolf is skinned?"

"You don't have to tell me if it hurts."

It would wound him far worse to keep his secrets from the woman he loved.

"I stood at the edge of the vampire encampment after following my parents' scents for miles. They were dead, strung up by their heels alongside a wood cabin with half a dozen other werewolf pelts. It takes only a few hours, though, before a werewolf transforms itself into a were."

Bella's gasp heated his chest. He clutched her, clinging, stopping his own tears only through force of will.

"I fled at the sight. I knew I had to protect myself. And yet I ran right into a trap. A bear trap clamped about my left ankle."

"That's why you limp."

"Yes, the bone never did heal right. They took me into captivity. I vowed that if I ever escaped, I would kill the men who had done this to my family."

"And Evie? Was it her family who did this to you?"

"Yes. Yet Evie's father was a mortal. The father took vampires for lovers and there were a few witches who served the family. They used their ability to tame us wolves as a power magnet for vampires. There would be days they'd set the vampires on us for fun. To torture us."

"Oh my God."

"It was Evie who asked that my life be spared when her father wanted to force me to shift and skin me alive. She begged for a plaything. I...knew she favored me, but she also couldn't understand that freedom was what I most wanted. I played along, bending to her desires, allowing her to think she was seducing me, preparing me to be the one who blooded her fangs."

"She bit you?"

"No. She didn't get the chance."

He cupped Bella's chin and held her as a most precious thing. He'd been given one more chance to have goodness in his life after Aby. He didn't want to lose it. But she needed to know everything.

"Weres come into their werewolf at puberty. The young ones are always the most difficult to control as the new skills of shifting are honed. Because of my uncontrollable rages, I was able to escape. I killed both the father and his vampire son, and left Evie crying on the porch of their home.

"I ran into her years later. Still she professed a pining love for me. I had never had anything but disgust for her and her family, yet, though I did not admit it to her, I was grateful to her for sparing my life. Still, I spurned her. She vowed revenge, which I deserved." He exhaled, tracking the swift beats of his heart in his throat. "So, yes, Bella, I have killed."

"You were only avenging your family. I can't imagine seeing your parents being tortured like that. You poor man."

He snarled. "It's been over seven decades. I take care of myself. Those who think to threaten my peace, or my former pack, have only to answer to the werewolf. Evie has every right to pursue a vengeance she holds to be just—but Seth was a cruel blow."

"He had no idea what he'd gotten into. Oh, Severo, what will happen now?"

"She's not coming after me directly. And that means she's playing a very dangerous game. I will protect you with my life, Bella. But I'd feel better if we spent some time teaching you how to handle a few weapons."

"I think that would be good."

Her desire to learn defense surprised him. Truly, she was as strong a mate as a wolf could wish to have.

The man actually had an arsenal in the storage room behind the garage. She was surprised only because it was so huge, not because he had one.

Bella lingered in the open doorway as Severo strode before the shelves and counters, selecting a few throwing stars and tucking them in the pocket of his leather jacket, hooking what looked like a medieval mace over his arm. He paused before a wall of pistols and rifles.

Over his shoulder, he grinned at her. A boy with his toys.

Last night had been sweet. She hugged herself at the memory of the quiet darkness and his soft breaths as they'd lain in bed. No sex, just tender kisses, strokes. Mostly they'd spooned into one another. They hadn't needed words.

After hearing how Severo had witnessed his parents' cruel deaths, Bella believed any vengeance he had taken had been just.

Now, more than ever, she wanted to meet Elvira.

"Bitch," Bella muttered.

"What's that?" He approached her with an armload of interesting weapons.

"Just thinking about what I'm going to say to the mistress of the night when I finally meet her."

He nodded as they exited, and pulled the door locked behind them. They headed outside. Crisp fall air necessitated that Bella wear a jacket, and she'd pulled her hair behind her head in a ponytail. All business. She wanted to learn.

"If all goes well," Severo said, "you'll never see Elvira. I want that bitch's head on a platter with as little collateral damage as possible. My grievance is only with her. Though, if any of those vampires who chased you are still alive, I'll take their heads, too."

They strode across the backyard and through a rusted iron gate that led them through the ten-foot wide hedgerow and out to the valley. The hill was clean of trees and cut a sharp line against the overcast sky.

Though it was the beginning of October, Bella guessed it would probably snow soon. She liked winter. But it would be colder this year without Seth to share a fall hayride or pumpkin carving.

She sniffed at a tear. Severo noticed, but he didn't say anything. She loved him for his ability to let her feel, to let her have a good crying jag if that was what she needed.

And that he'd softened and let himself feel last night, during his confession, meant the world to her. He hadn't cried, but Bella figured that letting down his defenses was probably the closest he'd get to an emotional breakdown.

He laid the weapons on the ground and picked up a huge pistol and showed it to Bella. "It's a big one, but it's your best protection against a longtooth."

"You've not talked at all about your breed." She made herself use his terminology. "Are all vampires and werewolves enemies?"

"Most. The vamps have difficulty stepping down from their self-imposed pedestals. They don't play well with others. Just ask the witches."

"Why? What did they do to the witches?"

"Enslaved them. Drained them of their magic. So much so that centuries ago witches created a master spell that made their blood poisonous to the vampires."

"Clever."

"Indeed. The spell was broken a few years back. The vampires and witches have come to an agreement. The one vampire I can tolerate is actually married to a witch."

"How does that work? If her blood was once poisonous?"

"Very careful sex? He's a phoenix, actually. If a vampire survives a witch's blood attack, he becomes indestructible. Anyway, the wolves get along with the witches for the most part. Here."

With both hands she took the pistol by the handle, and it still dropped heavily. "This must weigh ten pounds. I've never seen a gun with such a big spinning thingy before."

He cast her an incredulous look, wincing against

the sunlight. "You've never touched a weapon in your life, have you, sweet?"

"Nope. But I'm willing to learn. What are those?"

He displayed a bulletlike object before him. "Bullets made of Brazilian ironwood, one of the hardest woods available. Shoot one of these directly at the vamp's heart. It won't take the longtooth out, but it will set it back and give you time to reload or use something more powerful, like a thick, heart-exploding stake."

She examined the wooden bullet. A cross had been burned into the flat, round end of it. "And I'm supposed to be able to aim this thing long and sure enough to hit the target, which is likely coming at me at Mach speed, with fangs bared?"

"Exactly."

Severo placed a few wooden bullets in the chamber and spun it into place for her. Demonstrating a good grip, he helped her to hold the pistol properly with both hands.

"Longtooths, eh?" she said. "A nasty word for vamps?"

"You bet."

"What do they call you?"

"If they're smart, they run. If they have a death wish, they call me dog."

"Oh." Wincing, she offered him an apology, remembering how she'd jokingly called him dog and other derogatory terms when they'd first gotten together. "Sorry."

He kissed her cheek. "Call me what you wish, sweet. Just don't stop calling me. Now hold it up and aim."

"At what? The tree?"

"That's too far. You've only about fifty feet with one of these things. Hmm, what could you shoot at? We need to see if you can hit something, and it should be moving.… How about me?"

"No!"

"Oh, yes." He stepped back, his arms held out in challenge. "Wood isn't going to kill me. It will just smart a little. Aim for my shoulder or a leg. Not the face. I may be a dog, but I don't need any more scars."

"Severo, there's no way I'm going to shoot you. You said you aren't immortal!"

"That's right."

She lowered the pistol. "Then why can't you be killed?"

"I've explained. Silver is the only thing that does it."

He splayed out his hands and walked backward. His dark brown eyes twinkled menacingly.

Bella dangled the pistol with both hands. It

knocked her knees. "Come back here, please, Severo. I'll try for a bird that flies overhead or something."

He shed the leather jacket as he swiftly increased the distance between them. When he was hundreds of yards away, he turned and charged her.

"I'm not doing it. I'll miss and hit you in the eye! What if I hit you in the brain? You'll be a brain damaged wolf who can't die and is crazed for sex!"

"Do it, bitch!"

He was trying to rile her. She wouldn't fall for it.

A toothy snarl and suddenly the man racing toward her became something else. Bigger, hairier, more monstrous.

The werewolf.

Which she thought she loved. But she'd never seen it in daylight and—

Bella squeezed the trigger. The pistol didn't make a noise. The wooden bullet exited with a forceful kick that tugged at her shoulder sockets. She dropped both hands down, following the bullet's trajectory.

The werewolf took the bullet without flinching. Yet it stopped charging her, digging its feet into the ground and spinning about with a leap and a running dart up the hill, away from her.

"I hit him. Oh, no, I didn't mean it. Severo!"

When it had crested the hill, the silhouette shifted and took on the were shape. It happened so quickly, and he didn't shed any skin, or anything creepy like that.

Clothing lay abandoned on the ground forty feet away. He'd shed his shirt and pants as he'd changed, which meant he was now naked.

And likely wounded.

He ran down the hill, gaining on Bella with supernatural speed.

"There you go, sweet." He pressed the flesh on his shoulder and popped out the short wooden bullet. Blood oozed down his pale flesh.

"Oh my God, you're bleeding. I really hit you. I could have taken out an eye!" Bella wailed.

"Or rendered me brain damaged."

"You bastard!" She shoved the pistol against his chest and stomped away. "Don't ever do that to me again. You know I love the werewolf!"

"Yes, but you were frightened of it just now."

"Because I've never seen it during the day. I didn't know you could change like that. I thought it was only during the full moon."

"Surprised?"

She rounded on him, but the boldness of him standing there, bleeding and naked and strangely apologetic, messed with her need to remain angry.

"Come look, Bella. Please, it's fine."

She'd done it. She'd fired a weapon at another

being. And if she could fire it at someone she loved, then she could sure as hell fire it at some bitch of a vampire who wanted her dead.

The creep had done this for her own good, and damn it, she was thankful for it.

"Let me see." She stalked up to her lover, but by the time she touched his shoulder, the wound had already closed. She wiped away a streak of blood. "That's cool."

"I promise that'll be the only time I ask you to hurt me."

"Did it hurt?"

"'Course it did." He kissed her. "About as much as this might hurt you."

He pinched her nipple and she jumped, slapping at him playfully. "Stop it, or I'll try the throwing stars on you next."

He caught her and swung her over one arm, dipping her into a dramatic kiss that would have made a silver-screen rogue jealous. "You make it so difficult to be serious sometimes, sweet. I like that about you. You allow me to remember what it's like to just be."

"Have you ever laughed for the heck of it?"

"Yes, many times."

"With Aby." He nodded, and she decided that someday she was going to have to meet that enigma of a woman. "Okay, what's next, naked werewolf dude?"

"Another kiss right—" he tugged up her shirt and bent to her stomach "—here."

And with more and more kisses, and the quick removal of her clothes, the weaponry lesson was postponed for a few hours.

Chapter 16

They strode at Severo's quick pace through the marble hallway, checking windows and verifying security codes. Bella knew the routine, but she sensed it gave him greater peace of mind to do this than it did her. She trusted she would be safe, no matter what occurred, so long as Severo was here to protect her.

Not for a moment did she honestly believe she could wield that monster of a pistol, especially with a snarling vampire approaching.

If it came to that.

It was hard to imagine the war Severo sensed was

brewing. One person had died. And while Seth was a sad loss, Bella couldn't see the matter escalating to gangs of vampires versus werewolves.

Not that she'd seen other werewolves. Severo was a loner who had left his pack years earlier. He'd said the packs were slimming down and seeking shelter in the northern areas of Canada and Europe. The werewolves were not particularly social creatures, which didn't surprise Bella, considering what she knew of Severo.

"And the security code is four-nine-zero-eight-five-two," she repeated by rote when he looked to her.

The code increased by twelve with each door, starting with the front door, then the garage doors, the side doors, the patio door and various other exits. The windows were all on one central control, activated with a push of a button in the bedroom or kitchen.

"But you said the protection wards would be the first line of defense, anyway, right? What are protection wards, anyway?"

"They're magical shields, so to speak, against demons, vampires and other sorts. Designed by a witch for me when I moved in. I can't be too cautious. One never knows what those longtooth bastards have up their sleeves."

"I'm hungry," she grumbled. "I think I've got it. Let's see what Heloise has cooking."

He grabbed her about the wrist with his usual forceful squeeze, but a second later he let up. "Bella, you're not taking this seriously."

"I shot you and you don't think I'm taking this seriously? Severo, this *is* a lot to take in."

"You accepted vampires and weres easily enough. Why is it so difficult to want to survive?"

"I want to survive," she said on a surprised gasp. "I love you. I want to spend more time with you. As long as I can. Forever, or for the rest of your three-hundred-some years. I don't want to die, but… Just let me handle this my way, okay?"

"Yes. Sorry." Occupied with security, he wouldn't come down from the command mode for a bit.

He strode off toward the kitchen.

She followed, loving his no-nonsense gait, fierce and solid despite the slight hitch in the left leg—due to being caught in a trap. A tear pooled in her eye when she imagined her lover suffering.

It was a good reason to hold a grudge against the longtooths.

"So tell me," Bella said as Heloise motioned for them to sit and wait for the dinner she was plating, "if you're not immortal, then do you just drop dead at the big three hundred?"

Now more relaxed, he dragged her onto his lap in what had become their favorite chair to sit in and snuggle and make out. Bella pushed a thick hank of his hair over his shoulder and laid her head at his collar, where the heat of his blood brewed a delicious man scent.

"I'm guessing at the three hundred number." He skated a palm along her bare leg, inching up her skirt, but not so high that it was inappropriate in front of Heloise. "Weres can live hundreds of years. I think the oldest was around three hundred twenty-five."

"I can't imagine a life so long. It would be amazing."

"I was born in 1935. I'm still but a pup, I guess. Though there are days I feel I've lived these nine decades and died a thousand times over."

She palmed his abdomen under the brown sweater, which matched his eyes, and snuggled closer. "What's going to happen with us? I'm not getting any younger. And you certainly don't want to be dating an old woman in another five decades."

"You can't imagine how good that makes me feel when you speak of us in terms of decades, sweet. Doesn't matter how old or wrinkled you become. I'll always love you."

"Oh, please. When I'm eighty, and you're still looking like a sexy thing, you can't tell me I'll appeal to you. And when I die...?"

"I will wish to go with you."

"Don't say that, Severo. Maybe we should just concentrate on the now."

"You will always have my heart, Bella. Never forget that. It is yours. You stole it from me months ago, and I shouldn't wish it back."

The clink of a plate clued them in that Heloise had served the meal. She was respectful of the two of them and left the room to tend to household chores.

"Smells delicious," Bella said.

"Salmon, I think."

"I mean you." She licked under his chin, where his trimmed beard was sensitive to the slick touch of her tongue. "She won't come back in now. How about a quickie before we eat?"

"And you call me insatiable." His hand drove up her thigh and cupped her derriere. "Unzip me, sweet, and hop on for a ride."

Three weeks later…as the full moon mastered the sky, the werewolf sought its mate three nights in a row. Bella had learned to wear nothing but a robe, because otherwise the visits always entailed shredded silk and sometimes tangled limbs.

If she thought about what she was doing—with a werewolf—all sorts of moral and rational arguments could be conjured.

But she didn't think. She acted with her heart. She made love to Severo, and no matter what his form, at his core, he was a man who loved her and put her above all others.

She'd driven into town earlier that day and found a Realtor to sell her loft. While there, she drove by Seth's place. The small house had already been resold. She knew his parents lived in Florida, and that they had been distant the last three years. They knew her from when she and Seth had danced together in competitions in middle school. She didn't feel the need to contact them. Let them grieve, and hopefully their son's death had been explained to them in terms they could accept, like a car accident.

Not that she expected the coroner's report would list vampire bite as the cause of death.

She wondered now if the death had been reported. The cleaners Severo had called had made efficient work of mopping up the vampires he'd slain in her loft. It was likely that Seth had been erased from this world without a trace.

That thought had reduced her to tears as she'd driven the gravel road out to Severo's mansion.

Sniffing tears and whispering a blessing for her friend, Bella strolled through the marble foyer, calling out for Severo. He usually called to her or appeared at her side to sweep her into a kiss.

"Hmm, must be outside. Heloise?"

The sun was already a glow of red on the horizon. It glinted over the white plastic covering the yard crew had placed over the pool a few weeks ago. A scatter of leaves dotted the taut tarp. They'd had a light dusting of snow a few days ago, but it had melted.

Bella opened the patio door but didn't step outside. The breeze snuck into her pores on a shiver. Wind rushed through the trees, tugging the branches to a rocking-chair creak.

"Maybe he's in the arsenal."

He'd been spending an inordinate amount of time in that storage room to ready the weapons then place them all over the house. He was a one-man gang preparing for a war that Bella still didn't believe would happen.

It disturbed her, but not enough to frighten her.

Had she become complacent with him always close by to protect her? Had she forfeited the control she'd once so staunchly wielded?

"A bit," she said as her heels clicked down the hallway. "But it's worth the sacrifice."

She punched in the security code but found the arsenal dark. Walking inside, she traced her fingers over the monstrous pistol's cold metal barrel.

With a glance she took in the assorted weaponry.

Wooden bullets and holy water and gold crosses. A mace, a few swords and dozens of pistols and rifles.

She wondered what weapons the vampires would use against a werewolf. Silver, surely. Probably a silver dagger to pierce the organs and poison the blood.

Another tear dropped onto her thumb and slid cleanly over the pistol's barrel. "Please let us be safe," she whispered.

Something clanked against the steel door.

Bella gripped the handle of the pistol.

He strode across the hilltop that paralleled his land and plunged into the valley. Land was at a premium here in northern Minnesota, but he wouldn't give his estate up for a sweet little apartment in Paris or a penthouse in New York. He belonged to the land and didn't believe he could survive in a big city for long.

He had been born into this world the minority and was of a species forced to hide and protect itself from discovery. He accepted that. He'd learned to walk amid the shadows and keep to himself. The wilderness, freedom—and Bella—meant happiness.

And now his happiness had been threatened. If Elvira targeted Bella, that would be akin to ripping out his heart and slamming it against a wall.

He would protect his own.

Thinking about shifting to wolf form, he decided against it. He'd been out long enough. Bella was due from the city, and he missed her when he could not scent her nearby.

The air had changed as he'd tracked the boundaries of his property. The world was not right.

Standing upon the pinnacle that looked over his land, Severo stretched out his arms and tilted back his head. Sniffing, he took it all in.

The air touched his fingertips, cheeks and nose, imbuing his senses with a catalog of the now. Nearby a jackrabbit darted for an underground burrow thick with her younglings. Tree roots that stretched dozens of feet underground stirred minutely beneath his boots.

The acrid odor of gasoline, which he rarely sensed so far from the city, now made him turn toward the house. All was quiet. The sun had just set, so he could make out a few lights, one in the kitchen, the other illuminating the recessed window high on the basement-laundry-room wall.

Perhaps Bella hadn't yet returned.

He clasped a hand over his heart and smiled. That he had been given this gift of love did not cease to humble him. When he'd thought he could make a go of it with Aby, he had always known that

that was not the direction their relationship was meant to take. Still hurt like hell.

And yet, someone new had laid a bandage over that hurt, and he'd peeled it away to find the wound almost gone. He was ready to forget what might have been and to accept what he already had.

"Love," he murmured and smirked. It was grand.

Starting down the hill, he used the incline to hasten his steps into a run. Halfway across the valley, a force hit Severo on the back of his left shoulder.

He spun. There in the shadows emerged half a dozen vampires.

She pulled the trigger and the heavy pistol kicked, forcing Bella backward against the steel counter. She grunted at the impact. The steel edge dug into her hip.

The hulk of a vampire who filled the arsenal doorway took the wooden bullet in the heart. He clawed at it, but the bullet had penetrated deeply, as intended, and could not be drawn out. One hand ripped the front of his dark shirt. Clawing at his exposed, bleeding flesh, he staggered.

Her thoughts honing, Bella remembered what Severo had said about the bullets. They'd slow a vampire down but would not kill him.

She eyed the wooden stakes, which hung in militant rows; each stake was twelve inches long and as thick as a chair leg. She reached for one, then another and another. The titanium syringe filled with holy water lay on the table, but her hands were full.

Racing forward, she didn't care that she was a dancer whose greatest achievement was the double *golpe* with spin, or that the first time she'd touched a weapon, she'd almost cried.

Somehow a vampire had breached Severo's protection wards.

"And the freaking security codes," she barked out. How had anyone managed to decipher those?

The vampire struggled with the bullet in his chest and didn't expect a skinny mortal woman to leap at him with a stake held at the ready.

Gripping the one stake firmly while she clutched the other two in her left hand, Bella planted the thick piece of wood in the vampire's chest. It slid in easily. She didn't have to push hard to make it go in up to her curled fist.

The vampire spasmed. Hissing steam escaped from around the stake. The awful smell of burning blood entered her nostrils. Bella scrambled backward, into the open doorway, securing a stake in both fists.

The creature's agonizing yowl filled her ears.

She bit her lip and almost called out, "I'm sorry."
Jelly legs quivering, she sunk to her knees.

"Please," she begged. The thing staggered and
spouted smoke. It clawed the air, growling. "Just
die. Don't come back to life. Where is he? Severo!"

A burst of ash dust filled the air. The vampire dis-
integrated into a human-shaped heap of gray ash.
The stake rolled from the ash over to her knee,
blood staining her white slacks.

"I did it," she said, amazed. Was she supposed
to be horrified? The dread feeling didn't emerge.
Instead, adrenaline pushed her to stand and pump
her fist in triumph. "Yes!"

"Think you're quite the slayer, eh, pretty?"

Stake held at the ready for another attack, Bella
let out a throaty squeak as she spied the three
vampires who blocked off the hallway and any
chance of escape.

Chapter 17

Six unarmed vampires? No challenge to him. They'd been going at it for a bit. One vampire would charge, and Severo would strike at his shoulder or deliver a roundhouse and thrust him off him.

He was rolling on the ground now with a snarling beast of a longtooth, its long fangs bared. A bite from a vampire would piss Severo off, but it couldn't change him.

On the other hand, he'd never experienced a vampire bite. It would leave a permanent mark. And that was the last thing Severo wanted on his body. A vamp bite was a stigma he'd never bear.

The longtooth twisted Severo's arm around behind his back and yanked sharply, tearing the muscles. Severo could endure it. He needed a moment to flip and…yes. On his back, he struck his opponent in the chest with his heels and sent him flying.

Darkness had fallen, and the trees were silhouetted against the gray sky. Now two vamps charged him.

"Have at me," Severo muttered.

He could take them. For now. But the werewolf was beginning to rage. Then the stupid bastards had better run.

Surprisingly, none *had* tried to bite him yet. Odd. It was the vampires' best defense, weakening their opponent through blood loss.

What kind of idiots had Elvira sent after him?

And only six? Perhaps she wanted to toy with him. Give him a preview of the war yet to come.

Or maybe she needed to wear him down. The obvious reason was she wanted him alive for something.

He caught a charging vamp about the neck with a vertebra-crunching swing of his own. The vamp yowled, but his partner knocked Severo off balance by kicking his ankles. He hit the ground with a growl. Spitting blood from his mouth, he

rolled to all fours and decided the werewolf had
been kept at bay long enough.

Three more vampires had been destroyed in the
arsenal. Bella couldn't think clearly about how
she'd done it. But she now knew that holy water to
the eyes was no way to go. The vamp's face had
peeled away.

Kicking off her high heels, she ran out as fast as
she could, though she had no idea what to do, where
to go. Adrenaline sharpened her senses. In the
garage, the odor of gasoline seemed to hang in the
air. In the house, the smell of the wax Heloise used
on the floor rose in invisible waves. And her
perfume seemed far too strong.

As she checked the front door, her hands shook
and she dropped the stakes twice. It was locked,
completely secure. She stepped back and scanned
the three-story foyer. The huge skylight windows
lining the upper story were unbroken.

Where had the vampires gotten in? If not through
the front door or the garage…

"Heloise." Bella hadn't heard the housekeeper,
and surely the commotion would have alerted her.
Heloise insisted on using the servants' entrance near
the laundry room, much as Severo wished she'd
come through the front door. "Heloise!"

She ran for the laundry room, praying the house-keeper had had the sense to hightail it to safety at the first sniff of vampire. Or at least hide.

Bella had no idea if faeries could defeat a vampire, but if they possessed any skill against the threat, she doubted that squat and kind Heloise had the ability to keep back anything larger than a dragonfly.

Hugging the pistol, which was loaded with three wooden bullets, to her chest, she skidded up to the laundry room doorway. And fell to her knees in horror.

A clear, thick substance pooled about Heloise's head. Her throat had been torn out, and it leaked more clear liquid. An unfolded bedsheet, still clenched in her hand, soaked up the stuff.

Reaching out and squelching the need to scream, Bella bent over and gripped her gut. "Don't do this. Be strong."

She examined the brownie's neck. The clear liquid must be faerie blood, because it sparkled. Had to be. "Those bastards. She was an innocent."

Standing, her back skidding across the wall, she hugged the pistol to her chest and checked both ways down the hallway. It was clear.

"I have to get to Severo."

Nodding, because nothing else made sense at the moment, Bella ran upstairs to the living room.

Where three vampires waited.

"She's mine," growled the tallest, sporting a black Mohawk. A fang glinted brightly at the corner of his mouth. "Secure her!"

Bella fired, but the wooden bullet went astray, missing the vampires and ricocheting against the wall. The picture of Severo and Aby cracked and dropped to the floor.

Two vampires charged, and before she could again squeeze the trigger, the pistol was pulled from her hand. Her shoulders stretched painfully as, one to each side of her, they wrenched her arms behind her back.

"Nice," the Mohawked leader said as he approached. "And brave."

Bella spat at the vampire. In punishment she took a knee to her spine. Pain shot through her skeleton and she yowled.

"Gentle, boys," said the leader. The dark vampire's eyes were pale blue, and the pupils large.

Bella thought, for an odd moment, that his eyes appealed to her. She stopped struggling as he reached out and stroked her hair.

"Severo's mate," he drawled. "She smells like dog, doesn't she?"

The two vampires grunted.

"Let me go, and I won't sic my dog on you," she warned.

"I'm not at all frightened, green eyes," replied the leader.

The vampire loomed over her, his face close to hers, as if to sniff her, as Severo often did. And yet he maintained the stare that Bella could not look away from. Something in his eyes…provocative. Sensual.

"That's right. Look all you like. What do you see in my eyes? Freedom? Pleasure?"

Her mouth dropping open, Bella felt her eyelids flicker. Part of her wanted to kick the vampire in the nuts. He was in the right position. But a bigger part of her wanted to melt, to succumb.

"No, no, don't look away. It's only going to get better, pretty one."

Brilliant white fangs descended over the vampire's lower lip. So pretty. And long. They would sink deeply into her flesh.

And she wanted it.

As he began to shift, and his shoulder bones stretched and his flesh thickened and grew, the whip's icy lash of cold steel wrapped about Severo's biceps. The rigid yet flexible steel locked tightly, scraping the leather jacket. A jerk of the whip brought him to his knees, stopping the shift to werewolf before his human features began to fade.

He gripped the steel lash. It burned, eating
through his palm. With a hiss, Severo dropped it.
Not steel, but silver. In a flexible whip?

He struggled, but the silver drained his energy.
Heaving himself forward, he was thankful for the
leather jacket. It kept the silver from touching his
flesh, but the whip was sharply edged, so he knew
soon it would cut through the jacket.

If he didn't struggle, he could survive this.

The air darkened. Vampires crowded about him.
He could not see who held the whip, holding him
captive. There were more than a dozen now. All
men. Their scents made him want to retch, and he
was fast losing strength. Longtooths wielded
daggers and pistols, but they weren't pointed at him.

Bella's gorgeous smile flickered in his thoughts.
He jerked a look toward the house. More lights were
on. She was home? He must hold back these
vampires and keep them from her.

Unless they had already gotten to her?

"Severo." The gang of vamps parted and Evie
strode through the grass. A feat, surely, considering
the open-toed spike heels peeking out at the bottom
of her black gown. "We meet again."

"You think this will hold me back?" he growled.

"Appears to be doing the trick. Ian Grim stole it
from the Highwayman for me. Nice, isn't it?"

The Highwayman? Christ, that was Aby's husband. Had they harmed him? What of Aby?

He fought against the powerful silver. The bladed edge of the whip cut leather. He'd once trusted Ian Grim. Until he'd learned the man was a nasty witch who should be labeled a warlock for his crimes against the faith he claimed.

"Careful, dear. Wouldn't want to bring on your death as you kneel, humbled, before a crew of vampires," the vampiress hissed.

A few longtooth assholes chuckled.

Humbled, yes. But never defeated.

"I thank you for the show," she said. Ruby blood glinted at Elvira's throat, a thick droplet that seemed suspended there without a chain. "I could have watched my boys go at you all night. You can't be put back, can you?"

"So you came to watch me perform, is that it? A carnival freak show for the biggest freak of them all? Bring out your weapons. I'll match them all."

"Oh, so brave and proud, my bruised little puppy dog."

He snarled and snapped at her. A seam of his jacket tore but the silver did not touch his skin.

With the silver containing him, he could not complete the transformation. Instead, he was suspended in midshift. His shoulders and neck had thickened, as had his legs and torso, but the bones had not yet changed. Nor had he the weaponlike talons, which could cut the whip as if it were made of ribbon.

She leaned forward, coming face-to-face with him. The foul scent of her tweaked at Severo's senses. And yet he'd once remembered her scent as the perfume of his savior when he'd been held captive by her parents.

"I could remove you from this earth right now." She glanced aside to one of the vampires who'd eagerly stepped forward. "Back, all of you. He's mine."

"He's mine." Severo chuckled lowly and shook his head. "It's been so long since I've heard that from you, Evie."

"Yes." She stroked his brow, and he nudged her away, but she persisted, placing her fingers to his cheek. The edges of her nails were as sharp as a blade. His flesh opened and blood trickled down to his beard. "You know I was the only reason you were never bitten while my family owned you."

Yes, he knew that. Evie had been the one to plead with her father to save the young werewolf for her. She had wanted him. And her father had given him that lecherous sneer and had bent to his daughter's whim.

"So will you finally have that bite you've been dying for?" he asked.

For a werewolf, the stigma of a vampire bite was great. For while the bite would not turn the werewolf into some sort of vamp/wolf hybrid, it would increase the werewolf's blood hunger immeasurably. He would crave blood, which usually resulted in hunting humans to satisfy the need for a fix. Other werewolves could smell the taint on the inflicted wolf and would sooner kill the bastard than suffer his pitiful disgrace.

"Go ahead," Severo said in defiance. "I will wear your bite with pride, knowing I have made your family pay for the travesties visited upon my own."

She crossed her arms under her breasts and sighed. Taking in the surroundings, she twisted her head about and then said, "I understand what you did was just."

"Do you? Then why this war now?"

"Because you know revenge never ends." Splaying her fingers before her, Evie observed the blood on her nails. "One man takes revenge for the sins against his family, which then breeds new revenge, to be enacted upon his own. It continues on endlessly, Severo." With the tip of her tongue, she licked the blood from her nails. She had a discerning look on her face. Obviously it wasn't enough blood to serve any need. "You're not so foolish that you believe this can ever be finished?"

"It will end when one of us dies," he said briskly.

"Just so. You want to kill me now?"

He swallowed and jutted his chin. Were the silver whip not about him, he could swipe her with a taloned paw and take her head from her body. But it didn't feel right.

Truly, revenge only spawned further violence.

"Do it, then," he said, tilting his head aside to expose his neck. "Mark me, and take leave knowing you have the satisfaction of this gauntlet."

"Brave werewolf."

She leaned into his neck. The warmth of her nose slid down his tense muscles. The pass of her finger along the jugular tickled. Would she murder him?

"Over the years you've walked a wide path around me when you could have easily slain me," she whispered, so others would not hear. "I offer you the same regard."

Her eyes glinted with unnatural light, a silvery shard of hunger. "I wish you no harm physically. My mark would mean little for one so proud and one who walks alone. Were you in a pack, it would be different. I'd drink you until you moaned for me to satisfy you."

She spoke truths. A vampire mark would mean little to him now—unless he ever wished to start a new pack. Should she bite him, he would feel it as a human would. As an intense orgasmic draw at the core of his being, one that commanded he submit.

The idea of succumbing to this bitch's persuasion brought bile to his throat.

"Besides—" Elvira tilted up his chin "—there's another who'll wish to take a bite out of you soon enough."

She propped her hands at her hips. The pale globes of her breasts were the only discernible shape on her black-cloaked figure. "Come on, boys. Our work here is finished."

Turning, she marched off, her sycophants in tow.

The whip dragged across his shoulders, slicing his jacket and jerking him forward to the ground. He landed, digging his fingers into the pummeled grass and clutching dirt.

Severo could only repeat the words she'd said over and over until he understood them.

…another who'll wish to take a bite out of you…

"Bella!"

Rage twisted Severo as he made a quick shift. Within moments, the werewolf howled out its anger. Vampires had hurt it. Yet though it could sense that they were close, it did not seek to track them.

A stronger scent drew it into a loping race across the field, toward the house.

The patio door was smashed in. The granite coffee table lay on the patio flagstones, on top of the shattered glass.

The werewolf charged across the debris. Glass shards pierced its paws, yet it did not slow down. Barking at the fierce cuts to its flesh, it trotted into the living room.

A thin streak of crimson ran across one couch cushion. The werewolf knew that scent. It was tainted with cloves. The scent briefly calmed it. Her. Its mate. Where was she? Was she harmed?

Calm turned to rage.

Rushing through the kitchen, it followed a trail of broken dishes and a crack in the wall where a force must have punched through.

Moving quickly, it took the steps downstairs, scenting blood so strongly, it growled and punched the walls as it made it to the laundry room.

Not a wolf or vampire, but not a human, either.

Not your mate.

It loped upstairs. Closing its eyes, it twisted its neck, scenting the air. Longtooths. Three of them dead. Others, no longer in the house, had left a scent trail that led toward the front door, which hung on one hinge.

Another scent grabbed at it. Mate.

Down the hall.

Inside the room with a bed the werewolf found her. The limp, bloodied body of its mate lay across the tousled white sheets.

A howl birthed from its core and vibrated through its entire being.

Severo shook off the sharp tingles of the shift and became instantly alert on the floor before the bed.

He clutched his foot and gripped the glass shard that had penetrated all the way through the top of his foot. Growling as he pulled it out, he tossed it aside. Blood spilled from his foot, but he gave it no mind.

He spied a body on the bed—and let out a cry.

Clenching a fist, he wondered if Elvira's minions had finally done what they'd set out to do that night of the chase. Please, they must not have raped her. He would tear those vampires limb from limb, and then… But no, she'd been *placed* on the bed. Perhaps she had not been violated, after all.

She moaned, and he lunged to the bed and leaned over her. "Bella, I'm here."

"I did it. Killed…vampires." Her voice cracked and her head fell back as he lifted her by the shoulders.

A pile of ash on the other side of the bed startled him.

"Good girl. You got them. I'm sorry. I don't know

how they made it through the wards. I was outside. There were so many of them. Bella, you're bleeding."

He reached to flick on the lamp. Just leaning over her, filling his senses with her blood, sickened him. He should have been inside to protect her. What hell had she gone through while he was out batting around vampires?

What he'd thought a head injury was quickly revealed to be neck wounds when the light gleamed across her side. Thick, viscous blood glittered. It had begun to coagulate, but there was so much, he couldn't tell if she'd been slashed or stabbed.

His heart knew it hadn't been a weapon of steel that had harmed her.

Fingers shaking, Severo touched the blood. He winced when the nature of the two wounds was revealed. Teeth marks.

Gathering her into his arms, he rushed into the bathroom and deposited her in the tub. As water filled the tub, he tore her clothing from her and tossed it behind him. He tugged down a towel from the bar and plunged it into the water.

Scrubbing the towel over the wounds on her neck, he wasn't sure what he could accomplish. He only knew he had to wash away the blood.

Chapter 18

Emerging from a groggy dream of ash-filled air and snarling fangs, Bella blinked and groaned. Was she underwater? Her skin was wet, yet the pressure of the water did not pull her down. The steamy scent of lemons made her wonder if she was in the bathroom.

Opening her eyes, she saw her lover sitting there, his shoulders bowed, his hands hanging between his bent knees. There was such intensity in his eyes. They were what had held her since day one. A promise of truth, trust and honor lived there in Severo's eyes.

Beyond him, she saw a strange disaster. The doorway had a big bite out of it. A force had punched the wall and taken out part of the door frame and Sheetrock. Bloody footprints led from the bedroom to the bathroom tiles.

Every part of her ached and her muscles had been stretched beyond their capacity. But of course, after battling a houseful of crazed vampires, what did one expect?

"Oh my God, the vampires." When she tried to move, her hand slipped on the edge of the porcelain tub and she fell back into the water. "What the hell?"

Now she realized Severo sat on the toilet lid, not reacting to her distress, but waiting patiently. He wore only jeans. Watery blood pooled at his bare feet. His face was dirty and his shoulder had blood on it.

"Why am I in here?" she asked. "Why am I all wet?"

She followed his gaze over the floor. A pile of bloody towels sat heaped before the vanity.

"I had to clean the wound," he offered in a raw, quiet voice. "It's still bleeding. It was left unsealed. I…couldn't take it away. I'm sorry."

She shoved herself up but the slick tub kept her sliding to a reclined position. "Wound? Your shoulder?"

"No, sweet. You."

"Was I cut? None of them had weapons. I ran from them. Took a few out with those wooden bullets and a stake. They got Heloise. Oh, Severo, Heloise."

She slapped a palm to her forehead, and when she thought the tears would come, she realized she had gone beyond them. Her chest heaved. Sorrow for the fallen housekeeper prodded her sympathy, but she had abandoned tears sometime after that first vampire had been staked.

Among her thoughts she remembered what Severo had said.

"What do you mean, 'left unsealed'?" she asked him.

Why didn't he just hug her? More than anything she wanted him to hold her and make her know everything was all right. That the vamps were all gone. They were alive. That meant they had won, right?

"Saliva is necessary to seal the wound and prevent the vampire taint from rushing into the bloodstream," he explained. "You don't remember?"

Standing, he loomed over her. He had blood all over him—at the corner of his eye, on his shoulder and at his abdomen. Blood had dripped onto his jeans. Not from fresh wounds. Streaks of dried blood from earlier wounds that had rapidly healed.

"Bella..."

He sucked in a breath. His eyes shifted up and along the shower curtain rod, searching for something. The pulse of his jaw, which she had once thought so sexy, now disturbed her.

"You've been bitten. And there's nothing I can do to reverse the imminent change," he blurted.

She gripped her neck and flinched at the pain. Slippery blood coated her fingers. "A vampire *bit* me?"

She met her lover's tired gaze and he nodded. "I'm going to tend to Heloise. She should not be left as she is. You'll be fine until I return?"

Fine? What was fine? She'd been bitten by a vampire. Was she going to change? Would she die? Would she want to drink blood?

Severo awaited her reply. Why wasn't he holding her?

If she closed her eyes and opened them again, would this crazy nightmare go away?

"Bella?"

She nodded, though she couldn't meet his tired eyes. "Sure. Fine."

And he walked from the room without bowing to kiss her or offering to help her out of the tub.

Was he horrified by her?

"He hates vampires," she murmured. Sliding a

finger along her neck to feel at the gaping tooth marks, she now found tears. "Will he hate me?"

Severo jogged downstairs. A sense that he had been here recently—as the werewolf—put up his hackles.

As suspected, he did not find Heloise's body in the laundry room. The ichor pool glittered brilliantly, and he knew that, by some strange and magical means, her body had returned to Faerie, whence it had come.

He knelt before the devastation.

Sheets were shredded, some spattered with red. It could only be vampire blood. So Heloise had put up a fight? *Good girl.*

Closing his eyes and bringing his joined palms up to his face, he wondered what he could say, then knew it would be better to say nothing. Thanks for all she had done for him would be inappropriate. It was a bittersweet moment.

He slammed the laundry room door closed behind him and made a hasty retreat to the kitchen. Piles of vamp ash sat among the debris of broken furniture, of his life.

How many vampires had gone after Bella? There must have been as many inside the house as outside.

How had they breached the wards? And the locks?

Looking around, he realized he did not know where to begin. How did one make things right when they were so wrong?

She is wrong now.

Catching his balance against the kitchen counter, he gasped in a breath. Wrong? No, not his Bella.

"Please, let her be right."

He placed a call to the cleaners, who promised they'd arrive within the hour.

Well and fine. He should probably tend his own wounds. Not that it mattered. They'd all healed— save the gaping gash through his heart.

"Bella," he whispered. "Bella."

Not wrong. Never wrong.

The wards and locks would have to wait before he could figure out why they had failed. He wouldn't need them now. He sensed Elvira had gotten exactly what she'd wanted, and would not return.

And what had she won from this round of battle? She would turn the one thing Severo most loved into the one thing he most hated.

"Masterful revenge," he muttered, then kicked aside a bloodied couch cushion.

The patio-door glass clinked beneath his boot toe. Sunshine tickled across the shards of safety glass as if they were large pieces of faerie dust. Poor Heloise. She was an innocent.

As was Bella.

He snapped a finger against a shard stuck in the door frame. Soaring through the air, it landed and slid across the pool tarp.

"I should go to her."

She would want him to hold her, to reassure and kiss her, to give her proof of his love.

For a long time he'd sat in the bathroom after scrubbing furiously at the wound on her neck. If only he could have washed away any trace of damage, taken the bite from her with the cleansing water.

What now would he feel when he again looked upon her?

"I love her," he growled at his insensitive thoughts.

Could he love a vampire?

A minute possibility remained that she would not change. To do that, she had to survive till the next full moon. Elvira had planned this so well. The moon had been waning but a day. There were four long weeks till the next full moon.

"She'll never survive without going mad."

Exhausted, and knowing that Severo was busy with the cleaning and security crews, Bella slept through the day. After she'd showered, the wound had stopped bleeding. She crawled naked into bed and fell instantly asleep.

A fitful sleep. She'd been aware when the water in the shower again beat against the tiles, and then when Severo had carefully tiptoed about the bedroom, selecting clean clothes and leaving her alone.

All she craved was spooning against his body and knowing that everything was going to be all right. But the dread that their relationship would never be the same kept her in bed, even when her stomach growled for food.

When the noise from the cleaners ceased and the sun had again set, she decided to sneak out for a morsel. At least now she wouldn't have to see piles of ash or signs of the struggle she'd been through.

Pulling on a black silk robe, Bella combed her hair and leaned toward the mirror. The bite mark was swollen and red. She couldn't conceal it with makeup. It didn't hurt, only ached.

"How did you do it, Seth? This is not my idea of a good time."

Of course, when the wound healed, she could get on with her life. She suspected Severo was avoiding her for the very reason that she bore the mark of the vampire on her neck. It couldn't heal fast enough.

Answering her hunger pangs, she headed to the kitchen. It was spotless, with no sign of broken dishes or the wooden stool she'd thrown at a vampire and had broken across his shoulder. She opened the fridge and grabbed the plastic bottle of pomegranate juice.

When she closed the door, she dropped the juice. Tall and strong, Severo posed as if ready for a challenge, head lowered and fingers coiled, ready to fist. She thought she could smell the fury on him, and his eyes appeared even darker.

The vampire's eyes had been so beguiling. Blue, deep and seductive. She couldn't remember anything after looking into them.

"I'm sorry. I was hungry." She picked up the plastic bottle. To run into his arms felt wrong but she so desired it.

"How are you feeling?"

"Better. Much. I think this stupid bite mark will heal in a few days. I know how it must make you feel. I understand you haven't had time for me. You've been busy all day, I'm sure. Can I make you something to eat?"

His inhale stabbed her in the heart. Bella closed her eyes. *Please, touch me. Hold me.*

"We need to talk, Bella."

Call me sweet. I am yours. You won't abandon me after you realize this bite means nothing.

"Sure." She screwed off the bottle cap and took a slug. She didn't realize how achy her jaw was until she swallowed. "Let's sit over there."

Drawn to their favorite chair, she waited for him to sit and pull her onto his lap. "Severo?"

He nodded as if jerking himself out of busy thoughts. "Yes."

He sat, and when she wanted to climb onto his lap, he allowed it, but he didn't cradle her as he usually did, only sat stiffly, as if he wouldn't push her away but would like to if he could.

"Are you angry with me?" she asked.

"Never. No. I'm sorry, Bella."

"It's the bite, isn't it? It reminds you of them. It'll soon be gone—"

"It's going to change everything, Bella."

"No, it won't. When it's healed, you'll forget all about this stupid incident."

"It will heal. But you will not. You will be transformed."

She pushed against his chest and leaned back to study his face. He couldn't meet her eyes. How dare he not look at her, to make her feel as if she were contagious. Now she wished she would have found a scarf to tie around her neck.

"Transformed? You mean…? But Seth didn't change when he was dating Elvira. Not until she wanted him to."

"Because a vampire usually licks the wound after it takes blood from a mortal. The infusion of vamp saliva seals the wound and keeps back the vampire taint. A bite that isn't sealed introduces the taint to the mortal's system. It will stir up the blood hunger in you, Bella, and you will change with your first taste of human blood."

"No." She shoved off from his lap and paced toward the opposite wall.

The now glassless picture of Aby and Severo had been rehung there. In the ten years they'd been together, why hadn't Elvira gone after Aby? Was it because he'd never made love to her?

"I don't want to be a vampire. I don't want—" To be the one thing her lover despised. The thing that would always remind him of his family's tragic suffering. "There must be some way to stop it."

"There is."

The warm weight of his hand on her shoulder made her flinch. Bella did not turn to him. Aby's bright smile taunted her. She had had Severo for an entire decade. Would Bella lose him after but a few months?

"You can wait for the full moon." His voice hurt her heart. So calm. Yet not affectionate, as it had been. More removed, clinical. "If you don't drink human blood before then, you'll be in the clear. But you'll be mad from resisting the intense hunger. Damn it, Elvira planned this well. It'll be another month before the full moon comes again."

"But you said if I drink *human* blood. Maybe I could…drink yours?" She winced at the thought of doing something so reprehensible.

"Bella, listen. There are three options for a mortal bitten by a vampire when the wound has not been sealed. You can answer the blood hunger—which should emerge within days—and complete the transformation, thus becoming a vamp."

"What are the other two?"

"You could kill yourself."

She gasped.

Severo punched a fist into his palm.

"Door number three, please?" she asked softly.

"You could try to wait out the full moon. If the victim can go without drinking blood until the next full moon is over and the moon begins to wane, then the vampire taint will pass from their system, leaving them completely mortal."

"Well, that's my pick. See, this won't be so bad."

"One problem."

"There's always a but."

"Bella, I don't know of anyone who has been able to resist the insistent blood hunger. If they did resist the insatiable need, madness would generally take hold before they made it to the full moon.

"There is a legend of one man who survived until the full moon—at the expense of his mind. His family, after committing him, decided to attempt to have him bitten again, in hopes of curing the madness. He'd changed to a vampire and yet remained mad.

"Bella, what's been done to you is irreversible. You are destined to become a bloody long—" He stopped.

"Longtooth," she whispered. Then she spun about and insisted boldly, "Say it. I know you hate them. And now you will hate me."

"No, I love you." But she heard so little conviction in his tired tone. "I could never…"

"Never look me in the eyes again? You won't. You can't. My God, that bitch really did know what she was doing."

She paced the floor. Wanting him to wrap her in his arms wouldn't earn her the reprieve from the horror she could never shake.

The patio door had been boarded up, and the smell of fresh paint made her wonder which wall she had seen her own blood splattered on last night, as the vampire had bent to bite into her neck.

A bite she recalled wanting.

She shivered as she recalled a memory. "It was the same ones who originally chased me." Severo had been there that night to rescue her. Why hadn't he been there for her last night? "Where were you?"

He leaned forward, hanging his head.

"Severo?"

"I was out back. Elvira and a dozen vampires detained me with some kind of silver whip. I had no idea they had infiltrated the house, or that you were even home, until it was too late."

"A silver whip? Are you hurt?"

"No more than my pride."

His pride. And while he'd been suffering a pride-busting tête-à-tête with the mistress of the night, Bella had been getting her throat chewed on.

"I'm sorry, Bella. This would have never happened if I had not pursued you after that night in the warehouse. If I had not kept you in my life."

"Don't say that. Seth was already dating Elvira then. It would have happened much sooner, is all. I'm glad you followed me home and seduced me into loving you, Severo. Do you…"

She wanted to ask.

She could not.

He could not love her now. It would be cruel to ask it of him after all she had learned of his past.

"So what are we going to do?" she asked instead. "Do you want me to pack my bags?"

He narrowed his gaze but still did not meet hers. Did he look at Aby's picture?

"That's ridiculous. This is your home. I swore

you would be my mate—" He fisted his fingers and the air in the room shifted as if a ghost had just breezed through. Bella felt the chill. "We'll get through this."

"I want that. But I'd feel much better if you'd hold me and…and kiss me." She waited for his eyes to find hers. They did not.

"The security crew is still outside working at the terminal. I need to go out and check on their progress. I'll return soon, I promise."

"You don't want to touch me now, do you?" Tears slid down her cheeks. Bella resisted the shivers that threatened to shake her body uncontrollably. "Will you touch me when the bite has healed?"

"It's not like that, Bella."

"Yes, it is! Don't lie to me. Everything has changed between us now, hasn't it?"

He didn't answer. And that was answer enough.

Chapter 19

He was being a bastard. Two days had passed since the attack and Severo had used the excuses of installing new windows and rechecking the grounds and restocking the arsenal as means to limit his time with Bella.

Hell, he wanted to go to her. To hold and kiss her, to make love to her, and find his place inside her again.

But the vampire's scent lingered on her, and he didn't want Bella to know that. To sense that he was repulsed by her. He was, and he wasn't. Yet he was stupid to think she didn't already sense his reluctance.

Rationally, he knew nothing had changed

between them. She was the same woman he had fallen in love with and had wanted to mate with for as long as their days would allow.

Illogically, his brain found her offensive. He cringed every time the fading red bite mark on her neck was revealed as her hair swept over a shoulder.

Vampires had viciously murdered his parents and enslaved him. They had gone to war with the witches with little respect for human life. Vampires were filthy, nasty creatures.

And soon Bella would become one.

He couldn't push her away. And yet he knew ignoring her was far worse. She needed him as much as he wanted her. She wasn't yet a vampire.

If he could not accept her now, how could he possibly do so after she changed?

Because it was starting. Last night she had moaned in her sleep, a deep, wanting whine that wasn't sexual. The blood hunger had begun to infiltrate her system.

Each night, after she drowsed off to sleep, he'd sleep on the chair in the bedroom, or rather, sit there with one eye open. He hadn't slept for days, and though exhausted, he would continue to keep watch on her. For any changes. For her needs.

Kiss me.

She said it every night before slipping between

the sheets. But she wouldn't look at him, as if she knew he could not meet her gaze.

"Idiot!"

He would not fall victim to mere thoughts. Mind games. His brain had convinced him of something irrational. He would make the best of this. He must. The longer he separated himself from her, the further they would disconnect.

"I want her. I will go to her."

Yes, he'd kiss her. And it would be as it always had been.

Or he would sooner die.

Bella sorted through the negligee drawer. She normally slept in the buff, but she'd been wearing pajamas lately because it was cold in bed at night.

Severo had been sleeping in the chair so he wouldn't accidentally rub up against her. He probably believed she didn't know, but she was aware in the middle of the night, when her sleep grew light, that he watched her. From afar.

She shivered and swallowed a desperate need to cry.

"You're stronger than this, Bellybean." Using Seth's nickname for her, she released a teardrop, which slid down her cheek. "Suck it up. You have far worse things to deal with than a confused boyfriend." Like how to deal with what she was becoming. She could feel it.

She traced her throat and then her chest. There, at the base of her lungs, was where the pining had first surfaced. It was a burning, like heartburn, but not. It wanted. Craved. And it needed to be slaked.

"The blood hunger," she whispered, her lower lip wobbling. "I don't want to do this. I can't drink blood. It would be so much easier…" If she had support.

"Bella?"

Tugging the pink silk nightgown from the drawer and clutching it to her naked body, she turned to find Severo on the other side of the bed. Leather pants, chest bare, looking so handsome. So fine.

Yet no longer yours.

"Is something wrong?"

"Yes, everything," he replied heavily. A sigh lifted his shoulders. He prowled around the bed to her side. He hadn't stood so close to her in days. Tentatively, he lifted a hand and traced a finger down her arm. The heat of him, his musky male scent cloyed. Her skin tensed in anticipation. "I've been cruel to you."

The confession stirred her hope. But Bella was not quick to clutch it. "With good reason."

"No." He touched the silk fabric hanging over her

forearm. "I've succumbed to an ingrained belief. I should not look to the past. I must move beyond. My world, my beliefs and prejudices, are formed, but I need to think about what I am willing to accept. What I think I should believe. I need to change my thinking. You should not go through this alone."

"You really feel that way?" The heat of his body poured over her like a desert sun, warm and rich. Could she melt against him without fear of him stiffening and pushing her away? "I just need you…to hold me."

"I can do that."

He embraced her, drawing her against his chest. The thin silk garment slid to the floor, and they stood flesh to flesh. But Bella did not fool herself into thinking he did not flinch. He did. And the embrace was noticeably stiff.

But it was a start.

"You've been feeling the hunger," he whispered. "I can see it torment you at night."

He smoothed her hair, and she remembered how she'd felt so safe in his arms. She wanted to know that feeling again.

"The hunger will only increase," he said. "I've no means to understand or deal with what is going on inside you. I think I need to contact a friend."

"Someone who knows about the transformation?"

"A vampire."

"But you called him a friend?"

"That may be too generous a term. I've mentioned him before. He is the one vampire in this world I respect. He was once a brain surgeon, and though he heads tribe Kila now, he has fought for peace between the vampire and witch nations. I admire him for his values."

"So you can accept a vampire."

He tilted up her chin. "I *will* accept a vampire. And I love you, so don't think I could ever stop."

"I think you've already stopped." She lifted her quavering chin bravely. "You just don't realize it yet."

"That's cruel, Bella. I love you."

Hearing the words forced her to swallow back tears. She nodded. "But it will be hard."

"I won't lie and tell you it's going to be easy."

"And I won't push. I'm just happy to stand in your arms. Will you hold me until I fall asleep?"

"Yes."

"I'll talk to Bella and get back to you. Thank you, Ivan."

Severo clicked the cell phone off and swiped a hand over his face.

So he was going through with this. He'd given Nikolaus Drake a call, the vampire he knew he could trust with the situation, but he'd been away in Africa. Instead, his son Ivan had taken the call. He was in Minneapolis for another few weeks.

After Severo explained the situation, Ivan agreed to help.

Not that it was his deal to go through with. It was all about Bella. Or it should be. He'd put on a good face the past few days. He'd even slept beside her last night, holding her, kissing her. But not on the mouth.

How desperately he wanted to make love to her, but she'd told him it was all right. She'd read his reluctance.

Why could he not get past this?

If he didn't master his feelings now, they would not climb up from this chasm and when she did turn, he would never be able to accept her.

"What's up?" Bella asked as she strode through the kitchen, a book in hand. She wore loose-fitting white yoga pants and a tank top that showed her peaked nipples beneath the fabric, and her hair was swept up in a neat ponytail.

"I spoke to Drake," Severo said. "He's out of the country, but his son Ivan is in Minneapolis."

"Oh. And?"

"I trust the Drakes, Bella. You would be in good hands with either father or son. But with the son you have the added factor that his father is a vampire and his mother a witch. And that vampire father is a phoenix."

"Is that a good thing?"

"A phoenix vampire has survived a witch's blood attack and has an immunity to the sun. If you chose to accept the transformation, you will have that blood running through your veins."

"This is my choice?"

"Can't be anyone else's."

"But I thought there was no other option. I mean, madness doesn't ring any of my bells, nor does suicide. I don't want to do anything that's going to see you hating me."

He gripped the back of her head. "I love you." Teeth bared, he snarled out the words, "I will always love you."

"You can speak the words," she said, "but I don't see the truth in your eyes."

That made him rear back and slam a fist against the kitchen counter. "Bella, I'm trying!"

"It's okay. If you won't have me as a blood-sucker, then I'll have to learn to accept that."

"You won't do any such thing. How can I make you understand how I feel about you?"

"By being truthful." She set down the book and crossed her arms over her chest. "Severo, you're as scared as I am. Admit it. You're losing the woman you fell in love with. I'm not the same, and I'm never going to be the same. And every time you look at me, you will see the horrors of your past."

"It won't be like that."

"Just, please, look me in the eye."

It was such a simple request, and yet he struggled to hold her liquid green gaze for longer than a second. In her eyes he saw so much. Their shared love. The good times, when they'd spent days making love until they were both too exhausted to rise for breakfast. And the teasing play. And the jealousy he felt whenever another man got close enough to breathe her air.

She is yours. Look at her.

Bringing up his chin, Severo found Bella's pleading stare.

"You love me?" she asked.

He nodded.

"And you're afraid?"

"I am. I…want it to be as it's been, but it never will be. And what scares me the most is the werewolf will kill you first chance it gets."

"It will not. I love the werewolf, and it loves me."

"The werewolf takes off vampire heads with one swipe of a paw."

"You can control it." She hugged him and kissed his neck. "If you want to."

If he wanted to? So easy as that, she thought.
Yet *would* he want to?

Bella kept a firm grip on the passenger-side door
handle as Severo navigated the potholes on
Highway 35W, which stretched to Minneapolis. He
seemed unsure and frequently slowed to read the
signs.

"You've not driven this road before, have you?"

He cast her a knowing smile.

"You've run here," she decided.

"Saves on gas, and the wolf needs the exercise. I
can make this distance in half the time it takes a car."

"Well, aren't you speedy on four legs."

"Don't worry. I've a driver's license. I drive into
town on occasion to stay in practice."

"You navigated our small town pretty well." She
twisted on the seat and curled a knee up to her chest.
"So, you've told me about Ivan. How does this all
work? How long do you think it'll take?"

"Ivan suggested a few days. The initial bite can
take place right away, but you'll then need to drink
human blood. He intends to show you the ropes,
which is generous of him. You'll be in good hands,
Bella. You could have just ventured out on your
own, attacked a mortal, and found your own way."

"You'd never allow that."

He smirked. "Only because I want what's best for you."

"You are what's best for me, lover. Are you going to be there when we…do it?"

"I will not watch another man hold you in his arms and sink his teeth into you, Bella. I don't think it would be comfortable for either of us, do you?"

The man did have a ferocious jealous streak. "Yes and no. I mean, I want you there for support, but it would be kind of squicky for you, I'm sure."

"Squicky?"

"Yeah, squirm icky."

He turned onto a highway off-ramp. "I'll stay at a motel and pick you up when you call. Might be safer for Drake that way, too. I know if I get anywhere near him after the fact, I'll want to rip his head off."

Ivan Drake lived in a forty-second-floor penthouse in downtown Minneapolis. Bella swallowed during the elevator ride, because fast elevators made her ears pop.

As they waited before the door, she slid her hand into Severo's. He leaned in and kissed her on the mouth—slowly, like he meant it—and she didn't sense any disgust or repulsion. In a way, it was a goodbye kiss. Goodbye to the woman he knew, the woman *she* knew.

"It's going to be fine," he said and pressed his forehead to hers.

What she wouldn't give to have back the randy, charming Severo who had once seduced her with suggestive moves and aggressive will. That charm was still inside him, but she would never be able to touch that part of him again.

"Just tell me what you think of me."

"I love you, sweet."

The endearment went a long way in reassuring her. Superficially. "I love you, too."

Ivan opened the door to the vast penthouse. The foyer was stark white and modern, as was the living room beyond it. The man had to be rich, because, Bella thought, from what she could see, the place deserved to be in a magazine.

Ivan stood as high as Severo and was equally as built. What was with all these paranormals? They were all muscled and so sexy. He had dark hair that feathered about his ears and neck, a regal nose and piercing eyes, not to mention a friendly disposition.

Cripes, her lover was delivering her to a male model so she could suck on his neck and exchange bodily fluids. The rabbit hole kept getting weirder and weirder.

"You must be Belladonna Reynolds," Ivan offered

when Severo forgot the introductions. "Come in, the two of you, and sit down."

Severo put his hands on her shoulders, pulling her to him. "I won't be staying."

"Oh, of course. I could have a car take Bella-donna home," Ivan offered to Severo.

"No, I'll pick her up when…" Severo let the end fizzle.

When? she thought. When she had become what he most hated?

"I trust your father," Severo said to Ivan, his hold still firm upon her shoulders. He wasn't ready to hand her over, and that reduced Bella's anxiety. "He's promised me that the same trust should not be lost on you."

"I know your struggles with the vampires, Severo, and believe me, I appreciate the work you've done with the Council. If my father could have been here, he would have helped you. But I promise to be a complete gentleman, or my wife will come after me with some wicked magic."

"You have a wife?" Bella hadn't been aware of that. The squick quotient suddenly rose exponentially.

"Yes, she's in Venice right now with her friend Lucy Morgan. Truvin's wife," Ivan said to Severo. At the mention of the name, Bella felt Severo's body tense. "Truvin," Ivan said to Bella, "is not one of Severo's favorite vampires. But his wife is a charm. She's involved in a sort of paranormal debunking venture right now. Dez, my wife, has been helping her with it. They keep the myth a myth, so to speak. It is a project that is invaluable to the safety of all paranormal nations. And Truvin—" Ivan cast a wink at Severo "—has mellowed greatly since the Protection was dropped."

"The protection?" she asked.

"The spell that made witch's blood poisonous to vampires," Severo said. "So do you intend to take her out and show her the ways of your kind…after?"

"If Belladonna wants to stay an extra day or two, I would be glad to," replied Ivan. "If one can have a mentor, then it can make a difference for one's entire future."

"I agree." Severo hugged Bella. "So I guess I should leave. Do you feel all right about this, sweet?"

Who could feel right about being left alone with a stranger whose only intent was to make you a vampire? The one creature her lover could not stand. A creature who lived on human blood. A *creature*.

Was madness such a better option?

"Yes, I'm good about this."

She wished he would stay longer. Truthfully this

didn't feel anywhere near right. But what, since she had met Severo, *had* felt right?

Only him holding her in his arms, making love to her.

Would they ever make love again?

She slid around in Severo's arms. Sensing that Ivan had stepped away to give them a moment alone, she bracketed her lover's face with her hands, sliding her palms over his rough beard.

Remember this, the roughness of him, she told herself. *His earthy scent. His whiskey eyes. The mouth she could get lost in.*

"I haven't been away from you since the day we met," she said.

"That first full moon I was gone three days, sweet."

"I'm going to miss you."

"I will stay close by. Perhaps a few blocks away."

"Thanks, but don't worry too much. I'm a big girl."

She kissed him and it didn't matter who watched; she just needed to fall into him. One last time. Once more as a mortal woman who had crazily fallen in love with a werewolf.

Once more, and then forever.

Chapter 20

After a walk-through tour of the immense penthouse—there was even a lap pool—Ivan led Bella to the main room.

The living room had floor-to-ceiling windows that looked out over the city. It might be a nice view, but Bella avoided walking too close to the windows. She got a woozy feeling even when walking too close to the guardrails on the fourth floor at the Mall of America.

"Would you like something to drink?" Ivan asked.

"Maybe."

His smile was warm and not at all creepy. Not a hint of fangs, either. "Wine? Or I have Evian."

"I'm not sure."

He crossed the room so quickly, she didn't realize he'd moved until his presence loomed behind her. Bella didn't see any drinks in his hands, which made her frown.

"Let's get everything out in the open, shall we?" he offered. "I'm sure we're both feeling awkward about this situation, yes?"

She nodded but avoided looking directly into his eyes. Last time that had happened… She refused to recall it.

"We don't have to be comfortable with it, but know I do genuinely want to help you. My father reveres Severo and would do anything for him. You have nothing to fear from me. And if at any time you do start to experience fear or get uncomfortable, just say so. We'll take this at your pace."

"But I just have to drink your blood to make the change, right?"

"Right."

"So we should just do it and get it done with."

"I'm going to pour us some wine first."

Ivan padded toward the kitchen and Bella followed, to sit on a bar stool across from the counter. He opened a glass-fronted wine cupboard.

"I don't want it to feel like some kind of pseudo-seduction," he said. "Trust me, I love my wife, and I would never betray her. But we're going to be about as intimate as a couple can be without removing their clothes."

"Oh good." She blew out a breath. "I can keep my clothes on."

Ivan smiled and set two goblets before her. "I would insist you stay clothed. Do you know about vampires and their bites?"

"Just that it is what they must do to survive. And that it hurts like a mother."

"Yes, blood is the life."

She nodded, recalling how Seth had waxed lyrical over Elvira's bite. She didn't recall her own bite. Everything from that night was a blur, save those blue eyes.

"Do vampires hypnotize people? Make them *want* to be bitten?"

"Ah, the persuasion. It's not hypnosis, but an actual persuasion of the mind. Some call it the thrall. If you gaze into a vampire's eyes, you will be caught."

"Yep, I know how that one works."

"And when a vampire bites someone, the victim is not in pain for long. They experience the swoon, which is…orgasmic." He slid a half-full goblet toward her. "And when you bite me, well…I, in turn…"

"I see." He'd experience the same orgasmic swoon.

She looked toward the door.

"We can call him back and have him present, if you wish."

"No, that would be too weird. I want it this way. I just…"

"Need to relax and get comfortable with the place, surely. Why don't you step out on the terrace for a while. The view is gorgeous, and I have a heater out there so you can enjoy the view. Take your time and get your bearings. Come back when you're ready for this."

"Thanks, Ivan. I think I will."

Severo rented a gallery suite at the Chambers, a luxury hotel down the street from Ivan's penthouse, but he had to take care of something back home first. He made the hour-long drive to the northern suburb where Bella used to live and parked under a willow tree. He strolled along the boulevard, taking in the nightlife.

His cell phone rang. It was Bella.

"What's wrong?"

"Nothing. So you going to hang out for a day or two? Listen to some Skynyrd?"

"I have something to take care of tonight, but then I'll be sitting around thinking of you. Are you okay? Why the call? Is it Ivan? I left too quickly, didn't I? I should have lingered, but it felt awkward."

"Ivan's letting me get my bearings. And don't worry about it. We're both doing things we never in a million years thought we'd do. I just needed to hear your voice." She paused, then added, "It's never going to be the same, is it?"

"Bella, don't cry. Please, sweet, be strong. You can do this. And when it's done, you'll come home to me and everything will be fine."

He heard a heavy gasp, as if she fought to catch her breath. "You're lying."

He sighed. A quick and reassuring rebuttal wasn't so easy for him.

"Goodbye, Severo," she said and hung up.

He clicked off the phone and stopped in the dark shadow that crept out from an alleyway. He didn't want to lie to her. He didn't want to be the man who needed to lie because he couldn't overcome this one small issue.

It could be good between the two of them.

He hoped.

The night was cold, and the wine lushly warm. Bella inhaled the crisp October air. It was supposed to snow tonight. She hoped she wouldn't miss the first flakes.

Resolute, she turned to face a future that she would likely manage on her own. She didn't want to do it alone, but she was a big girl.

Ivan sat in the living room, on a white sofa, an empty goblet on the coffee table. Soft jazz music played in the background. His bare feet tapped, his head was tilted back and his eyes were closed.

She approached cautiously but knew he was aware of her entrance. "What is it with all you immortals and the white furniture?" she said. "Do you have a great cleaner, or what? I mean…blood spots, anyone?"

Ivan smirked and nodded toward the black leather chaise opposite the sofa. "I don't usually hunt on my sofa. But believe me, the wife has tried to get me to change the furniture here dozens of times."

"Smart girl. We women look at furniture and wonder how it can be kept clean, not how aesthetic it is. So, will you tell me about your wife?"

Well-worn and riddled with scratches, the leather chaise was soft and Bella found it more welcoming than her and Severo's chair had been lately.

"Dez is a witch who is twelve hundred years older than me," Ivan offered. "She swept me off my feet a few years ago and succeeded in releasing me from a pact with the devil Himself."

"Wow. Sounds like an incredible woman."

"Amazing. But I suspect you may rank alongside her. Severo speaks highly of you."

"I think I'm the first relationship he's had since Aby."

"I don't know about her, but if the werewolf is willing to allow his mate to transform into a vampire, then you know you've got yourself a keeper."

"Willing or simply has no other option? I'm not much for madness. Oh." Bella doubled over, clutching her ribs. Stronger than it had been previously, the ache eroded her insides.

"It's the blood hunger. It will only increase. You've done well so far."

"It's not in my gut. It's right here." She tapped her chest, just below her diaphragm. "Will it always be like this?"

"Not so strong. It'll become instinctual."

Instinctual sounded animal. Animal sounded like her lover. *Oh, Severo, don't stop loving me.*

"Let's do this, please. Before I change my mind," she said.

Ivan stood and knelt before her, touching her knees comfortingly. His wide hands, traced with thick veins, were beautiful. "You can change your mind."

"Have you seen someone who went mad?"

"I have."

"Not pretty?"

"Not particularly." He clasped one of her hands. "This life, Bella, is wondrous. You should not fear it. The idea of drinking blood may repulse you now, but trust that it will quickly become second nature. You will be gifted with immortality, so you may live with your mate as long as he lives."

"But he has only a few centuries left."

"And don't you want to spend that time with him?"

"I do. If he'll have me."

"Give him a chance to adjust. Severo has been wounded."

She nodded. Vampires had stolen his family. That was a wound she doubted anyone—even mortal—could get over. "Do you have enemies? What about werewolves?"

"I grew up during the height of the war between the vampires and witches. My mother actually killed my father once. But he rose from the ashes as a phoenix and then managed to fall in love with her."

"That sounds weird, yet wickedly romantic."

"I imagine it was. So no, I've never been prejudiced or hated any particular species or breed. I have the blood of both witches and vampires in my veins. And you will have that gift, as well. You will be a rarity among vampires, Bella. Very strong."

"I like the idea of being strong. And I don't ever want to call another species my enemy, either. Hell, a species? You can't imagine how my life has changed these past few months."

"I can't, actually." He smiled. "I was born this way, so humanity is a curiosity to me."

"But you're humane."

"We all are, so long as we don't succumb to the darkness that threatens us with every sip of blood we take. We vampires are called the Dark, but it's only a label. It's nothing we have to embrace. Witches are the Light. Though I have my doubts about that one at those times when my wife is angry with me."

His smile shied from his lips as he looked aside.

"So what do we do?"

"You need to drink my blood." He tugged his sweater off and held up his wrist. But Bella didn't notice his wrist, because the hard pecs and washboard abs distracted her.

"I thought you said we didn't have to get naked?"

"Oh, sorry. I didn't want to ruin the sweater. I can put it back on."

"No. It's fine. Just show me what to do."

"I'll bite into my wrist and then you drink. Simple as that. But don't pause, because I heal quickly."

"H-how much?"

"You'll know. Ready?"

"Wait." She gripped his wrist, holding it over her lap.

This is your last chance to run away from it all, Bella, she told herself. *You can end it. Not have to face drinking blood for a freaking eternity.*

No.

She wanted to live. With Severo. And she'd be damned if she was going to allow him to use the longtooth defense to weaken their love. She was in it for the long haul. The werewolf was going to have to accept her.

"I'm ready."

Crimson blood bubbled on Ivan's wrist like candy beads. It didn't smell awful; in fact, it smelled delicious. Bella didn't pause. She took his arm and pressed her lips over his bloodied flesh.

The vampire moaned, but not out of pain. It stirred Bella from her intent sucking. God, this tasted good. It filled the aching hunger that had been clawing at her for days.

"More," she murmured.

He'd told her the swoon would affect the victim, but it took hold of her, as well. Bella dropped Ivan's wrist. Thrusting her head back, she smiled and drew up her knees as she twisted on the leather chaise.

She was sated.

"Rest," Ivan whispered near her ear. He put a blanket over her. "Your teeth should come in quickly. We'll take the next step then."

Bella closed her eyes to dreams of Severo taking her in the pool, his strong arms holding her against the cement wall, his hips bumping hers as he thrust deeply into her.

She slept, or maybe it was a reverie of sorts. Either way, Bella came to clarity with a prick at her lip. She touched her mouth. The spot of liquid wasn't saliva.

"Oh, hell."

From around the corner Ivan popped his head. "Ah, your fangs have descended. How do you feel?"

Like she had a bad toothache. "Not sure."

"Come look in the mirror," he suggested. "It'll help you to acclimate."

Bella followed Ivan down the hallway. The bathroom was another all-white, blinding splendor of modern-day privilege.

He hung back at the door as she approached the mirror. Dark circles had formed beneath her eyes. Her skin looked faded, in need of a tan. *What a wreck,* she thought. But there, glinting in her mouth, were sharp fangs.

"How am I going to do this?" she said with an open mouth, not wanting to bite herself.

"You can will them down when you need them.

Most often when the hunger strikes, they will descend automatically. You might cut yourself a time or two until you become accustomed to them. They're pretty."

She shot him a look over her shoulder. "Pretty? You think?"

She bent toward the mirror and touched the fangs. They were small, about twice as long as a normal tooth. And pinpoint sharp.

Severo would not like this.

And yet he sported fangs that were much the same in his werewolf form.

Bella sighed and leaned against the counter to face Ivan. "I'm losing him, you know. You and he both say he can accept me, but he's fooling himself."

"I wouldn't be too sure about that, Belladonna. Sure, Severo's hatred for the vampire goes back many decades. But it is a focused hatred, which he has allowed to expand for reasons that have no tie to the original hate. There is no reason he cannot love you exactly as he has."

"You talk a good game, Ivan. Your wife is a lucky lady."

"I'm the lucky one. So how do you feel?"

"The same. Still have that strange ache below my lungs."

"You need to drink more. Then the change will be complete, and you can learn to stalk a human victim."

"Peachy. So I'm no longer human?"

"You, Belladonna, are now a vampire."

He pronounced it with such grandeur, as if bestowing an honor.

Oh hell, what would Seth think of her now? Or her mother? Probably she could keep this secret from her mother. They were distant at best.

"So let's get on with it," Bella said. "Shall I do the other wrist?"

He rubbed his neck and raised his brows.

"Ah. The neck. Suppose I need to learn the routine, eh?"

He nodded. "It would be best. You know the difference between the carotid and the jugular?"

"Nope."

"Then let's get you up to pace, because I don't want you biting into any arteries."

"On the bed?" Bella gripped her throat.

The fangs already felt natural. And after a quick lesson on discerning veins from arteries, she was ready for this. But Ivan stood before his king-size bed, covered with rich emerald damask, as if it was the most natural thing to expect her to climb on with him.

"Do you prefer the chaise?" The narrow chaise longue in front of the window was covered with pillows. "The bed's going to be more comfortable."

She climbed on the bed, needing a lift from Ivan because it was so high.

Not wanting to wait awkwardly for the right moment or signal, she pushed him against the pillows and dove toward his neck.

Canines to skin. The act felt natural. Her sharp teeth easily penetrated his flesh. Blood pooled in her mouth.

Ivan didn't flinch, and she thought to ask him if it was all right, but then put that worry aside. Of course it was all right.

Then again, nothing would ever again be right.

Dashing her tongue over the bite mark, she licked up his slowly flowing blood. She would need to suck to make it come out easily. The first bite was more delicious than the one in the living room.

The more blood she drew from him, the headier the taste. Bella lifted his shoulder and head to bring him closer to her.

He made a noise of satisfaction. His hand palmed her back—not stroking, nothing overt—but she took it as a sign to continue. Closing her eyes, she drank until she thought she could drink no more.

And when Ivan let out a moan and tilted his head,

his body shuddered against hers. The swoon. An orgasm.

What he must feel, knowing his wife was off in another country while a stranger was literally getting him off. Bella realized Ivan had sacrificed much to help Severo and her.

Drawing away from her, he pushed up to sitting position. "Did you lick the wound?"

"Yes. But I don't need to for you, do I?"

"No, but you should get used to it. How did that feel?"

"Great. You, uh…"

"It felt awesome." He slid off the bed and offered her a hand. "Let's go talk semantics."

Good. He was keeping this businesslike. And while she'd much prefer to loll in bed and slip into a heady reverie now that her soul had been fed with blood, she followed him out to the living room.

He stood in the entry to a mansion east of the city. Elvira's limo had driven here an hour earlier. Severo had hung back under an elm tree, watching as a crew of vampires followed her inside. Four of them. He recognized one who had chased Bella that fateful night of their first encounter. He hadn't seen his face, but the longtooth's foul scent lived in his brain.

He snarled. His teeth descended as the wolf

fought for release. There was no need to completely release the werewolf. He didn't need that strength. But he'd go halfway. Enough to ensure swift and final death.

The foyer was empty, and the front door had been left unlocked. Careless vampires. Loud rock music blared from somewhere beyond the doors at the end of the vast foyer. One vampiress and four slobbering minions? He could imagine what sort of debauched play went on in there.

Something stirred in his periphery. As soon as the vampire sighted the werewolf standing in the entry—stripped to the waist and half shifted, with long, muscular arms and taloned claws—he charged Severo.

Severo swiped the air. His talons cut through the flesh and bone at the neck, removing the vampire's skull in one leathery tear. Severo tossed the head. The vampire ashed, all except the head.

The music stopped, and two male vampires sped toward him. He made quick work of them, not moving from his position.

Letting out a howl that had been birthed deep in his chest, Severo stomped forward, scenting the final longtooth. This one cowered behind a marble column. Severo grabbed him by the head and swung him across the floor. The vampire slid through two piles of bloody ash and landed at the front door with a crack of bone.

Severo pounced, landing with his forepaws upon the vampire's chest. He beat down once, forcefully with fisted talons, penetrating the vampire's rib cage and slicing through pulsing heart muscle. He ripped out the beating organ and tossed it behind him.

The vampire gnashed his fangs before Severo ripped off his head and threw it to the wall, not a foot from another staring head.

Huffing and heaving, Severo stretched tall, shedding the werewolf and resuming were form. Since he'd only half shifted, he still wore his leather pants. He shook off the blood from his hands.

The scent of another vampire made him bring his head upright, his ears pricking.

Stilettos crossed the marble floor, one heel slightly worn and creating a louder tone upon landing. Severo swung to face her, arms arced out at his sides. He breathed with triumph. A bittersweet win.

Elvira regarded her fallen comrades with a bored sigh. The still-pulsing heart elicited a small sneer from the vampiress. "Does this mean we're even?"

Severo snorted and punched his fist loudly into his opposite palm. "As even as the two of us will ever be."

"I can accept that."

As could he. He had no intention of harming the one individual who had been responsible for his remaining unmarked while in captivity. But he would never forgive Evie her indiscretions toward Bella.

"My bags are packed." She pouted. She couldn't shift her dark-shadowed eyes away from the heart, not five feet to her left. "I think Berlin will be lovely for a time."

"Good riddance." Severo turned and marched out.

Chapter 21

"I don't need to kill? Whew."

Ivan drove a black BMW around the city. Bella sat on the passenger side. Though it was midnight, she hunted a human victim because the blood hunger had not relented.

"Vampires don't need the kill. A small sip often or a larger drink less often. You choose," he explained. "But to kill takes the nightmares of your victims into your soul. You will relive those nightmares in what we call the *danse macabre*. It's not pretty. And those vampires who kill indiscriminately usually go mad from the nightmares."

"There seems to be a lot of madness associated with vampirism. So do we have a connection now? I took your blood, so do I know things about you?"

He cast her a smile. "Do you?"

"I don't think so."

"And you won't. I am considered your blood father, but our only connection is that my blood runs through your veins now. There is a theory that vampires exchange pieces of their soul when the transformation is made. I'm not so sure about that, but I wouldn't rule it out."

"Huh. And you'll show me how to enthrall a victim?"

"It's easy once you accept that your mind is a powerful tool."

"I see." She looked out the window when he was about to turn. "No, not that alley. It's too dark and creepy."

"We want dark and creepy, Belladonna." Ivan pulled the car into the alley.

"Yeah, but I don't think I can do dirty homeless guys or drunks."

"For tonight, you will take what we can find." He scanned the street as the car rolled smoothly over the tarmac. There weren't any flesh-and-blood humans out and about.

"What, besides being a vampire, do you do, Ivan?"

"I serve on the Council."

"Severo said that is some kind of council of vampires, witches and werewolves that oversees the paranormal nations."

"In a nutshell, yes. We have members from all species on the Council, but when there is an issue, it's usually only the representative nations that show."

"So are they discussing the divide between the werewolves and vampires now?"

"There have been suggestions of ways to bring the two nations to terms. Perhaps arranged marriages between principle players in each nation. Nothing's come of it yet. Of course, if Severo openly takes a vampire as a mate, that can only be a good thing."

"So we're to be an example?"

"Only if Severo chooses to allow it. He's very private."

"He is. Says his kind has to hide from humans. But you seem outgoing. What do you do beyond serving on the Council?"

"I'm a philanthropist."

"Are all immortals rich?"

"Depends on how you manage your money. If you're going to live forever, you'd better learn, because I can't imagine doing the homeless thing for long. What is your profession, Belladonna?"

She liked that he used her complete name. The man was too charming for a creature. *Nix that,* she thought. He was no creature. He was a kind man who happened to be a vampire.

"I work from home designing Web sites. It's enough to get by. And I also dance flamenco."

"A dancer? I figured you for some kind of athlete. You have a gorgeous body."

"Thanks." And she accepted the compliment for what it was. Not a flirtation. She did feel a connection to Ivan, but nothing sexual, despite their intimacies.

"So tell me how you and Severo met. I bet he didn't find you dancing in a club. Don't think the guy does the scene all that much."

"A gang of vampires was chasing me, and Severo pulled me into hiding while they searched for me. He intended to do exactly as the vampires wanted once they found me. But he didn't."

"The werewolf is an interesting breed. But fiercely devoted to their mates."

"You say that, but how can they remain devoted to those not their breed?"

"Give him a chance, Bella. What do you say about stopping by a dance club before we find your next donor? There's an underground tapas bar close by. If you like flamenco, it'd be your kind of place."

"You want to dance instead of hunt?"

"Might take the edge off your nerves."

She clasped her shaky fingers together. "You noticed?"

He smiled. "Let's stop in and see what's up."

She was dressed for the club. A knee-length black velvet skirt with ruffles down the back that spilled to her ankles. And a leotard top, also in black. It was the only stuff Bella had taken to Ivan's, and it had felt right to go all black for her first hunt.

The club was underground, very small and dark like a cave. Ivan led her in, but Bella eagerly followed the music, which already had her snapping her fingers and rotating her wrists with the urge to dance.

"The atmosphere here reminds me of the Caveau de la Huchette," he said to her. "A little underground club in the Latin Quarter of Paris. Tourist trap, but they play some great jazz and swing. I'll get us some wine."

"I'll have water, please."

She didn't need the wine to loosen up. Just walking into the room relaxed her. Here were her kind of people. Besides, Bella wasn't so sure wine wouldn't make her sick. She'd not eaten for days— except for the blood. And that suited her fine.

Ivan returned and pressed a cool glass into her hand. "They're all vamps," he said. "Save the faerie over in the corner."

She spied the grizzled old man, his front teeth missing, enthusiastically doing *palmas*. A faerie? She would never look at people the same again.

It was a comfortable crowd and they all took turns on the small dance floor. Right now a couple danced *sevillanas* to a quick beat. Castanets trilled and the singer encouraged *palmas*.

She tilted back the water and licked the cool liquid from her lips. "Do they know I'm a vampire?" It felt surprisingly empowering to say the word.

Ivan's soft chuckle carried over the Spanish rhythm. "Vampires don't know one another unless they touch."

"Then how do you know they're all vamps?"

"Because I've been here before, and the faces are familiar."

He touched her arm, clasping his fingers around the flesh. A thrilling shiver traveled her veins. Not a sexual shiver, but one of…knowing. "Feel that?"

"Yes. What is that?"

"We call it the shimmer."

"Appropriate. So unless I see fangs or touch another vampire, I have no way of knowing? Nor does the other vamp?"

"Exactly. Comes in handy once in a while."

"Good to know. So do you dance at all?"

"Not this stuff. I'm more a waltz kind of guy."

"Romantic. I'm going to have to meet your wife someday."

"I know she'd like meeting you."

The rhythm wasn't about to release Bella from its hold. She twisted her free hand before her and stomped her feet to the beat. The guitarist strummed a *bulería*. Bella loved this fast, demanding rhythm.

"Hold this," she said to Ivan. He took her glass, and she headed out to the dance floor.

The air in the cavelike club expanded and caressed at the same time. Bella did a *golpe* across the stone floor in her high heels. Not the best shoes to perform flamenco in, but they would serve in a pinch. Raising her arms, she rotated her wrists and played the sensual music through her body.

For a while she danced by herself, beating out the rhythm with a tilt of her hip or an exact heel-toe. One man joined her. He was older, probably sixty, but fit and tanned. He approached, stiff and cocky, a bullfighter striding up to challenge the bull. And she was his cape.

Bella loved the game of the dance. She circled him, fingers lifting her skirt only slightly, because it was already so short in front. Elbows high, she spun her back to him and clicked out a few beats before they both spun to face one another.

He smiled and winked. She tried to keep a solemn face, but she was enjoying this too much and let out laughter as the two of them spun and repeated the move the opposite way.

Dancing with a fellow vampire. How surreal had life become?

A glimpse of Ivan found him doing *palmas* with half a dozen other men who stood by the walls. Vampires, all of them? Yes, the room hummed with a presence she felt a part of.

As an introduction to her new life, this night rated high on the scale. How wise of Ivan to bring her here, to a place where she would feel comfortable and safe.

She didn't understand Spanish but knew from her dance studies that the singer spoke of love, loss, struggle and renewal. It was how all the flamenco songs were. Tragic, sorrowful, but always expressing a lively connection to life.

Bella fancied she could feel the blood rushing through the veins of each and every person in the room. It invigorated her. It made her feel alive.

She wanted more of it in her mouth. The pulse of hot blood danced a beat upon her tongue, at the back of her throat. In her body.

Suddenly she was tugged from the dance floor. A firm hand about her upper arm took her captive. She butted up against a hard body but did not feel the shimmer.

The male dancer stomped up to whoever held her, his arms held defiantly back so his chest puffed up in a challenging pose.

"She's mine," growled the one who held her.

"Severo?" He was supposed to be in a motel, waiting for her. "What are you doing?"

His breath hot near her ear, Severo whispered harshly, "You never dance for me, sweet."

He pulled her from the dance floor, past Ivan, who did not make a move to intervene, and up the stairs outside. Nondescript brick walls sandwiched them in darkness. Snowflakes fluttered softly.

"How did you know where to find me?" She tugged from his grip and walked away a few paces. The air was cold tonight. She could see her breath, yet she was flushed with warmth and the adrenaline soaring through her system. "That was rude!"

"I scented you."

"Tell me something I don't know. Am I forever destined to unfinished dances with men?"

He bowed his head and ran fingers through his hair. "Sorry. I... He was so close to you."

"Here's a reminder for you. We were dancing.

You *know* that. You've seen those same moves before. Jeez, jealous much?"

"I am." He stepped in front of her, without touching. Dark eyes held hers, searching; then he looked down and stepped away. "I thought you'd call to come home this evening. When you did not, I wanted to find you. Quite a surprise to discover you dancing when you are supposed to be learning a life skill."

"Ivan thought it would relax me."

"And did it?"

"Severo, don't do this. Hey, Ivan. Sorry about that little scene."

The vampire stopped in the doorway and leaned a shoulder against the frame. He didn't say anything. Wine tainted his breath. But nothing could overwhelm the scent of Severo's rage.

Suffering humiliation was no way to end the evening.

"I'll be in the car," Bella said and stalked down the alleyway.

Both men listened, heads bowed, as the click of Bella's heels took her to the end of the alleyway. Severo breathed in heavily through his nose and shook his head.

He owed Ivan an apology. He owed Bella one,

too. But he'd been taken off guard. He'd expected her to tag along behind this vampire, learning how to drink blood. Then to find her dancing so suggestively with a stranger?

Okay, so it was not suggestive in Bella's mind. But to him, any closeness she experienced with another male disturbed him. Would he never learn?

And yet she had never danced for him. Would she ever give him a private concert? He'd love that. It was a part of her that still belonged to the mortal realm, a part he wanted to preserve as much as she probably did.

"I need to apologize," he started.

Ivan stepped into the street. "It's fine. It's not going to be easy."

"You were supposed to teach her."

"After she mentioned she was a dancer, I thought this little aside would relax her. She was very nervous."

"Yeah, well, I'll take her home now."

"She hasn't taken human blood yet. I'll want to supervise. Why don't you come along. We'll find a donor and she can get over her hesitation."

"I can't do that. I can't…"

"Watch? You don't have to. But having you close by may mean more to her than you can imagine."

* * *

Ivan pointed to a lone man walking down the alley. He looked young, in his twenties—perhaps he was a college guy—and clean. Bella's only requirement.

She glanced to Severo. He approved with a barely perceptible nod.

The threesome loitered at the alley entrance, Bella between Severo and Ivan. She hadn't spoken to Severo since he'd dragged her out of the club. Now, though, she looked to him and gave him a not-quite smile.

"You're not going to watch?"

Severo shook his head. But he was glad to sense that she was as uncomfortable with this as he was. And then he admonished himself for such thinking. Of course she was uncomfortable. She was new at this.

And here he stood, participating in something so far from his comfort zone. It opened the doors of memory to another vampiress, dressed all in black, looking pale and hungry.

But Evie had once saved him.

He knew Bella would never harm him or his kind. He had to look beyond the past. Give her his presence and be strong for her.

"I'm ready," she said to Ivan and stepped down the alley.

Though his arms reached out to pull her back,

Severo did not call out. He would simply be here, in case she should need him. A witness. A supporter.

"I can do this," he murmured.

The skirt swung from her hips and about her knees. Long legs in spike heels put Severo in instant lust mode. Those legs should be wrapped about his hips right now.

Yes, even as he fought the repulsion, he craved the woman he had fallen in love with. She was sashaying so sexily toward another man. A human she would put her hands on and talk to sweetly. She would take a part of the mortal stranger inside her. So deeply. The act of drinking blood was wickedly sexual.

Severo shifted his shoulder around the corner and pressed his back to the wall so he could not watch. He knew Ivan would step in if Bella needed assistance.

"She takes to this so easily," he said hoarsely.

"The hunger overwhelms the most rigid inhibitions," Ivan told him. "I know you don't want to be here, Severo, but you need to watch. It'll show you what she is."

He knew what she was. Severo had seen vampires drink blood from victims time and time again. And he'd seen them murder and maim for no reason other than for the macabre joy of it.

What of the blood on your hands?

Those vampires he'd killed tonight had deserved to die.

"She's not like those you hate," Ivan whispered. "She never will be. I'm going closer. She needs guidance."

His back against the wall and his eyes closed, Severo listened, trying to hear beyond his own pounding heartbeats.

Bella cooed to the man, who said things like, "You're hot" and "My place is close."

Jerk, Severo scoffed.

It was a strange departure from that first night he'd rescued her, while the vampires had searched the warehouse. Her heart had pattered like a bird's. Then she'd been so frightened. Now she was so eager.

Releasing his clenched fists, Severo reminded himself that this was part of the deal. She had to come in close contact with humans, unlike him, who put as much distance between them and himself as possible.

And now he had a vampire in his life. A *longtooth*.

The taint of blood carried to him. Beer and fast food littered the human's scent. Unappetizing. He wondered if Bella liked the taste. It would kill him if she did.

Turning, he crept around the building. Bella was silhouetted before the man, whose legs buckled.

Ivan stood on the other side, his hand to Bella's shoulder.

It was like some kind of twisted sex scene. A *ménage à trois* Severo had no desire to join. And yet...

When she tilted her head back in pleasure and the moon glinted on her pale neck, he wanted to know that pleasure. *Her* pleasure. To touch the luscious rise of her breasts. And perhaps to be the one to kick the other man aside.

As it was, the man slid down the wall and collapsed. Bella began to topple as one of his legs twisted between hers, but Ivan caught her. She tugged free and swung about to walk away.

As she approached Severo, the drunken grin on her face bemused him. A trace of her forefinger wiped away a drop of blood from the corner of her mouth. She thrust the finger between her red lips and sucked, smiling as she came upon him.

A strong blood scent forced Severo backward. Yet arousal had widened her pupils. God, she was gorgeous.

Bella grinned a sloppy smile. "I'd kiss you," she said, "but you wouldn't like it."

She wandered off, swaying but sure-footed, toward his Mercedes.

"She's drunk," Severo hissed as Ivan joined his side.

"It'll be that way the first few times she takes human blood," the vampire said. "It's overwhelming in so many ways. She is not used to it and needs to be cautioned not to take too much, or she might accidentally kill."

"Christ."

"If you love her, you'll go with her the next few times."

"I can't do that."

"Then she will kill." Ivan strode off.

And Severo beat a fist against the brick wall.

Chapter 22

For the first time in ninety years he was prepared to welcome a longtooth into his home.

Not exactly prepared. How *did* one prepare for such a thing? Since his hatred against them was so ingrained, he wasn't sure it could ever be truly siphoned from his blood.

Severo drove the Mercedes toward home. On the passenger seat, Bella lolled in a blissful state as the blood swoon lingered. Her skirt was hiked high on her thighs—another inch and she'd reveal things only he should see. He liked those long, slender gams. Better, he liked imagining what lay beneath the flirty ruffles.

And that image gave him hope that it was all going to be all right. He still desired her. *Nothing has changed,* he repeated silently.

"Ivan said you should drink once more before going home tonight. That it would sate you for at least a week."

"Sounds good to me," she offered sweetly.

She was no longer silly drunk, but relaxed and in a strangely heightened state, what he'd normally call arousal.

"This may be cruel, but I have to ask," he said. "Do you get off on it?"

She sighed. So much pleasure in that sigh. "You know vampires swoon from the blood."

Yes. He also knew the swoon was orgasmic. And surely she and Ivan must have shared some swoons. His grip tightened on the steering wheel.

"But get off?" she said. "No. That would imply I get some kind of thrill from a stranger. It merely serves a need. Though I had wished you were standing beside me instead of Ivan."

For a moment, he had wished the same thing. Because standing at the end of the alleyway, listening to his lover's sweet coaxing and the human's moans, Severo had gotten hard. From the temptation Bella offered with her sighs and touches. From the kiss he'd struggled to label sweet when he knew it was now dangerous.

"Let's go down Poplar." She pointed out the street. "It's not far from where I used to live. It's quiet, but we may find a college kid walking around this late."

In the quiet neighborhood, they found a new development. Bella approached an acceptable candidate with the same sensual daring she'd exhibited downtown.

Severo parked and followed, but by the time he gained on them, Bella was holding the man close in front of a green Dumpster in an alleyway. Blood scent filled the air. Both her hands on the rim of the Dumpster, she sucked at his neck. The guy initially stroked his hands over her hips, but quickly his hands dropped to his sides and he let out a long, appreciative moan.

His jaw tensing, Severo forced himself not to interfere. The guy was giving blood, so he deserved the swoon. And he wouldn't get far with Bella if he did try to put the moves on her.

Was this what his life had become? He must accompany his lover each time she sought blood in order to ensure no one touched her overtly?

Hell, he'd have to get used to it. He couldn't go along every time. It would kill him. And it wouldn't be fair to her.

Bella needed this. And he grew hard as he

imagined stroking the hair away from his lover's face to reveal her blissed-out expression.

Yet he could not touch her. He didn't want to disturb her. He didn't want to touch what he could not approve of.

Christ, but he breathed as heavily as she did. When the unconscious victim slipped from her and settled onto the ground, Bella remained, leaning against the Dumpster, hands fitted to the rim, her legs spread.

She smirked and licked her lips. There was no blood. She was surprisingly neat.

"Ivan taught me the persuasion," she said. "Makes them forget I was ever here."

Looking over her arm at him, she sent him an air kiss.

"Don't look at me all judgmental like that," she said.

"I'm not judging you, sweet." It wasn't worth the wasted thought. Besides, he'd gone beyond that. Her bold and sexy position had made him consider taking her from behind. "I'm admiring you. A gorgeous vixen of the night."

"You're turned on?"

"Yes."

Before she could react, he stepped up close behind her, bumping her, and placed his hands over hers on the Dumpster. He fit his erection against her derriere, pressing, making her know what watching her had done to him. Kissing down the back of her neck, he bit at the thin fabric covering her torso and licked along her shoulder.

Sliding a hand up her thigh, he swept his fingers across her silken skin and found her panties. The lace, crisp and barely there, gave easily at his tug. She wasn't wet—which pleased him; the act of taking blood was not so sexual, after all—but with but a few flicks of his fingers, she was there.

Stroking her and rubbing his erection against her, he brought her to a swift orgasm. Her quiet murmurs entered his ears as music. Her shudders he drew into his body. He hadn't come, but he didn't need to. Experiencing her bliss did it for him.

"I'll take you home now," he said, and lifted her into his arms and carried her away.

A light dusting of snow whitened the brown grass behind the mansion. Bella had headed right for the shower, mumbling something about brushing her teeth.

He'd done it. Watched his lover take blood from another man.

And it had turned him on. How sick was that?

Or was it sick? He'd shared an intimate new part of Bella. Something she would keep private from the world, except for him. He could only love her for allowing him to witness her new ritual.

And he did love her. That would never change. But right now it felt tenuous. Yes, he was unsure. Would she want to bite him? And how could he refuse her when he knew the one thing vampires required to become close to their mates was sharing blood?

The notion of being bitten or sharing blood did not appeal to him. The werewolf did enough of that for his taste.

So she had become the animal he already was, and *he* was having trouble dealing with it?

Lifting his head, he sniffed the air through the open patio door in their bedroom. The snow cleaned the fall rot from his senses and his focus immediately found her. She was behind him, sweet with lemon shampoo and minty toothpaste.

Yet he wasn't confident he truly wanted to be here.

Yes, he was.

Probably.

"Hell, pull it together, man," he muttered.

She smelled like the Bella he remembered. But there was something else. Some undertone he didn't want to translate into thought. Yet his mind processed the scent and reacted to it before he could argue. His body stiffened, his fingers arching into claws. A defensive tickle ran up his neck.

Vampire.

"Severo?"

Shaking out his hands at his thighs, he cursed his instincts and put on a smile as he turned to her.

The white silk robe clung to her nipples. Like a bride marching down the aisle for her groom, Bella stepped up to him. Winter's blossom—with a taint of blood.

He hated that he could not make this perfect for her. For himself.

You can. Just put off all doubt. See her for the woman you first fell in love with. Remember you savored her fear?

He could scent that same fear now. And he hated himself for making her feel that way.

"You look great, sweet. Two days away and I'd almost forgotten how bright your eyes were. Come here."

Yes, he could do this. He wanted to do this. He needed to make the effort of stepping into the usual, with the hope that it would erase his rising doubts for the future.

Her body fit against his. The scent of lemon in her hair and the silk threads briefly overwhelmed her clean smell. And yet she was no longer clean or human.

Her chest melded with his. He buried his nose in the crown of her hair. She might be tainted, but she was his mate.

"I missed you," she said. "I didn't know if you'd welcome me into your arms. I know this is hard for you."

"Nonsense," he murmured and stroked her hair down her back.

The feel of her made his body react as it always did. He hardened and the lust surfaced. Good, then. He hadn't lost the desire. The quick interlude out in the alley had simply been a reaction to something so intense. This was different. They were alone now. No secrets. No lies.

"You're mine, Bella. My mate. Forever. Did you learn what you needed from Ivan?"

"He was a perfect gentleman and showed me the ropes. I've blooded my fangs, as Ivan called it." She smirked. "I like that. Sounds so decadent."

She was different. Not so uptight, easier with him. Accepting of what, he imagined, was an incredible change in her life.

A stroke of her finger along his beard, accompanied by sad eyes, made him look aside. "It made me feel good that you took me in the alleyway, after watching," she said.

"I needed you. It was an instinctual thing."

"It felt great. Like it always feels when I'm with you. You controlled me. I belong to you."

"As I am yours."

"Will you kiss me now?"

A kiss?

Why the hell had this been done to him and Bella? They had been so perfect. His future had been designed with her at his side. Even the werewolf loved her.

All that had changed now. The werewolf would never accept a vampire. Never.

"I won't bite," she whispered, a touch of hope lifting her voice.

A nudge of her nose along his jaw sweetened the lust, which predominated over the all the emotions he'd rather not deal with right now. Maybe she had the right idea.

Just let go. Concentrate on the now.

Severo kissed the corner of her mouth. She tasted like Bella. Soft, salty, clean.

Things would be fine. This kiss bonded two souls. It drew the two together, wanting and needing and giving.

They hit the bed stripped of their clothes. Bella couldn't have dreamed of a better welcome home than this. He had accepted her. The werewolf had welcomed a vampire into his home.

He'd once said to her that she would always have his heart. And she did still.

Severo's hand glided up her back as he pulled her on top of him. She bent to lick his nipple, a small, hard jewel. His satisfied groan heartened her. A familiar tune, yet one she could listen to over and over.

His fingers massaged her breasts. Her loins tingled, aching for his entrance. He flipped her on the bed so she lay on her stomach. He trailed kisses down her spine as he slipped a finger inside her.

"So ready," he growled. "So hot. I've missed this, Bella."

"Quickly, please," she cried.

Gripping the pillow, she spread her knees as he lifted her under her hips and brought the backs of her thighs against his. His favorite position.

He pushed inside her and she gasped as his length filled her. Fast and frenzied, he worked them both up to a spectacular climax. Bella gasped and reached for the headboard. He drew her up against his chest. She wanted to wrap her arms around him. This position gave her an incredible orgasm, but it always left her aching for face-to-face contact.

It was the wolf in him that liked to take her this way, and she loved it for that reason. When his body relaxed, he dropped onto the sheets by her side.

Bella kissed him along his torso, licking the sweaty moisture and reaching to grip his semihard shaft. A lick to his bicep, and she trailed her tongue upward and kissed his neck. Opening her mouth wide, she leaned in—

"Bloody hell!" Severo shoved her off him and scrambled away. The palm of his hand, held before him to keep her back, hurt worse than a slap. "No fangs, Bella."

"What?" She ran her tongue along her teeth and a sharp canine pricked it. "Oh hell, I didn't realize. I would have never—"

He stood. The back of him, naked and muscled, flexed as he gripped his fists.

"I wasn't thinking," Bella offered. "I didn't feel them come down. I don't know why—"

"Because your kind have sex and they want to take blood. And vice versa." He spun on her. "Didn't Drake teach you that?"

"Well, yes, but like I said, he was a gentleman. We didn't do anything…sexual."

Though the swoon *had* been sexual. She couldn't deny that. Ivan had explained about the blood and sex desires being intertwined, though at the time, she'd thought it incredible. Every time she had sex, she'd want blood?

That wouldn't be good for this relationship.

"I must need more time to get a handle on things. I'm so sorry, Severo. I didn't mean to freak you out."

"Well, you did." A heavy sigh lifted his chest. "I don't want your bite."

His confession hurt. Deeply. He was denying her. Denying her very nature.

He approached the bed to sit at the edge. "I mean, I love you, Bella. And I know you can bite me, and nothing untoward will come of it, save an increase in blood craving, but…there is a stigma attached to wearing a vampire's bite."

"You were never bitten, and if you were now, it would mean you'd succumbed to the captivity once again."

He winced.

"I won't do that to you, lover. I don't need to bite you. I think. I may need to give Ivan a call." She rubbed a palm down her leg and shivered. Sex was over. But was the relationship? "Can we make this work?"

The ferocity of his gaze chilled her. Once she had admired that look, so intense and ever focused only on her. Now it made her scared for what he might never share with her. He put up a good front, but the truth was Severo might never be able to accept her.

"It's not what you think," he said carefully, so gentle. "Bella, I can accept you as you are now.

And those fangs, which fit so prettily over your bottom lip? They're kind of sexy."

He reached to touch her mouth, and only then did Bella realize her fangs were still down. She willed them back up.

"Mine are bigger," he said with a smirk.

"What about the werewolf?"

"The werewolf." He pulled her so she sat with her back against his chest. The touch of his hair on her shoulder tickled her. "That is what is keeping me from surrendering to you, sweet. I know the werewolf, and it doesn't like vampires."

"It loves me."

"Bella, the werewolf takes off vampire heads for entertainment. Why do you think it would be any different with you?"

"Because it does love me. Aren't you willing to find out? If the werewolf could accept me, could you?"

"Of course I would, but I'm not willing to set you out as bait for a vampire-hating beast. I won't do that. I can't."

"The full moon is in two weeks. You can't stop me from trying to seek out the werewolf. No matter how far away you go."

He hugged her tightly. Bella wanted him to break her, to fit her into his soul and keep her there forever.

"Don't ask me to sacrifice you," he whispered. "Please, sweet. Just accept what we have now."

Accept him as a lover, but never as a soul mate?

"It's my sacrifice, as well. Don't you think I make a sacrifice when I'm out in the yard with the werewolf? A facsimile of you takes me quickly, and to fill a need, and then later, when you are a man, you have no recall!"

"It hurts to hear you say that. I never asked you to make such a sacrifice."

"You wanted the werewolf to accept me so I could be your mate. Well, I'm asking a sacrifice of you now. Let the werewolf come to me. Give it the opportunity to decide if I truly am the mate it desires. I know it will harm me only if *you* allow it to."

"Bella, you know I have little control over it."

"But you can influence it."

"Yes, in small ways. But what if something goes wrong? What if…"

"It tears me apart? That's a chance I'm willing to take."

Severo stood abruptly. "Vampirism has made you bold, Bella. Perhaps stupidly so."

"It's freed me, lover. It's made me not care about the past. Not care what others think. Give me this one small gift, please?"

He grimaced but nodded. "I'll think about it."

It was all he could offer, and Bella accepted that. But she fully intended to go out wandering when the moon was round and high in the sky.

Two weeks later, when the moon was full, Severo did what he had to do.

He'd hated to do it. To lure her into the arsenal on the pretense that he wanted to lock away the weapons he used against vampires—as a sign of acceptance. But while Bella had collected the wooden bullets he'd purposely dropped on the floor, Severo had locked her inside.

She'd pounded on the steel door, pleading for release. It had cut into his heart to hear her tearful pleas. She would be safe from the werewolf for the night.

Now he tore away his shirt and stepped out of his pants. The air was cold and fat snowflakes fell like down from the heavens. He shivered and shifted into the furred wolf.

Taking off through the backyard, the wolf loped into the valley, intent on tracking that rabbit Severo had sighted earlier in the day.

Chapter 23

"Bastard!" Bella kicked the steel door for the third time to no avail.

She paced.

Here she'd thought Severo had resolved to make this work. And the only way she could possibly foresee that happening? *Let the werewolf decide.*

If it accepted her, Severo could banish his apprehensions and worries that she'd never be safe around it. And if the werewolf tore out her throat... Well, there wasn't much of a way to argue if that happened, was there?

Rationally, she understood his fear. So much had happened to them since coming together. He could have never anticipated that his girlfriend would be transformed into a vampire. And then to face losing her should the werewolf protest?

This might be the safest place for her during the full moon, but having blooded her teeth, Bella had lost all trace of fear. And she was hungry.

She gave the door one more good kick but succeeded in only denting the steel.

Shouldn't she have superpowers by now? she thought. The other vampires were so strong, they'd rip this door from the hinges.

Though she had noticed many changes since the transformation, Ivan had said it would take until the next full moon before she was completely a vampire. Whatever that meant.

Right now her senses increased. She could smell the gunpowder in the plastic containers at the back of the arsenal. And though night had fallen and she hadn't switched the light on yet, she could see very well.

Stalking to the table's edge, she grabbed hold of the stainless steel. The corner of the table bent. "So I am stronger." She glanced to the door. "But not strong enough for that mother."

Maybe if she pried out the hinges?

Searching for a tool, she grabbed a crowbar and hammer and went to work.

A ghostly howl outside made her stop pounding. Another howl sounded closer to the house.

"He must not have gone far away. Is he coming for me?"

Bella leaped onto the counter and peered out the ten-inch-high glass-block window. It was impossible to see through the distorted blocks.

She jumped down and resumed pounding at the door. One hinge pin popped out and clanged onto the cement floor.

She positioned the crowbar beneath the next hinge pin but paused. "Do I really want to do this? Do I think I'm some kind of big bad vampire now who can take on anything in my path? I don't think I can win against a werewolf."

But she didn't have to win; she just had to seduce.

Glass crashed to the ground. Bella guessed it was the patio door that Severo had only just reinstalled a week earlier. The werewolf had entered the house.

She worked at the second of three hinges, but it wouldn't budge no matter how hard she hit it with the hammer. Instead of creating more noise, she set down the tools and bent before the door to listen.

Snorts and huffing breaths sounded. Far away.

The werewolf was probably walking through the kitchen. Talons scratched across marble. The thunder of each footstep—it was not running, but was slowly taking the foyer's measure—rocketed her heartbeat to her throat.

He was looking for her. He must smell her. Hell, the werewolf could smell her from miles away. Now his head must be filled with her scent.

Her vampire scent.

"There must be deodorant for hiding vampire pheromones," she muttered. "Just…let him be calm, to see *me* before he rages."

And she closed her eyes and pressed her fingertips to the steel door. *See me,* she repeated over and over. *Know me.*

The wolf stalked the hallway toward the arsenal. A bang outside the room shook the wall. It seemed angry, impatient to find the creature it scented. It was on the hunt.

On bent legs, Bella twisted to eye the arsenal. What kind of weapon would work against a werewolf? Not a lethal weapon, one that contained silver, but something to hold it back if it intended to take off her head. Something to pin it to the ground while she ran for the garage and hopped in the car to speed off to China.

She didn't want to die. And to be ripped apart by her lover was not on her top-ten list of adventures.

But she did want it to recognize her—if only for a moment—and know that she had not changed. Sure, she now needed blood to survive. But her heart had not altered. Her soul needed Severo...and the werewolf.

A bang against the door pushed in the steel in the shape of wide knuckles. A chilling scrape of talons down metal sent a shiver up the back of Bella's neck.

The werewolf howled. Bella did not recognize it as that "I see you and want to mate with you" kind of howl with which he usually greeted her. This one was low and menacing.

A prick to her lower lip made her jump. "Now is no time for the fangs." Try as she might, she could not will them back up.

The vampire she had become was prepared to fight for survival.

Two more fist marks bulged in the door. The middle hinge, partly released, cracked in half. A kick brought the door down inside the room.

The bullets and guns and knives sitting on the counter behind Bella clattered to the floor as she backed into it. Her hip bone hit the steel, and she winced but did not take her eyes from the approaching threat.

The werewolf seethed, its fangs descending along its extended jaw and glistening with saliva. It howled at the sight of her and stalked up in two long strides, forcing her to jump onto the counter and crouch defensively.

"It's me," she cried. "Severo, see me!"

It snarled and tossed back its head. The muscles strapping its shoulders pulsed as it did a caveman chest pound. Powerful thighs flexed. It stomped. One paw swept across the counter, to Bella's right, tearing the steel in four jagged lines.

Blood drooled down her chin. She'd bit her lip. *The blood scent must enrage the wolf beyond measure,* she thought. "Hell, I can't sit here and take it," she said aloud.

She dropped to the floor and thought to crawl away, but a hand connected with her side. One blow swept her across the room and out the door. She skidded along the waxed marble floor and slammed into a wall with a groan.

Blood seeping from her thigh, Bella scrambled along the floor. Behind her the werewolf stalked at a distance, as if it planned to play with her, exhaust her before the killing.

"You're not playing fair!" she shouted and scrambled to her feet.

Dashing toward the front door, she reasoned that outside the werewolf would have her at an advantage. The garage door was behind her, behind the werewolf, so reaching the car was out of the question.

Veering right, Bella headed toward the bedrooms. Perhaps the smaller rooms and the furniture would impede the werewolf. For a few seconds.

"Severo, I love you!" she called back. Gripping the door frame, she swung herself into a bedroom.

She slammed the door and locked it, knowing the gesture was futile.

In proof, talons ripped through the wood as if it were fashioned from mere leather. Bella stumbled backward, her spine colliding with the bed. She scrambled across it to the other side. The werewolf pushed the door into the room. On all fours, it lifted its head and sniffed.

With one leap it soared across the bed and knocked her on the floor, its deadly taloned fingers on her shoulders and its knees pinning her feet.

Bella screamed.

She was beyond caring about hurting Severo's feelings. Obviously she'd been wrong. The werewolf did hate vampires. It didn't matter if its alter ego was screwing one and claimed to love her. All that mattered was instinct.

"Please," she said, her voice reedy and shivering with fear. "Please."

Just...please.

The werewolf sniffed her body. The graze of its teeth over her breast shocked her. Its canines didn't break the skin, but it wasn't a sexual touch by any means. Panting and emitting a low growl, it sniffed along her neck. Its tongue swept out to lick under her jaw.

Tasting her? Why not get it done with? And please, if she were to die right now, she much preferred losing her head to being...munched.

Oh, Bella, don't even think it.

Turning her head, she winced as the fingers curled and talons dug into her shoulders. Not deeply, but it wasn't aware, obviously, how easily it could damage her tender flesh.

Feeling her heart finish the race, she whined miserably and shook her head. The scent of her own fear was like bad cologne wafting in the room.

But the werewolf's earthy scent was sweet to her. Her lover.

Don't forget it is your lover. The man who claimed you as his mate.

"No!" She bashed her elbow across the werewolf's snout and scrambled away. The werewolf snarled and leaped for her. It gnashed its teeth but halted abruptly, short of biting her on the cheek. "You know me. Remember me? I'm the same Bella. The same one."

She dragged herself up over the edge of the bed, kneeling, and stepped off the other side. Slowly, she backed away. The werewolf would not kill her before she could give it her all. This vampire was willing to fight to win her lover.

"You once said you loved the smell of fear on me. Recognize it now, Severo. And know I am yours."

Something clicked in her brain. Bold courage. A willingness to die to achieve her greatest desire. *Trust*.

She trusted this man would make the right choice, no matter his form.

Bella drew her shoulders straight and lifted her chest. Drawing in a breath through her nose, she found a strange calm amid the chaos.

"Very well, wolf boy." She bowed her head and looked up through her lashes. "You like it rough?"

The werewolf slashed the bed, taking out some cotton stuffing.

"You think you're such a beast? All he-man and stalking me?" Tracing her tongue over her fangs, she smiled widely. "Come to me, werewolf. Take me if you can."

Unzipping her pants, she slid them down and tore open her shirt. The werewolf licked its maw.

Slowly, she slinked around to the end of the bed.

Tilting her head, she put back her shoulders. The shirt slid off, leaving her naked. Her breasts sat high and her nipples hardened.

A throaty growl signaled her lover's desire. She loved that growl.

Turning, Bella bent over the bed, placing her palms flat on the sheets. "Take me. I am your mate. It's death or mating. Your choice."

A heavy hand slapped the back of her neck, shoving her face against the bed. A sharp talon cut into her skin. And then it entered her and gratified its instinct.

Bella cried out at the pleasure of the intense friction. If this was to be her last breath, she would breathe it gladly.

The wolf howled its familiar boon of triumph, and then it was gone, leaping over the bed and dashing out through the patio door.

Bella collapsed on the bed. She breathed heavily. Her heart still had not started. And her lips were slick with her own blood.

But she had won back her lover.

Severo shivered and came fully awake with a start. He was naked, lying on the icy flagstones by the pool. As he moved something slashed his ankle. It was glass, scattered everywhere.

The werewolf had broken into the house last night. He'd tried to hold it back but not even he could stop his beast.

"Bella."

Rushing inside, he didn't want to think of what he might find. Blood put a metallic taste in his mouth, and the scratches on his arms and palms indicated a struggle.

"Please be alive. I'm so sorry, Bella!"

He jackknifed as he rounded the corner to the bedrooms and ran right into a white towel, stretched out to receive him.

"Thought you'd need this," she said. A sweetly wicked smile curved her red lips. "Cold out there last night?"

"You're…" He eyed her up and down as he wrapped the oversize towel about his waist. She was dressed in a sheer pink negligee that revealed the tawny areolae on her breasts and the thatch of dark hair at the apex of her thighs. "Okay?"

"Peachy." She strode past him into the kitchen and straightened a stack of mail he'd been avoiding for days. "And you?"

"Besides being frozen, I'm… The werewolf didn't get to you? You were safe in the arsenal?"

She pointed over his shoulder. Hard to miss the havoc in the foyer. The front door had slashes through it. The walls had been clawed and Sheetrock was busted everywhere. He couldn't see the arsenal door, but a memory of last night flashed before his eyes.

The steel door clattering to the floor…Bella's eyes flashing wide with fear… The werewolf approaching…

"Tell me," he said, fighting against the horrid vision.

She leaned in and kissed his jaw, then tapped his chin. "The werewolf loves me."

"It…didn't harm you?"

"I got a nasty slash down my thigh, but I don't think it was intentional. The werewolf was initially out for blood. But then it calmed down. I dared it to take me. Then I offered myself to it."

"Offered yourself?" he said, his voice falling.

"We had sex. Just like old times." She kissed him again, this time pulling his head in for a long, deep, hard connection, mouth to mouth. "Mmm, you taste good the morning after, you know that?"

"So the werewolf…"

"Could care less that I'm a vamp."

Severo shook his head, taking it all in. It was wondrous. It was astounding. The werewolf had accepted Bella. Which meant he need not fear for her. Not ever.

"You're so brave. I'm sorry I didn't trust the werewolf. Sorry I locked you away."

"I think that might have been a good thing. It made it difficult to get to me. Might have given it a chance to think. Anyway, I look forward to tonight. What about you?"

"Tonight?" He lifted her in his arms. "We've some catching up to do, sweet. No time like the present."

"What happens if the fangs come out to play?"

"One rule. No biting."

"Severo, I've sacrificed everything for you. Is a little bite too much to ask of you?"

This time he did not stiffen in her embrace, as expected. Instead, he hugged her tighter and buried his face in her hair. "It isn't."

"I want to taste you, lover."

"Feeling your teeth enter my flesh may just turn me on. But I honestly need some time. Please, Bella, can you love a man who is willing but wary?"

"I already love you. Nothing changes that. And I can wait until you're ready, until you ask me for the one thing that will bond us completely."

"It won't be long. Promise."

Epilogue

"Soon," was Severo's rote answer every time Bella asked when she could bite him. She would never stop asking. One of these days his answer would be "Now."

It had been a few months since she'd become a vampire. The world was amazing as viewed with her heightened senses and newfound confidence. She'd always been confident, but now she was strong. And standing beside her werewolf lover made her feel powerful.

She enjoyed walking by humans on dark streets, drawing in the scent of their blood. There were as many scents and flavors of blood as people, and she loved to indulge. Severo waited in the car sometimes for her return to him. She would be woozy from the swoon and eager to make love.

Life was good. And it only promised to get better.

Now Severo parked and gestured to her to grab the whip from the backseat. They both got out.

A couple held hands near the hood of a black Mustang. Bella didn't know a thing about cars, only that this one was cool. The man was tall, lithe, and wore his hair tousled about his handsome face. He had movie-star good looks.

The woman holding his hand was petite and red-haired, and when she saw Bella and Severo approach, she bounced on her heels and stretched out her arms.

Severo let go of Bella's hand and rushed up to meet the woman. He pulled her into a hug that lifted her feet from the ground.

A prick on her lip alerted Bella. She willed her teeth—and her jealousy—back to the shadows. This woman was no threat to her. She had a man. And Bella was now willing to fight any woman who thought to lay hands on *her* man. Unless it was a friendly hug.

"Bella." Severo set the woman on the ground and held out his hand to her. Bella took it and kissed him on the cheek. "This is Aby Fitzroy. Aby, my mate, Bella. I love her. We're going to marry in the spring."

"It's such a pleasure to meet you." Aby's green eyes twinkled as she pumped Bella's hand. "This is my husband, Max."

The man leaned in to shake Bella's hand and offered a wink to Severo. "Nice to meet you, Bella. Marriage? Congratulations. I wish the two of you as much happiness as Aby and I have."

The man, after releasing Bella's hand, stared at it, and then brushed his own off, as if he'd touched dirt. He winced.

"Wondering what she is?" Severo asked the Highwayman. "He has a sixth sense for paranormals, though the man is mortal himself," Severo said to Bella. "My future wife is a vampire."

Bella did not miss Aby's gasp.

"And I love her." Severo wrapped Bella in an embrace. "Do you have the whip, sweet?"

Bella held out the coiled silver whip and handed it to Max.

"I happened upon this a few days ago," Severo said. "I believe it's yours."

"Thanks. I thought I'd lost it. Ian Grim stole it."

"That bastard needs to be taken down," Severo growled.

"I agree," Max said.

Aby rolled her eyes and reached for Bella's hand. "Let's go inside the restaurant and get a table. We'll leave the menfolk to growl and plot to take over the world. I love your shoes. Manolos?"

"Louboutins." Bella clasped Aby's hand and they wandered away from the guys.

"So you can walk in the daylight?" Aby asked.

"Yes, I have phoenix and witch blood in me."

"Interesting that Severo chose you."

"I wasn't a vampire when we met." Bella opened the restaurant door. "He's accepted me."

Aby halted at the threshold. "I know he has. I've never seen that man smile so big." She turned to Bella, her green eyes sparkling. "You're the one, Bella. I know it. I'm so happy for both of you." .

* * * * *

In the third instalment of the WICKED GAMES *series, find out if the vampires and werewolves can overcome their differences and unite in peace when a sexy vampire lord marries a sassy werewolf princess. Watch for* Her Vampire Husband *by Michele Hauf from Mills & Boon® Nocturne™ in October 2010.*

® NOCTURNE™

Coming next month

THE VAMPIRE'S KISS
by Vivi Anna

Vampire CSI Olena is mystified by a recent bank robbery.
When sexy human agent Cale arrives, her suspicion that all is
not as it seems is confirmed. As Olena and Cale are thrust
into a dangerous battle between species, they learn that
love is their strongest weapon.

RED WOLF
by Linda Thomas-Sundstrom

Tory understands exactly what kind of monster is stalking
the streets. She, too, is a werewolf and is ready to bring the
rogue shifter to justice. What she isn't prepared for is Adam
Scott, the sexy detective whose investigation crosses
paths with her own.

On sale 17th September 2010

HER VAMPIRE HUSBAND
by Michele Hauf

Werewolf princess Blu won't allow her husband to
consummate their marriage with his vampire bite, marking
her forever. But when Blu uncovers her pack's secret
plot to destroy the vampire nation, she is forced to
confront her growing feelings for Edward.

On sale 1st October 2010

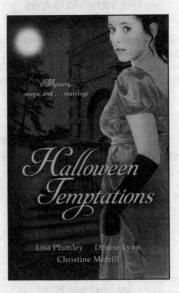

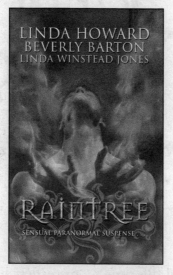

INTRODUCED BY BESTSELLING AUTHOR KATIE FFORDE

Four fabulous new writers

Lynn Raye Harris
Kept for the Sheikh's Pleasure

Nikki Logan
Seven-Day Love Story

Molly Evans
Her No.1 Doctor

Ann Lethbridge
The Governess and the Earl

We know you're going to love them!

Available 20th August 2010

www.millsandboon.co.uk

M&B

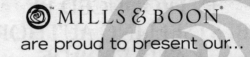

2 FREE BOOKS
AND A SURPRISE GIFT

We would like to take this opportunity to thank you for reading this
Mills & Boon® book by offering you the chance to take TWO more
specially selected books from the Intrigue series absolutely FREE!
We're also making this offer to introduce you to the benefits of the
Mills & Boon® Book Club™—

- **FREE home delivery**
- **FREE gifts and competitions**
- **FREE monthly Newsletter**
- **Exclusive Mills & Boon Book Club offers**
- **Books available before they're in the shops**

Accepting these FREE books and gift places you under no obligation to buy, you may cancel at any time, even after receiving your free
books. Simply complete your details below and return the entire page
to the address below. You don't even need a stamp!

YES Please send me 2 free Intrigue books and a surprise gift.
understand that unless you hear from me, I will receive 5 superb new
stories every month, including two 2-in-1 books priced at £4.99
each and a single book priced at £3.19, postage and packing free.
am under no obligation to purchase any books and may cancel my
subscription at any time. The free books and gift will be mine to keep
in any case.

Ms/Mrs/Miss/Mr _____ Initials _____

Surname _____

Address _____

_____ Postcode _____

E-mail _____

Send this whole page to: Mills & Boon Book Club, Free Book Offer
FREEPOST NAT 10298, Richmond, TW9 1BR